Indiscretions

A NOVEL

JESSICA TILLES

XPRESS YOURSELF PUBLISHING

Xpress Yourself Publishing
eMail: publisher@xpressyourselfpublishing.com
www.xpressyourselfpublishing.com

ISBN: 978-0-9852484-9-9 (paperback)

Library of Congress Control Number: 2024938764

First Xpress Yourself Publishing trade paperback printing June 2024
10 9 8 7 6 5 4 3 2 1

Editing, Book Cover, and Interior Design by:
TWA Solutions & Services
www.twasolutions.com

Ordering Information:
Our books may be purchased in bulk for promotional, educational, or business use. Please contact us at publisher@xpressyourselfpublishing.com.

Worldwide Distribution by:
Ingram Content Group
www.ingramcontent.com

Acknowledgments

When I began writing this book in 2015, its title was *Trespassing*. My rough draft was far from perfect, and I nearly abandoned it—several times. Honestly, I was ready to give up.

However, two people refused to allow me to do so. Their input proved to be a turning point. Bill Holmes and Ann Jeffries—thank you, thank you, thank you! Your suggestions were invaluable, helping me refine the manuscript into something that felt like a book and showed my growth as a writer.

Your encouragement and insights were crucial in bringing this story to life, and I am deeply grateful for your unwavering support. This book is as much yours as it is mine. Thank you for believing in me and in *Indiscretions*.

I'd also like to acknowledge Cinnamon, Chelsea, Chanel, and Piccachu—my beloved furbabies. Thank you for keeping me company during my late-night writing sessions. Your gentle snores and dream-induced twitches under my desk were music to my ears, providing comfort and companionship throughout the process. Your presence made those long hours more enjoyable and less lonely.

To you—the one holding this book—thank you for reading my books over the past twenty-four years! Your support means more to me than words can express. I appreciate you more than you will ever know.

Love,
JT
May 23, 2024
2:03 p.m., EST

ALSO BY JESSICA TILLES

**Raven Ward Series
(in paperback and ebook)**
Anything Goes
Sweet Revenge
Unfinished Business

**The Howard Sisters Series
(in paperback and ebook)**
In My Sisters' Corner
Crossing Sisters

**Standalone Books
(in paperback and ebook)**
Apple Tree
Fatal Desire
Loving Simone
Loving You
Native New York
(with Adrienne Lilliette Harris)

**e-Short
(in ebook only)**
No One Has To Know
(with William Fredrick Cooper)

**Anthology
(in paperback and ebook)**
Erogenous Zone

On Audiobook
Loving You, narrated by Kelley Hazen
Loving Simone, narrated by Kelley Hazen

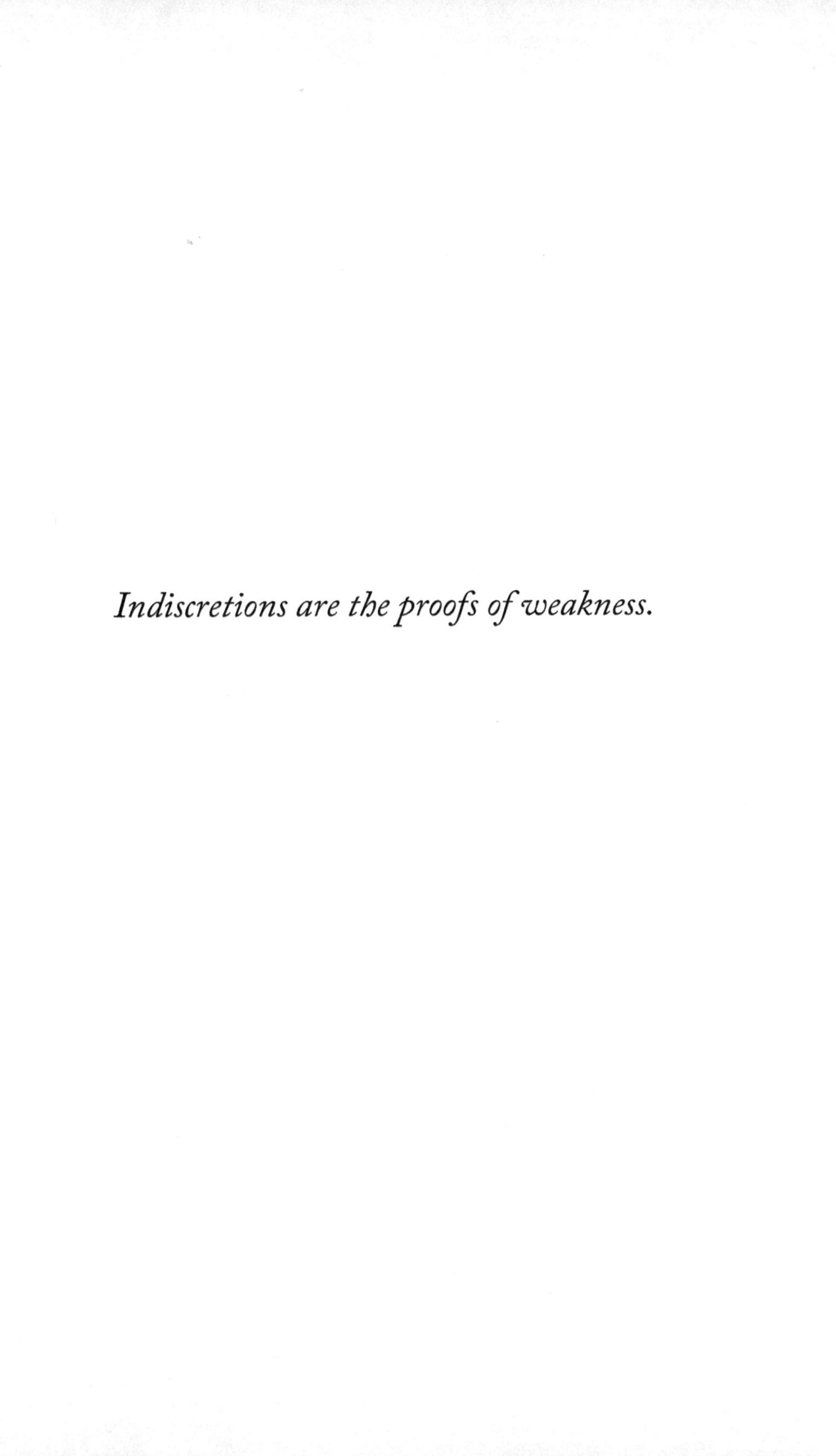

Indiscretions are the proofs of weakness.

PROLOGUE

Entering the dimly lit pub, she exuded an undeniable beauty. Flowing chestnut tresses cascaded down her back in gentle waves with curled ends, complementing her ivory complexion perfectly. Azure blue eyes twinkled, while her high cheekbones and full lips formed a soft, welcoming smile.

Gliding gracefully through the room, the knee-length hem of the floral print Diane von Furstenberg wrap dress swayed as leather peep-toe platform heels emitted a soft click with each step, turning the heads of the few men sipping drinks.

With a pleasant and inviting expression, the bartender turned toward the approaching woman, a friendly smile stretching across his face. The sparkle in his eyes twinkled with anticipation, ready to offer a delightful experience. Pausing for a moment to observe her presence, as she hiked her curvy hip on the swivel stool, the bartender spoke in a congenial tone. "What can I get for you?"

Behind the counter, a symphony of bottles stood tall against a wall-to-wall mirror, showcasing an array of spirits waiting to be crafted into delectable concoctions.

Tucking the strands of her hair behind her ear, she warmly smiled. "Cabernet Sauvignon."

Observing her surroundings, her gaze landed on a man seated at the bar a few stools away.

His wide shoulders relaxed as piercing hazel eyes complemented his butter biscuit brown complexion. He had an alluring ruggedness about him with a neatly trimmed beard and stylishly tapered dark hair. The fitted black Lacoste polo shirt hugged his muscular frame, paired with beige khakis.

As he sipped from the snifter, the tendons in his forearms flexed. His self-assured demeanor and magnetic presence exuded an aura of quiet power.

While he was sitting there, lost in his thoughts, she dismounted her stool, nodded toward the bartender, and moved toward him, taking the stool next to him.

He observed her features and offered a polite smile, revealing a row of pearly white straight teeth. Experiencing a flutter in her chest, her heart skipped a beat, and she looked away, feeling a blush creeping up her spine.

Setting the drink on the smooth surface, the bartender presented it with a sense of pride. With a warm grin, he gestured toward the beverage, inviting her to indulge. As a final gesture to their brief interaction, he casually flung the white towel over his shoulder, an emblem of his expertise and attentiveness. The bartender then gracefully stepped away, leaving her to savor the drink and the man beside her.

With a sideways glance, the stranger leaned over and struck up a conversation, asking her about herself and making her laugh with his witty comments. As the hours passed, they drank more and talked more, and shared stories.

As she spoke, her voice was reminiscent of music, smooth and melodic. Her radiant laughter flooded him with joy and warmth. He couldn't resist being drawn to her, captivated by her beauty and charm.

More than simply another pretty face, she had a kind heart and a sharp mind. Her range of conversation went from her beloved bulldog and peaked to the highest level of politics. Her demeanor caused him to feel comfortable in her presence, a sensation he'd previously experienced with someone else.

"I Wanna Be Closer" by Switch was the musical backdrop for this impromptu rendezvous. The lights dimmed more, casting everything in a subtle, romantic glow. With her eyes closed, she swayed and pursed her lips. She opened her eyes to see him staring at her.

"I love this song. Want to dance?"

He shrugged. "Sure."

Leaning, she extended her hand, palm up, and gazed up into his eyes.

Glancing down at her turned-up palm, he smiled. This was a first. With an inner chuckle, he placed his palm on hers and she led him to the middle of the empty dance floor.

The soft strains of the 1978 romantic ballad filled the room as they swayed, pressed close, falling into a gentle rhythm that felt as natural as breathing.

His hands were strong and warm as they encircled her waist, pulling her in closer. She felt his breath on her neck as he leaned in, and she shivered with pleasure. His scent was intoxicating, a heady mixture of cologne and cognac that made her vagina moist.

As they swayed, moving in perfect sync, she felt a sense of peace wash over her. The world outside faded away as they lost themselves in music—in each other.

He whispered sweet nothings in her ear, his voice low and husky, sending shivers throughout her. She turned her head to look up at him, and their eyes met, each gazing deeply into the other's soul. She parted her lips. He did not partake in tasting them. She felt a moment of disappointment.

The dance was languid. As the song ended, he held her close, and they continued to sway, unwilling to break the spell. The air grew thick with anticipation as they basked in a silent exchange of desire. They had been flirting all evening, and the tension between them had grown almost unbearable.

Stroking his back, her hands moved down to his buttocks, causing him to kiss her with a hunger that took her breath away. She responded to him, her heart racing as his hands roamed over her waist, down to her round bottom, caressing and squeezing. It was like nothing she had ever felt before, a mixture of passion and tenderness that left her dizzy with pleasure, and a moist panty crotch.

The world around them fell away as they lost themselves in the feelings, entwined in a dance of desire. The kiss was a revelation, a reminder that this was what it meant to be truly alive.

Looking into each other's eyes, she knew she had met someone special who made her feel alive, wanted, and desired.

With a tilt of her head and a frisky smile, she entwined her fingers in his and led him out of the bar and to the bank of elevators at the Hyatt Regency, as he watched her hips tease him with every sway. After she pressed the call button, they stood side-by-side, holding hands, him stroking her palm. The heat between her thighs was growing into a raging fire. She wanted him—badly.

He wanted her, too, as the throb in his groin was tightening and needed a release.

When the elevator doors opened, they hurried inside, frantically groping each other before the doors could close. He slipped his hand under her dress and eased his finger inside her panty, playing with her moisture. *Damn*, he thought, as he was hard as concrete. He had one thing on his mind: blow her back out—nothing more, nothing less.

Clinging to each other for support, the pair stumbled out of the elevator, down the corridor, and into her hotel room. After having their fill of libations, they were beyond inebriation and feeling one another.

Almost unbearable was the prolonged anticipation, as they stumbled toward the bed, collapsing in a heap, fondling and kissing until he couldn't hold back any longer. Standing, he pulled up her dress and ripped off her panty.

The room was spinning, and she felt as though she were on a merry-go-round, watching him unharness his beast, his pants dropping to the floor. Her mouth fell open at the sight of the gargantuan penis. *Wowser*, she thought as he looked into her eyes, lay on top of her, pushed her thighs back, impaled her wetness, and began punishing her cave—humping and pounding with vigorous force. No kissing. No hugging. Straight sex. As the urge built inside him to explode inside her, he stiffened, released a deep growl, then his seeds, and rolled over onto his back.

Panting, he rubbed his abdomen, looking up at the ceiling. "Damn, I needed that."

She stared at the ceiling. "I didn't come."

"No?"

"No."

He rolled over onto his side and pulled up on his elbow. "Well, we can't have that now, can we?"

She remained quiet.

He leaned in, tongue-stroked her neck, and vigorously rubbed his middle finger against her clitoris as if starting a forest fire until she came so hard that he quickly covered her mouth to keep the entire eleventh floor from hearing her cry of ecstasy.

Sitting on the edge of the bed, he looked at the digital clock on the nightstand: 1:35 a.m. "I need to get some sleep." He stood, picked up his trousers, and ambled toward the bathroom. He flipped on the light and stepped inside.

She looked up at the ceiling, unsure of how she felt. This was the first time in her life, she'd had a one-night stand, especially with someone years younger than she. However, she hoped for more. She was really digging him.

"You're welcome to stay here."

He turned on the water, washed his hands, and rinsed out his mouth. He pulled a clean washcloth from the metal rack on the wall, wet it, and cleaned himself up.

"Thanks, but I'm good."

"Will I see you later?"

After putting on his pants and adjusting his clothes, he exited the bathroom and moved toward the bed.

She stood up and stroked his back. "Will I see you again, baby?"

Baby? He smiled with an inner chuckle.

She smiled. "How about breakfast in the morning?"

"I can't."

"Well, lunch, maybe dinner?"

He twisted up his mouth, as if in contemplation, and then shook his head. "You get some rest." He pivoted and walked toward the door. He faced her, blew her a kiss, and walked out of the room, allowing the door to close behind him.

Well, damn. With her head still spinning, and feeling a headache coming on, she pulled back the covers, climbed into bed, and felt some kind of way—like a prostitute who'd given up the goods to a customer at no charge.

The next morning, she awoke to a bright new day, hung over and feeling a hot mess. She was not ready to face whatever challenges lay ahead. Thinking about the handsome man who had bedded her hours earlier, she desperately wanted to see him again. She wouldn't mind a repeat performance, either.

Sitting on the edge of the bed, she thought of calling the front desk to inquire about him, then realized hotel policy would prohibit it.

Heavily sighing, she stood up and padded to the bathroom, silently beating herself up for sleeping with a stranger, with no protection.

Exiting the bathroom, she turned on the television and moved toward the bed, her eyes casting downward.

"What's that?"

Bending down, she picked it up and opened it.

A smile grew on her face. Happy as a lark, she sat down and perused his wallet: credit card, debit card, an upcoming appointment card for the doctor, and—her brows rose. *What's this?* A small photo of a beautiful woman who looked to be in her early twenties. *Sister maybe? He didn't mention a wife, and I saw no ring. Oh well.* She tossed the wallet on the nightstand.

Using the complimentary pad and pen on the desk, she noted the details from his driver's license. After showering and dressing, she gathered her things and left out of the room, heading for the lobby.

The front desk clerk saw her approaching. She wreathed a smile as bright as the sun. "Good morning."

She returned the smile, but not as bright, and set the wallet on the counter. "Will you please see he gets this? He left it in my room last night." With the tilt of her head, she winked, pivoted, and walked to the door, exiting the hotel.

CHAPTER 1

Twenty-one years later...

From the curly bush nestled between powerful thighs, his masculinity beckoned her. Malcolm Linton Ellis stood in the pocket doorway to the en suite bathroom leading to the master bedroom he shared with his wife, Kennedy Rhodes Ellis. Fresh from the shower, as he approached her, the hungry fire in his eyes matched her equally aroused smile.

Kennedy could not help but smirk and look into his hazel eyes as her bosom heaved behind the periwinkle silk and lace negligee hanging off her shoulder.

Their love flight took off several hours earlier and had yet to descend. After he tongue-stroked her top lip, she eyed the love of her life from the top of his thick, curly head to his strong, bare feet. She exhaled. Everything about him she adored—his natural smell because he was passionate about what he consumed, his sweet breath, the softness of his skin. It all drove her insane. Basking in the warmth of his embrace and resting her head on his broad shoulder, with his muscular arms encircling her, was her favorite pastime.

Sexy and confident in her skin, and despite a slight belly bulge, body dimples, and stretch marks afforded to a seasoned, five-foot-seven-inch woman, Kennedy possessed an insatiable libido. Early morning, four-mile runs with Malcolm kept her toned. They met their freshman year at Columbia University, and he was the sexiest man in the world then, and her feelings remained unchanged. Early in their relationship, Malcolm learned to push her buttons the right way. Twenty years of marriage, and she was still in love with Malcolm. He gave her butterflies each time she set eyes on him. There was a craving in her belly for him that had never left since college. To everyone who knew them, their love and friendship were the embodiment of marriage. Though many men have tried, their attempts to distract her from the man she loved were futile.

Malcolm stopped short of her mouth, the mushroom head of his tool gracing the fullness of the lips that only an hour ago welcomed his shaft. When they were dating, she exhibited oral skills that were unmatched, and nothing had changed. She knew how to make his toes curl each time she sucked seeds from his sack.

Eyes lowered, with puckered lips, she craved rest, but the tensing of her jaw betrayed her building frustration. It was routine for her to fellate him at a moment's notice, but it was time for the changing of the guard. Malcolm needed to revisit the South with an extended stay, to tickle, tease, and drink from her fountain.

Failing to see her hesitancy, he smiled and caressed the back of her head. "Taste it, babe." The corner of his mouth formed a sexy smirk, his hazel eyes peering into her brown ones.

He was irresistible, but Kennedy pursed her lips and shook her head. Rolling her eyes upward, she was not giving any more oral gratification. Hell, she had met her quota for the night. She wagged her finger at him and tilted her head. He needed to catch up, and he had a long way to go. She reclined on the bed and raised her legs, spreading them apart, her toes pointed, as her center called out to him. Pouting, she mocked him with a smile. "Taste it, *babe*."

Beaming, he relished the games they played. Enjoying the challenge and eager to comply, Malcolm lowered to his knees, meeting her center. Casting his eyes upon her flesh, he pressed his palms against her inner thighs, pushing them wide as her knees touched hour shoulders; he loved her flexibility. She still had it. His tongue, long and wide, hid behind the straightest row of pearly whites only a dentist could appreciate. Leaning closer, he inhaled, her natural essence marinating in his nostrils.

He licked his lips. Anticipating tongue-to-clitoris caused Kennedy to shiver. Wanting to make sure his animated creature delivered ecstasy and connected perfectly with her, she pressed her manicured fingers against her full vaginal lips, exposing something delectable and always delicious to Malcolm.

He looked up at her and smiled. "Oh, now that's a beautiful picture."

Winking at him, with her index finger, she pulled back the tender flesh. "I think my portrait needs its paintbrush, sweetie." Her excitement building, she would surely climax from expectancy alone, as she felt a pending explosion building behind her fleshy mound.

Malcolm licked beneath the fleshy hood, savoring the salty sweetness of his wife. Wanting to arouse every nerve in her, the fluid flickering of his lively lizard grew into sucking and nibbling.

Whew, shit, she thought, moaning. Circling her hips to match the tempo of his tongue, she loved his guttural sounds as he dined in her drenched forest. To her, that meant he wanted to experience her orgasmic contractions just as much as she did.

Knowing every trick in the cunnilingus handbook, Malcolm used indirect stimulation of her heaven by rubbing his chin against her entrance, driving her crazy. Next, his nose descended upon her, as that talented tongue swirled in a circular motion at the space between her honey spot and the anus.

As he loved her labia, involuntary wails left his woman, who pled for even more pleasure. Eyes rolling back in her head, Kennedy went crazy.

Wanting to form words, to tell him she loved him, and she wanted more of what he was giving her, was so hard to do as Malcolm locked his lips on her triangle, mixing magical movement with munching; the object at his brim fluttered out of control as he moved from cunny-to-clit-to-cunny.

"*Ooh*, Malcolm, please don't stop."

Spiraling into a place where panting met colors and sounds, a series of climatic convulsions escaped her. Grinding hard and steady against his mouth, the momentum had Kennedy writhing as she flinched and shivered from an orgasmic burst comparable to a spaceship blasting off for orbit. Sensuous sensations shot through her as she tried to resist the oh-so-wonderful feeling, but Malcolm's oral persistence had her pounding the mattress as she reached the summit of sexual satisfaction. Quivering and quaking, she stifled a scream as her waterfall cascaded over his chin.

Releasing her triangle, Malcolm planted several soft kisses on her inner thigh and excused himself from her staggered breathing. He looked over his shoulder and winked at her. "We're not done."

Before Kennedy could question his actions, she peered at him as he disappeared into the bathroom. For two minutes, she heard running water, before he returned to her with a warm, soapy water basin. Now, leaning up on her elbows, Kennedy looked puzzled as she watched him place the items on the floor. Then, for the first time in recent memory, she saw his handsome face blush.

Malcolm's brow rose, and his lips pouted. "Can a good boy bathe the kitty?"

Now it was her turn to blush. How could she say no to the way he massaged her treasure, as he rubbed the warm, sudsy cloth between her thighs, reigniting her carnal impulses? She couldn't express no when he pecked her labia after gently cleansing it. No way would she deny her man after he cleaned her with precision and plunged his face into the most intimate part of her once more, doing things to her kitty he couldn't do to her mouth.

According to the sounds escaping his wife, she didn't mind his refueled appetite. Malcolm didn't just stay on the clitoris like he was mending a broken button, making her shudder and gyrate. He licked and probed every inch of her sexual territory; he wanted his honey to be warm, wet, and welcoming, ready for something bigger than his tongue, which was driving her insane.

Trembling, anticipating his hooked seven inches, she couldn't take his teasing. Malcolm kissed every inch of her gorgeous frame, then met his queen with an affectionate peck on the lips.

The building up to nirvana was driving Kennedy crazy. She eased her hand between their abdomens.

Malcolm moved her hand and shook his head. He did not need help. Smiling, her husband eased inside of her. Starting with shallow strokes, he made slow harmony with the eager gyrations of her hips.

Shrieking in delight, she marked her pleasure across his back with her fingernails.

Obliging her, from tip to thick, hooked shaft, their movements synchronized as their tongues tangoed.

Malcolm gyrated left, Kennedy right, and they met as one in the middle. Soon, their mutual joining turned into an unchained animality. Thrusting and retreating within her, Malcolm fought his arousal as she clamped her vaginal muscles around his member. His orgasm building, he slowed the tempo, then sped up once more, nearing nirvana.

Wanting to bring her over the edge and determined to see it, Malcolm kept stroking with vigor, and Kennedy loved it. As she studied his face with a look of love one second and muffled screams the next, another Earth-shattering orgasm spilled from her. Trembling as she leaned up to his mouth, she loved making him taste her tongue after her orgasm.

With a glassy-eyed look of rapture, she kissed him with all the passion she could find at that moment and tweaked his nipples.

Malcolm always peaked when she did this, and this time was no different. He panted, as unrepressed growls and ragged breaths had him shuddering when his hips stiffened, then loosened to prepare for his release. Grunting, he felt a thrill as four more warm spurts shot from his groin.

His orgasm brought yet another from Kennedy as her eyes closed, her back arching.

Finally, they both collapsed in bliss.

Leaning over her, sweat decorated his chest. "I love you, wife."

"I love you more, husband."

Exhausted, she rolled over onto her side, inching her rear end into her husband's groin. She, as well as her core, craved rest.

As the gentle morning sunlight poured through the expansive window, filling the room with warmth, Kennedy stirred beneath the covers, stretching her limbs. Propping herself up on her elbow, she leaned over and softly pressed a kiss on a sleeping Malcolm's cheek. Rising from the bed, she sat at its edge and raised her arms, interlocking her fingers and elongating her torso. With closed eyes, she inhaled deeply and rolled her neck, savoring the tranquility of the moment.

Following her customary routine, Kennedy padded across the oak wood floor as she retrieved her cell phone from the dresser. She slipped into the en suite bathroom and gently slid the pocket door shut. Standing before the full-length mirror, she admired the elegant curve of her hips that tapered into long, shapely legs. The fruits of her and Malcolm's daily runs were showing. Although running held little appeal for her, she willingly supported her husband's endeavors. Malcolm's passion for scuba diving prompted her to hold her breath, both figuratively and literally, as she joined him in exploring the ocean's depths. Similarly, she knew Malcolm would reciprocate her support. She reminisced about the time when she yearned to take belly dancing lessons, and to her surprise, Malcolm set aside his reservations, wearing a cropped top and belly beads, and undulating his abdomen with the finesse of Shakira in a room filled with women. It was a testament to their unwavering commitment to each other.

Seated on the toilet, she positioned herself comfortably with her knees bent and toes touching. As she attended to her personal needs, she activated Siri on her device.

"Hey, Siri, call Zora."

Calling Zora mobile.

Turning onto her side, Zora extended her arm and retrieved her ringing cell phone, promptly answering the call. There was no need to glance at the caller ID since there was only one person who would reach out to her at such an early hour—her beloved best friend.

"Morning, sis."

Kennedy smirked. "Girl, I don't think I've had thirty minutes of sleep, and—"

"Y'all are just nasty."

Kennedy burst into laughter, and in her amusement, she quickly covered her mouth to stifle the sound, not wanting to wake Malcolm. "Girl, hush."

"Y'all be humping twenty-four-seven?"

"Listen to the pot calling the kettle black!"

Zora giggled like a schoolgirl, which was how she felt each time she talked to her bestie. "I know, right? We just finished."

"See!" Kennedy shook her head. "Slut!"

"Listen, pole hoe, I have to get it when I can." Zora looked over her shoulder at Maceo Hicks, her devoted companion of ten years, snoring beside her.

Kennedy frowned. "Wow, is that Maceo?"

"You can hear him?"

"Honey, yes. Get that man a C-pap, like yesterday! Sounds like a goddamn bear in hibernation."

"Well, he is exhausted." Zora beamed with pride that she had sexed him into a deep sleep. "So, sis, today is the day, huh?"

A resounding sigh escaped Kennedy as emotion welled in her throat. "Yes. I'm going to miss my baby."

"I will, too. I'll miss all the eye-rolling, sass talk—"

"Now that, I won't miss!"

In perfect harmony, the sister-friends erupted into soft laughter. They shared striking similarities. While Zora boasted a slightly taller stature by a few inches, both possessed lustrous dark auburn hair, untouched by any trace of gray, with elegant facial features, particularly their full, alluring lips.

Zora's physique exuded a noticeable tone and definition, thanks to regular visits to LA Fitness. In contrast, Kennedy's body had a different build. However, their fashion preferences aligned closely, and they shared a mutual love for hand dancing at the VFW Lodge.

Ever since their high school days, Kennedy and Zora had been inseparable. Graduating with honors, Zora pursued her education at Howard University, where she graduated cum laude, with a bachelor's in management, while Kennedy excelled at Columbia University, graduating magna cum laude, with a bachelor's in engineering, further solidifying their impressive academic achievements.

Competition had always been an underlying theme in Zora's life. When Kennedy completed her college education, her parents pleasantly surprised her with a candy-apple red BMW 318i. To outshine Kennedy, Zora accumulated debt to gain her own candy-apple red BMW 850i. Deep down, Zora nurtured a silent desire to outperform Kennedy in various aspects of life, or so she believed.

Kennedy was acutely aware of Zora's persistent desire to surpass her, yet she ignored it. Embracing unconditional love and the ability to acknowledge and appreciate the goodness in others, Kennedy cherished Zora not only as her closest friend but as a sister. Her mother had instilled in her the wisdom that jealousy and envy lived within everyone.

With a sigh, Zora rose from the bed and slid her feet into red and white two-toned faux-fur slippers. She made her way toward the bedroom door. However, before her foot could cross the threshold, Maceo stirred beneath the sheets and patted the space beside him. "Hey, love?"

Zora moved the phone away from her mouth. "I'm here, baby. On the phone with Kennedy. I'll be back."

"Yes, she'll be back, you horn dog." Kennedy turned on the multi-head shower and adjusted the water temperature to her liking. "He sure loves your dirty panties; worse than a puppy dog sitting at your feet while you pee. Won't leave your side for a hot minute."

Smirking, Zora rolled her eyes. "I hear you talking, kettle. What time are y'all leaving?"

"Soon."

"What time will you be back?"

"I don't know."

"Well, you think y'all will stay overnight?"

"What's with the questions, Zee?"

"Shut up, just asking."

"I'll call you when we get back. Is that better?"

"Yes. You know I worry about you."

"I don't know why. You know Malcolm will let nothing happen to me."

"That's true. Kind of like that little puppy dog that sits at your feet and won't let you wipe your ass in peace."

"*Ha-ha!* I can't stand you sometimes, pot."

"Ditto, kettle. Let's have lunch when you get back. I need sister time."

"I would love that. Is everything all right?"

"Yes, everything is fine. It's just been a while since I've seen my sissy."

"Okay, we'll do lunch."

"Great. Love you, girl. Y'all drive safe."

"Love you, too. We will."

Ending the call and placing the cell phone on the luxurious marble vanity, Kennedy piled her thick tresses on the crown of her head and wrapped a towel around it like a turban. Stepping into the glass-encased shower, water cascaded over her, spraying from all directions.

Smiling, Kennedy remembered the first time she talked to then-fifteen-year-old Lindsay about avoiding sexual encounters on the night she attended the high school pep rally. It had been an uncomfortable dialogue, but she believed it was necessary and ultimately effective. Lindsay was now heading off to college, with her innocence intact. The recollection of Lindsay's teen years brought forth a chuckle from Kennedy. Perhaps she had been strict with her daughter, but it was her way of ensuring Lindsay didn't end up young, pregnant, and uneducated. Kennedy wanted her daughter to embrace the wondrous adventures of life. She longed for Lindsay to live life boldly and on her own terms. Traveling and experiencing the world were among the desires Kennedy had held for her daughter. She yearned to provide Lindsay with everything her heart desired and more. As she contemplated the remarkable young woman she and Malcolm had raised, Kennedy couldn't contain her happiness as she broke out in song. "She'll be living her life like it's golden! Yeah, yeah!"

Once finished with her shower, she delicately dried herself off and slipped into a soft white terrycloth robe, ensuring the belt was snug around her waist. Discarding the towel, she finger-combed her hair, gently massaging the scalp. *An appointment at the salon with Siggy is in order*, she reminded herself.

As she stepped over the bedroom threshold, Malcolm's eyes lit up with a smile. He sat propped against the headboard with his hands interlocked behind his head.

"Good morning, beautiful."

She pursed her lips and blew him a kiss. "Hey, sunshine."

He patted the space beside him.

Smirking, she side-eyed him, shook her head, and rolled her eyes. "It won't take long."

She moved into her dressing room. "That's what you always say. Anyway, we've got to get on the road."

Fixing his gaze on the digital clock perched on the nightstand, Malcolm let out a sigh. "Yeah, I guess you're right."

Peering around the doorjamb, she smiled at her husband. "I know for certain I am right."

"Do we have time for a run?"

Within the expansive master suite's enormous modern closet, characterized by gender-neutral beige tones, wall-to-wall white cabinetry with brushed chrome handles, and elegantly curved bullnose drawer and door fronts, she removed her robe and carefully hung it on a chrome hook on the back of the door. Moving toward the central marble-topped dressing island, she retrieved a tube of Elizabeth Arden's Sunflower lotion. Squeezing out a quarter-sized amount into her palm, she massaged the fragrant lotion into her skin, relishing the rejuvenating sensation and fragrance it provided.

"Do we, babe?"

Slipping into a pair of well-fitted khaki pants and a crisp white button-down cotton shirt, she complemented her attire with a pair of beige and brown-trimmed Coach slip-on shoes. Making her way toward the bedroom door, she paused, leaning against the doorjamb. Folding her arms across her chest, she tilted her head. "No, we can't squeeze in a run. I'll meet you downstairs for breakfast." Blowing him a kiss, she swiftly pivoted out of the bedroom, traversed the hallway, and descended the back staircase, heading straight for the kitchen.

CHAPTER 2

Now standing in the doorway of her bedroom, Zora watched Maceo pull back the covers, exposing his hardened phallus with a full smile on his face. With a devilish smirk, she said not a word as she sauntered to the bed, climbed on it, straddled her man, and lowered onto his beckoning steel. She palmed his chest and tweaked his nipples, causing his hips to react, pumping into her, bucking her with each thrust. She loved it, and she loved him.

Peering into her eyes, Maceo gripped the hips of the woman he'd loved for ten years and enjoyed his flesh inside the soft warmth of her. In Zora's presence, the Earth stopped still on its axis. There was no time, no wind, no rain. His mind was at peace around her. She was his peace.

Peering into his eyes and determined not to orgasm, Zora bit down on her bottom lip. Even though Maceo was bringing her closer to the edge, she refused to let him push her off the cliff. She wanted them to orgasm together. The harder he stroked, the harder she tweaked his nipples.

"Jesus, Zora!"

As if on cue, she kissed his open mouth and humped him until he cried out her name and his throat dried like the Sahara Desert. It was a wonderful hard thing driving inside her core, feeling it bathed in her juices, and as he drilled up inside her, sending ecstasy washing through her, chills of a pending explosion coursed through them both. Maceo's thrusts came faster, and she, too, cried out as her breasts pressed against his muscular chest, his lips against her lips, their bodies molding together.

She raised her hips, eased off of him, and rolled over onto the bed. Turning to his side, with her back to him, he spooned his woman and finger-stroked her belly button.

He nuzzled his nose into her neck and gently kissed her on the shoulder. "Damn, you wore a brother out."

She chuckled.

With his face buried in the back of her head, he loved the smell of her hair. "I love you, Zee."

Zora nibbled the inside of her mouth. Torn between the desires of her conscience and the sentiments of her heart, she found herself at odds. Though she loved Maceo, she grappled with the realization that loving him and being truly in love with him were two distinct realms altogether.

She closed her eyes and thought of someone else. A smile grew on her face. "Ditto."

Zora was fast asleep, as Maceo lay in bed staring up at the ceiling. The only sound was the faint ticking of his old clock on the bedside table. He couldn't sleep. His mind was racing with thoughts and worries that refused to let him rest. He didn't know what he would do if anything happened to his Zora.

As he lay there, Maceo thought about his life and all the choices he had made. Mainly, moving from his hometown, New Orleans, Louisiana, to be with the woman he loved.

With a smile on his face, Maceo took a trip down memory lane. Admittedly, he was feeling quite cocky that day when he saw her across the quaint restaurant.

Daisy Mae's Southern Fried Chicken & Breakfast in downtown New Orleans swelled with loyal diners. Oblivious to all, Zora sashayed into the establishment, with a briefcase in hand, a Lorra Rivers satchel hung over her shoulder, and her head held high. The day before her travel to the Big Easy, she had her shoulder-length tresses chopped short, tapered, colored a rich, glowing auburn, and easy-breezy. She was in love with the new look her stylist of twenty years, Siggy, had given her. Sitting her purse and *The New Orleans Tribune* on the table, before setting the briefcase on the floor, she removed the black Elie Tahari single button blazer, exposing toned arms, a fitted white ribbed knit wrap cross sleeveless top, with booty-

and hip-hugging white slacks. Resting the blazer on the back of the chair, she smoothed her hands over her hips and eased down onto the chair, gracefully crossing one leg over the other. She lightly feathered her hair, stroking the back of her head; the hairstyle was so punk rock, a little spiked at the top, but she loved it.

Before she could catch her breath, the young woman approached her table. She looked like Pippi Longstocking—the fictional main character in an eponymous series of children's books by Swedish author Astrid Lindgren—with red hair in two pigtails and freckles. Her ivory face had a musk-rose flush on the cheekbones, her lips pouty, and her eyes sparkled like Caribbean water.

"Good morning!" She smiled at Zora, bright-eyed, with pen and pad in hand. "I'm Lizzy. I'll be your server today. Can I start you off with something to drink?"

Zora looked up, smiled, and nodded. "Yes. Coffee, please, Lizzy." Though Zora had noticed the young woman darting from table to table, she didn't appear weary.

"Coming right up." She rushed off to the next table.

Zora pulled her iPad from the briefcase and turned it on. She eyed the small diner, taking in the New Orleans paraphernalia covering every inch of wall space.

"All right, here we go." Lizzy set the cup brimming with hot java on the table, startling Zora, who whipped her head around to face the Pippi lookalike.

"Oh, that was quick. Thanks." Zora picked up the menu and quickly perused it.

"So, do you need a minute, or do you know what you're having?"

"I'll have the alligator omelet with fried green tomatoes on the side, and an unsweetened iced tea, please."

"Excellent choice."

"I've never had alligator."

"No? You're not from here, are you?"

Zora chuckled. "You can tell?"

With a shrug, she smiled. "Most folks from here eat alligator."

"Oh, yeah, well, I'm from Maryland. We eat crab, shrimp, and Alaskan crab legs. Alligator is not on our menus."

"Welcome to the Big Easy. How long are you here for?"

"Just for the weekend."

"Make sure you go to the French Quarter."

"Yes, I plan to."

"Alrighty, I'll put in your order. Be back shortly."

Zora pulled her earbuds from her purse. As she pressed them into her ear canals, and as if on cue, her FaceTime rang on her cell phone. She accepted the video and smiled.

"Hey, bestie!"

Kennedy beamed at her best friend. "Hi, honey—oh my God, Zora, you cut your hair!"

Nodding, Zora held up the phone as if she were looking into a mirror, turning her head from left to right, posing. "What do you think? You like it?"

"I love it! It definitely takes ten years off you. Is that Siggy's handiwork?"

"Yep, and honey, I need all the years back I can get." They both laughed.

Kennedy leaned into her phone as if she were trying to come through it. "Where are you, and who is that behind you?"

Zora's brows furrowed. "Well, I'm at this quaint spot, Daisy Mae's, about to have breakfast, and who are you looking at behind me?"

"Girl, that fine dude looking at the back of your head."

Zora started to turn.

"No! Don't turn around."

"Why not?"

"Then he'll know we're talking about him."

With an eye roll, she smirked. "Ken, really? Okay, I won't look. So, what do you want?"

Kennedy frowned. "Eww, don't be unkind, Zora. Just checking on you to see how you're doing."

"Sorry, don't mean to be unkind, sis. I'm good. I haven't had the chance to visit the city much, and I'm leaving tomorrow. The waitress here told me to visit the French Quarter, so—"

"I don't know, Zora. You're there alone. Do you think you should traipse all over the city by yourself?"

"Well, no, you're right. Maybe I can get someone from the conference to go with me."

"Or you could get Mr. Fine-As-Wine, who can't keep his eyes off you, to go with you."

"A stranger?"

"Girl, you need dick in your life!"

Thank God for earbuds, Zora thought. "How about I call you tonight and we can talk about that, okay?"

"I'll be here. Let me know how it goes with Mr. Fine-As-Wine."

Zora rolled her eyes. "Girl, I ain't paying that dude no mind."

Kennedy sucked her teeth. "Girl, you're single. Get your feet wet in the Big Easy!"

"Bye, girl, bye!"

Kennedy chuckled. "Talk later, chick! Love you."

"Love you more."

Smiling with an inward chuckle, she ended the call and set the iPhone on the table, picked up the iPad, and checked her email and social media. Her friendship with Kennedy had been the best relationship of her life. As long as she had her bestie, she didn't need a man.

As if her eyes could roll around to the back of her head, Zora tried her best to see the man behind her, without turning around. *This is silly*, she thought, shaking her head.

However, he couldn't take his eyes off her. Sitting with elbows on the table, and a coffee cup to his lips, Maceo's eyes roamed Zora's curvy figure. A smile graced his full lips. That she could sit alone in a full establishment told him she was confident of being alone, which was a trait he liked in a woman. He peered at her voluptuous rump that filled the wooden chair with no overlap. Biting his bottom lip, he liked what he saw. He wasn't like most men he knew, who couldn't be with a woman unless her hair flowed down her back. He loved her short haircut. *Kudos to her stylist*, he thought as a tingle shot through his groin.

Looking up and turning, Zora scanned the venue. Their eyes connected. She bit her bottom lip. He smiled and nodded toward her. Her heart skipped a beat. Something about the stranger stole her breath. His beautiful caramel skin looked smooth and flawless. His curly textured hair waved around the perimeter of his perfectly round head. He was the finest specimen she'd seen since she landed in New Orleans to be the keynote speaker at the 10th Annual Black Professional Women's Conference.

Maceo, who favored the actor Colman Domingo, rose with a cup in hand and maneuvered through the table of diners toward Zora. She watched him. His swagger was smooth as Tennessee whiskey. His smile was as bright as the rising sun.

Towering over her, he relaxed his stance. "Hey."

Feeling his presence, even though she saw him coming her way, she pulled her earbuds out. "Hey."

He nodded at the vacant seat at her table. "May I?"

Pondering his request, there was an initial apprehension. After all, she didn't know this man from Adam. Alas, she relaxed her posture and smiled. "Sure."

Pulling back the chair, he set the cup on the table, nodded at the server for another refill, slowly sat down, leaned on the table, and clasped his hands. "So, where are you from?"

She blushed and shook her head. "Is it that obvious?"

He nodded, with a slight hand gesture. "It's okay." He took a long pause and peered into her eyes, losing himself completely. For a moment, it was the most wonderful feeling in the world for him. Clearing her throat, she broke into his short daydream fantasy about her. He extended his hand, palm up. "Maceo Hicks."

Eyeing his palm, she wasn't sure what she should do. His hand was large and would surely cover hers. *You know what they say about men with huge hands*, she thought, as she eyed the gorgeous specimen from foot to head. *Have mercy.*

Feeling awkward staring at him, but unable to redirect her stare, her eyes wandered below his waist. His worn denim hugged his thighs and caressed his bulge. *Damn.* Smiling, dirty thoughts were running rampant in her head.

Noticing her eyes undressing him, his smile was warm and inviting, giving her a warm and fuzzy feeling.

Embarrassed, Zora looked down at her iPad and closed her eyes. *What an idiot. I may as well hang a sign on my forehead that reads: desperate.*

"So, you're just going to leave me hanging?"

She placed her tiny hand in his. "Zora."

"Hi, Zora. It's nice to meet you. Now, I gave you a last name."

"Well, I don't know you."

"I don't know you either, but I gave you mine."

"Vaughn."

He watched her mouth as her name fell effortlessly from her lips. "Where are you from, Zora Vaughn?"

"Maryland."

"Well, Zora Vaughn from Maryland, you're stunning."

He's really pouring it on thick. Just when she thought she had come across a nice guy, he ended up being a simple game player. Zora's demeanor changed from bashful to not-in-the-mood. She smirked at him. "Not today."

"Corny, right?"

"Right."

Lizzy returned to the table with Maceo's coffee refill. "What can I get you, Maceo?"

"I'll have whatever she's having."

"The alligator omelet with a side of fried green tomatoes and an unsweetened iced tea?"

Zora looked up at the young waitress. "Aww, you remembered. Any chance I'll be getting that soon?"

Lizzy smiled at Zora. "Yes, it's up now. Let me grab it for you."

As she was walking away, Maceo changed his mind and called out to her. "Lizzy, I'll have my regular instead."

"Okay, got it!"

Zora placed her iPad on the table.

"Listen, I'll stop beating around the bush. I believe in being upfront. This way there will be no confusion and if you want to roll with it, then cool."

"I beg your pardon?"

"I find you sexy. I want to make love to you."

Zora broke into hysterical laughter. "Yes, you're corny and full of shit."

"You obviously find me attractive because your eyes damn near pierced a hole through my crotch."

"You're okay. I mean, you look okay." She chuckled, her eyes freezing on the smile that formed his beautiful, thick lips. He was a sight to behold, that's for sure. That smile, shining brighter than a full moon. She was feeling a little froggish and was wondering what she'd get if she were to leap. It had been a while since her last sexual encounter, and his energy had ignited her pheromones. She had run down her last two double-A batteries, so her silver bullet was out of commission until she made her weekly visit to the Dollar Tree. "So, let me see if I understand what you're proposing. You don't know me, know nothing about me, and you want to have sex with me? I may have leprosy."

"No, I don't want to have sex with you. I want to make love to you. I seriously doubt the leprosy part, although anything's possible."

She sipped her now lukewarm coffee. "There's no difference."

"Oh, there's a difference between having sex and making love."

"Yes, except you don't love me. So, it would be sex."

"I don't need to love you to make love to you. Besides, 'having sex' is so impersonal. Don't you think?"

There were touches of humor around his mouth and near his intriguing eyes. Twenty years earlier, she would've jumped his bones without so much as a blink. However, these days, she wasn't jumping on anything without a few tests and a thick-ass condom.

Zora leaned back in the chair and rested her elbow on the back of the seat. "So, uh…what do I get in return? How are you going to make me come?" She was willing to play his game because she had no intentions, whatsoever, of having sex, making love, fucking, screwing, or doing anything else with a man she just met.

"What you'll get in return is the best love you've ever had." He leaned closer, as what he had to saw was for her ears only. "The kind of love that will have your pussy twitching for days. The kind of love you will want over and over. The kind of love you won't have to pay for. The kind of love you can have forever, if you act right."

"Honey, you have no control over whether a woman falls in love. I don't even care about any of that—"

"Sure, you do."

Zora stood to her feet. "No, I don't. Now, if you'll excuse me." She grabbed her belongings.

"But you haven't had your breakfast."

Just then, Lizzy returned with both of their meals.

"Honey, I need that to go." Zora propped one hand on her hip.

"Listen, I'm sorry. Lizzy, set the plates down. We're going to stay and—"

"What the hell? Lizzy, what did I tell you?"

Poor Lizzy looked beyond confused and didn't want to be in the middle of whatever was happening.

Maceo stood and took the plates from Lizzy, who smiled and whisked away. "Zora, please, I apologize. Can we start over?"

Her heart was racing, not from fear, but from the anticipation of giving in to him. He had piqued her curiously, but it was silly. She wasn't in Maryland, on her home turf, where she knew the rules, and knew how and where to escape if she needed to do so. She was in New Orleans, Louisiana, and the only soul she knew at that moment was Maceo Hicks.

Zora sat down and gathered her composure. "I don't do that narcissist shit."

Ignoring her comment, Maceo sat their meals on the table and took his seat next to Zora. Lizzy returned with their drinks, silverware, and linen napkins.

"Thank you, Lizzy."

Zora remained quiet, picked up the silverware, and focused on the delicious omelet before her. After all, she was starving.

"Again, I'm sorry, Zora. I was out of line and—"

"Yes, you were, totally. A sister would prefer dinner, conversation, a few dates, an AIDS test, your mama's and daddy's first names, and anything else you can think of before you invite me into your bed. Your ass might have bedbugs."

"Ooh, feisty, just how I like it."

Zora stood up. "To hell with this meal. I don't need no damn alligator. Shit is probably nasty."

Maceo stood up, his appetite now ruined, reached into his pant pocket, pulled out a fifty-dollar-bill, and tossed it on the table. "I will not keep apologizing. I'll let you be. Take care, Zora. Enjoy New Orleans."

When Maceo turned to walk away, Zora opened her mouth, as if she were going to speak. Still standing, she watched as Maceo Hicks walked out of her life. She was interested, but he was coming on a little too strong for her taste. She had never experienced someone approaching her in such a manner, and it made her feel uncomfortable. Where she'd come from, men didn't just walk up and say, "I want to have sex with you." Well, not grown-ass men, anyway.

What the hell, she thought. She grabbed her things, pulled a fifty-dollar bill from her jacket pocket, and tossed it on the table.

As she exited Daisy Mae's, she saw him crossing the street. She called out to him over the passing traffic. "Can we start over, Maceo?"

He reached the other side of Poydras Street and turned toward her. "Yes, I would like that." He smiled. Her apprehension abated somewhat under the warm glow of his smile. The beginning of a smile tipped the corners of her mouth. "You have a beautiful smile."

"Thank you."

He held up a finger, motioning for her to stay put, as he maneuvered the traffic, crossing back to the other side of Poydras Street. His lips curved into a smirk. He walked up beside her. "Let's go to my place."

"Now see!"

He bowled over with laughter. "Just joking. Do you have any plans tonight, Zora Vaughn?"

"No, I'm free."

"Great. Have you been to the French Quarter yet?"

"No, but Lizzy suggested I go."

"If you don't mind my asking, what hotel are you staying in?"

She smiled and looked across the street. "Le Pavillon Hotel."

"Great. The Quarter is only a short walk from here. How about dinner?"

"I would love to. Where?"

"The Tableau on St. Peter Street."

"Great, I'll meet you there, say about seven-thirty?"

"Seven-thirty it is." He peered into her eyes. "Until then, Zora Vaughn." He pivoted and strolled away, leaving her to watch him disappear around the corner.

As the sun was setting over the French Quarter, Zora nervously waited outside of The Tableau.

Zora had never been to New Orleans before, and the vibrant colors, lively music, and delicious smells that filled the air had already enchanted her. As she waited, she watched the street performers and listened to the sounds of jazz music coming from nearby venues.

Suddenly, she spotted a handsome man walking toward her. Zora was wearing a light blue sundress and matching sandals. She had a bright smile on her face as he approached her, and Maceo felt a wave of excitement and nerves wash over him when he spotted her.

"Hi, Maceo. It's so nice to see you again."

Maceo couldn't help but notice how her eyes sparkled in the evening light. "Likewise." He tried to sound confident, but he was nervous as hell. Earlier, when they met at Daisy Mae's, he was confident, bordering cocky, but she'd left an indelible impression on him that had him thinking of her every moment of the day, so now he felt like a teenage boy on his first date.

The two of them walked into the restaurant and the host sat them at a small table near the window. They ordered drinks and chatted about their interests, their families, and their travels.

As they ate their meals, Zora noticed how much Maceo seemed to appreciate the food and the atmosphere of the restaurant. He spoke with such passion about the history of New Orleans and the French Quarter.

After dinner, Maceo suggested they take a walk around the Quarter. They strolled through the narrow streets, taking in the colorful buildings, street performers, and art galleries. They walked hand in hand, occasionally stopping to listen to a band playing or to admire a piece of artwork.

As they walked, Maceo realized he was having an incredible time with Zora. She was easy to talk to, and they seemed to have so much in common.

Finally, they stood in front of Jackson Square, formerly the Plaza de Armas, a historic park in the French Quarter. The moon was high in the sky, illuminating the Square.

Maceo turned to Zora and took her hands in his. "I've had an amazing time tonight. I feel like we have a real connection."

Zora couldn't help herself, as she leaned in to kiss him. It was a gentle kiss, full of promise, and it felt so natural. "I agree. I feel like we have a lot of potential."

Maceo felt a surge of happiness as he hugged her tightly. Surrounded by the magic of New Orleans, he felt anything was possible.

Now spooning his woman, with her softly snoring, anything was possible. After ten years, he figured it was time they solidified their relationship with a marriage certificate, but the time and moment had to be right. Soon, though.

CHAPTER 3

Aserene stillness filled the room, occasionally broken by the chirping of birds outside their bedroom window. Keith stirred first, his eyelids fluttering open as he gradually noticed the golden rays beaming against the wall. With a contented sigh, he stretched his limbs beneath the cozy embrace of the duvet, a lazy smile gracing his lips as he welcomed the new day.

Beside him, LaTonya stirred as well, her breathing deep and steady. As the sunlight filtered through her lashes, she slowly blinked awake, a soft yawn escaping her lips. Stretching her arms above her head, she savored the warmth that enveloped her.

Turning toward each other, their eyes met in the soft morning light, exchanging silent smiles that spoke volumes of their shared love and contentment. With a tender touch, Keith brushed a stray lock of hair from LaTonya's face, his fingers lingering against her cheek.

Embracing her, Keith traced his fingers along his wife's bare back, causing her to shiver with pleasure. Without a word, he pulled her closer and their lips met in a passionate kiss.

Their hands roamed freely over each other's bodies, rediscovering every curve and crevice. The familiarity and comfort of their touches made their hearts beat faster with desire.

Gently, Keith trailed kisses down LaTonya's neck, causing her to let out a soft moan. He knew all her sensitive spots and how to make her feel loved and cherished. She ran her fingers through his coarse hair, caressing his scalp. Turning on her side, she pressed her naked bottom against his erection. Positioning himself, he eased inside his wife and loved her until they both climaxed, which was a morning ritual since the day they married.

Their lovemaking was slow and sensual, with each touch speaking volumes of their deep connection. They moved in perfect harmony, their hearts beating in sync.

As they reached the peak of their passion, they whispered sweet declarations of love to each other. At that moment, nothing else mattered except the love they shared.

As they lay in each other's arms, basking in the afterglow, Keith kissed the back of his wife's head. "I love you, sweet thing."

With a smile, she took his hand that was draped over her hip and kissed it. "I love you."

Keith patted her on the hip. "Ready to get our run on?"

As Keith and LaTonya laced up their running shoes, the air buzzed with a silent challenge. The sun's gentle rays filtered through the canopy of leaves overhead, painting the sprawling greenery and winding pathways with a golden hue.

As they set off on their daily run, their footsteps fell in sync with the rhythm of their shared stride. Keith's athletic frame moved with purpose; his determination evident in the steady pace of his gait. Beside him, LaTonya's lithe form glided effortlessly, her long strides carrying her with grace and ease.

Their route took them along the winding trails of the park, surrounded by towering trees as she whisked by him. The sweet scent of nature filled the air, invigorating their senses as they lost themselves in the peaceful tranquility of their surroundings.

"Bet you can't keep up, sweet thing." Keith flashed a grin over his shoulder.

LaTonya shot him a playful smirk. "You wish. I'll leave you in the dust!"

The only sounds were the rustle of leaves in the breeze and the steady thud of their footsteps echoing in the morning air.

With each passing mile, the intensity of their rivalry grew, driving them to push themselves harder and faster than ever before.

"You're falling behind, Keith!" LaTonya called out, a competitive edge creeping into her voice.

Keith chuckled. "Just warming up, honey. I'll catch you on the home stretch!"

Beneath the friendly rivalry simmered a deep-rooted bond, a shared love for the thrill of the challenge and the joy of pushing themselves, and each other, to their limits.

As they rounded the final bend and sprinted toward home, their laughter echoed through the park.

In the end, it didn't matter who crossed the finish line first. What mattered was the exhilarating rush of the race, the shared laughter and camaraderie, and the unbreakable bond that united them as husband and wife, partners in both life and competition.

CHAPTER 4

Nestled within the vast expanse of five acres in National Harbor, Maryland, the gourmet chef kitchen of the magnificent seven-thousand-square-foot colonial exuded sophistication. Adorned with impeccable craftsmanship, it boasted top-of-the-line cabinetry, sleek marble countertops, state-of-the-art appliances, and elegant light fixtures. The thoughtfully designed layout of the kitchen facilitated the joyous experience of meal preparation for the Ellis family, offering multiple stations for their culinary pursuits. These included a dedicated cooking area, a spacious prep island, a convenient carving/serving cart, a built-in fifty-bottle wine refrigerator, and a well-appointed butler's pantry, despite the absence of hired household staff.

Perched on one of the six stools surrounding the expansive twenty-foot island, Kennedy leisurely savored a goblet filled with freshly squeezed orange juice. Engrossed in her morning routine, she casually perused the pages of *The Washington Post*. Shaking her head in a mix of disbelief and resignation, she folded the paper with a sense of nonchalance and cast it aside. "Same old story, just a different day."

Kennedy raised the lid of the sixteen-inch MacBook Pro and powered it on. As she patiently waited for it to warm up, she strolled toward the base of the dual staircase positioned next to the in-law's suite. "Lindsay, are you awake, sweetheart?"

Lindsay emerged from her bedroom, reaching the top landing, and peering down at her mother. "I'm up."

Glancing across the hallway to the wall-mounted clock in the home office, Kennedy let out a sigh. It was already 8:30 a.m., and she felt the urgency to hit the road much earlier. Time was slipping away, even though her morning with Malcolm had been wonderful. They needed to leave the house and embark on their journey within the hour.

"We need to get moving, babycakes."

With arms folded, Lindsay leaned over the upstairs banister. "Hey, Mom."

"Yes."

"I've never lived on my own before."

A warm smile crossed Kennedy's face as she propped her hands on her hips. "Well, you won't be alone. You'll have a roommate."

"I know, but you know what I mean, without you and Dad."

Resting her arms at her sides, Kennedy lowered her head, contemplating how to ease her daughter's apprehension. She looked up and locked eyes with Lindsay's beautiful brown gaze. "You will be just fine. You know why?"

Lindsay shook her head, awaiting her mother's words of reassurance.

"Because you're my daughter. You possess strength and resilience, just like me. Besides, your dad and I are only a phone call away and a four-hour drive. Don't forget, you have family there as well."

"Okay."

"Will you please get dressed for breakfast so we can leave?"

Kennedy observed Lindsay move away from the banister and head toward the hallway bathroom. Her emotions were all over the place, thinking about her daughter's college journey, but fear wasn't a part of it. Her baby had blossomed into a young woman, and she fervently prayed that she and Malcolm had instilled the values and guidance needed for Lindsay to navigate the right path. So far, their efforts had been fruitful, and Kennedy held onto that assurance.

Kennedy returned to her laptop and sorted through emails, responding to those that required her immediate attention. As the Chief Operating Officer of Ellis Enterprises, she held the responsibility of overseeing the organization's operational and strategic leadership, business development, negotiations, and asset acquisitions. She was the right hand of her husband, Malcolm, who served as the Chief Executive Officer. Together, they had founded the investment conglomerate one year after graduating from Columbia University with a mere five thousand dollars in their bank account, thanks to Malcolm's parents. Within five years, they had transformed that initial investment into a multi-million-dollar company. Malcolm's bachelor's in business proved beneficial.

Turning the corner and entering the kitchen, Malcolm greeted his wife with a tender kiss on the back of her neck. "Morning."

"Good morning, honey." Kennedy patted him on the behind as he moved around the kitchen island. She couldn't resist the allure of her forty-two-year-old husband, who resembled a shorter version of Rick Fox at six-foot-four, complete with curly black hair and a sexy five-o'clock shadow.

Lindsay observed her parents' affectionate interaction as she descended the staircase and joined them in the kitchen. "Oh, God, give me a break." She positioned herself beside Kennedy, draping her arm around her mother's shoulders. "It's kind of early for that, don't you think, Mom?"

Kennedy shook her head, with amusement twinkling in her eyes. "Don't be so grown." She pecked her daughter on the cheek.

Malcolm smiled proudly at his daughter, appreciating her beauty. Lindsay was more valuable than gold and possessed the same stunning features as her mother.

"So high," he belted, though lacking the melodic finesse of John Legend. "So high on cloud nine."

Lindsay glanced around the kitchen, her brows furrowed, and her mouth twisted in confusion. "Wait, do you hear that?"

Kennedy and Malcolm exchanged glances. They were curious about what would come out of her unfiltered mind next. Lindsay had always been an independent thinker and wasn't afraid to speak her mind.

Kennedy prepared herself for whatever was about to be said. "Dare I ask?"

"Don't you hear the dogs howling in the distance?"

With a tilt of his head, Malcolm flashed Lindsay a smile. "What do you know about John Legend?"

"He ain't no Drake."

Frowning slightly, Kennedy regarded her daughter with a touch of annoyance. "Is that the grammar you'll be using in college?"

Jokingly, Malcolm rolled his eyes and sucked his teeth, feigning exasperation. "She's ghetto fabulous." He and Kennedy burst into laughter.

"Your father has no sense." Kennedy stroked her daughter's shoulder-length burgundy tresses, pondering when she had given permission for Lindsay to dye her hair. "Are you hungry? When did you color your hair?"

"Yes, I am. I did it last night. French toast?"

"Already taken care of. The plates are warming in the oven."

Since Lindsay was five years old, she had adored Kennedy's French toast. Kennedy would dip slices of bread in pancake batter, creating French toast slices as large as freshly baked bread. Generously sprinkled with cinnamon, melted butter, and warm maple syrup, a side of hickory-smoked bacon, and a bowl of fresh seasonal fruit on the side topped it off.

Malcolm leaned in close to Kennedy's ear. "I missed you this morning."

Kennedy's lips curled upward in a flirtatious smirk. "Do you ever get enough?"

Malcolm expelled a guttural moan. "Of you? Never." His lips grazed her ear, and she shuddered. "You know I can't get it down without your help."

Kennedy looked down at this crotch, up at him, and leaned in close, speaking for only his ears. "Is it still up?"

That question also landed in Lindsay's ears. Rolling her eyes at her parents' loving antics, Lindsay had long gotten over being embarrassed or uncomfortable. "I think I'm going to be sick. You two old farts and this foolishness."

"Oh, hush and eat your breakfast." Kennedy chuckled. "'Don't hate,' as you're always putting it."

"Ha! I guess you told her, honey." Malcolm beamed at his daughter, popping a piece of bacon into his mouth.

Lindsay mumbled something inaudible under her breath.

Kennedy whipped her head around. "What was that?"

"I'm going to eat in my room so I can finish packing."

"You should have finished packing days ago."

Lindsay headed up the steps with her plate of breakfast. "Yes, Mom. Shoulda, woulda, coulda…"

"I heard that, Lindsay! We're leaving here in less than one hour."

"Is there any coffee, babe?"

She smirked at him, raising an eyebrow in amusement. "Yes, in the coffee pot."

The aroma of freshly brewed coffee filled the air, making her wonder why he would ask such a question. Kennedy let out a deep sigh as Malcolm moved toward the Nespresso Vertuo and poured himself a steaming mug of java.

"You know, that girl is growing up too fast for her own good. I hope she understands that her time at Hampton won't be all fun and games. If she thinks otherwise, she's in for a rude awakening. I expect her to focus and work hard."

Malcolm took a sip of coffee, shaking his head as the music from Lindsay's bedroom grew louder, enveloping the entire house. "She's just like her mother. She'll handle it well."

"If her grades slip, she's coming back home. We won't let our money go to waste."

"She'll do more than fine, trust me." Malcolm looked at his wife and ran his tongue over his lips.

Peering over her coffee cup, she shook her head. "Uh, no."

Malcolm put down his cup and strode toward Kennedy, who sat perched on the wooden stool at the kitchen island. His hand rested on her knee and crept up her thigh, his fingers slipping inside the waistband of her khaki pants, toward her warm, fleshy mound. "You're not wearing panties."

"My goodness, man, do you ever rest?"

Smiling, he played with her naked pubis, dipping his finger in her wetness. "Can't say that I do."

She removed his hand. "Go get dressed, please." She kissed him, dismounted the stool, and moved toward the home office.

CHAPTER 5

With the saddle-brown, leather Lorra Rivers Nia Hobo bag draped over her shoulder, Kennedy stood in the grand marble foyer, her hands resting on her curvy hips. Her mouth fell open in astonishment at the sight of the designer luggage that filled the immaculate space. She gently tucked loose tendrils of hair from her elegant upsweep behind her ear, shaking her head in disbelief just as the doorbell chimed.

Glancing back over her shoulder, Kennedy observed the footsteps echoing down the staircase. "Are we expecting any guests?"

Freshly showered and clad in Burberry from head to toe, Malcolm descended the T-shaped staircase, with Kennedy's satchel slung casually over his shoulder. "Nope. Do we have everything?"

Trotting down the staircase, Lindsay joined them in the foyer. Kennedy chuckled and turned to Lindsay. "Why are you talking all of this stuff with you?"

Holding the door open, Malcolm teased Lindsay. "You do know you're going to have a roommate?"

At that moment, to their surprise, Helen Ellis and her husband, Lionel, appeared before their son, wearing bright smiles. Malcolm hugged his mother tightly, as if they hadn't seen each other in years, despite his parents' regular visits. "Hey, Mom! Dad. What brings you here?"

Helen Ellis moved past Malcolm and planted a loving kiss on Kennedy's cheek. "We couldn't let our granddaughter leave without saying goodbye."

Lionel Ellis followed closely behind, stopping to embrace his son. "Absolutely right, sweetheart. This is a momentous day for our grandbaby."

Lindsay beamed with joy at her grandparents. "Hi, Pop-Pop and Gigi!"

Helen enveloped her only granddaughter in a warm embrace. "Hello, sweetheart."

Lionel playfully ruffled Lindsay's hair. "Pop-Pop! You're messing up my hair."

Lionel chuckled and surveyed the foyer. "My goodness! Are you leaving for good?"

Side-embracing her father-in-law, Kennedy joined in the light-hearted banter. " Hey, Dad. That's exactly what I asked her. I don't understand why she needs so much stuff."

Lindsay propped her hands up on her hips. "Mom, I need all of this."

Helen Ellis playfully swatted Lindsay on the backside. "Take your hands off what you think are hips, baby."

With a smirk, Malcolm stood beside his wife. "Might have to take the Navigator."

"No! Lindsay, you need not take your entire bedroom with you." Kennedy picked up two heavy suitcases. "Lindsay, what in the hell? Did you pack rocks? This is crazy!"

"Funny, Mom." Lindsay breezed past her and out the front door.

Kennedy dropped the suitcases to the floor. "Excuse me, young lady. Get back here and grab a bag!"

Malcolm leaned in and kissed his wife on her neck, causing a slight chill to course through her. "I've got it, babe. I'll take everything out."

"Are you sure, Malcolm? You need a moving team for all this stuff."

Malcolm nodded and smacked Kennedy on the backside as she walked away from him.

"Hey." Kennedy's lips formed into a cute pout. "You're always starting something, Mr. Ellis."

"I always finish it, too." Malcolm licked his lips, stirring up something inside her, once again.

Helen Ellis never missed a beat, seeing the loving interaction between her son and his wife. "Have some respect for your mother, son."

Malcolm kissed his mother on the cheek. "Always, Mom."

Lionel Ellis picked up two suitcases. "I'll help you, son."

"Now, Lionel, you know you have a bad back."

"I'll be fine, woman." Lionel walked out the front door and set the suitcases on the ground, at the rear of the Navigator.

Leaning against the SUV, with her arms folded across her flat chest, and her legs crossed at the ankles, Lindsay caught every smile, smack, and kiss her father gave her mother. Although she would hate to admit it, she was going to miss two grown folks acting like two horny teenagers. Watching her parents interact was her blueprint for how she would allow a man to treat her. Her father loved the ground her mother walked on, and she planned to have it no other way by the man with whom she would fall in love.

In the winding driveway, flanked by a lush, manicured lawn and wintergreen boxwood shrubbery, Lindsay followed her father to the driver's side of the black Lincoln Navigator with tinted windows. "Dad, may I drive?"

"Drive what?"

Lindsay eyed her father.

He shook his head. "This isn't Mom's Jaguar, sweetheart. Do you think you can handle it?"

"Yes, Dad, I believe I can."

Standing at the rear of the SUV next to her mother-in-law, Kennedy smirked. "I hope all that believing doesn't end us up in a ditch."

Helen Ellis nodded and chuckled. "I second that. I think this is too big for you, Lindsay. It is too big for me."

"There's always a first time for everything." Malcolm closed the rear lift door and moved next to his wife, caressing her shoulders, and looking at his mother. "I'll sit shotgun."

"Mom, Dad, you want to ride with us? There's room."

"No, thank you, Kennedy. We have plans today. We just stopped by to say goodbye to Lindsay."

Lionel Ellis reached inside his jacket pocket and retrieved a white envelope. "Yes, and to give her this. Here, honey."

Rounding the rear of the SUV, Lindsay took the envelope and lunged into her grandfather's arms. She loved him so much.

"Don't you go spending it all in one place, you hear?"

Eyes wide, and with her mother looking over her shoulder, Lindsay quickly opened the envelope and shrieked at the crisp, ten one-hundred-dollar bills inside. "Thank you, Pop-Pop!" She adored her grandfather, and Lionel Ellis would climb the tallest mountains and cross the hottest deserts for his family, especially his only grandchild.

"You're welcome."

"Mom, Dad, that's too much for her. One hundred dollars or less is enough."

"Nonsense, Kennedy. She's going away from home, and I want to make sure she won't have to ask anyone for anything at all."

Malcolm looked at his wife. "How much is it?"

"One thousand dollars."

"Yeah, Dad, that's way too much for—"

"What's done is done, son. Stop stressing over it."

Lindsay lunged at her grandmother, wrapping her arms around her neck. "Thank you, Gigi!"

"You're welcome, honey. Now, listen, I want you to enjoy yourself. Campus life is a wonderful experience, but don't forget you're there to learn, too. Think it through before you react. Make wise choices. If you're not sure about something, call your parents or you can call me."

"Yes, ma'am."

Piling the last of Lindsay's carry-on luggage in the back seat, Malcolm took his wife's hand, helped her inside, and closed the door.

Kennedy opened the door. "It's too hot in here for a closed door."

Malcolm jogged around to the driver's side to his daughter. He opened the door, took her by the hand, helped her climb up into the cab, and instructed her on adjusting the driver's seat, the rearview mirror, the side mirror, and the seat belt.

"Are you straight, baby?"

"Thanks, Dad." She smiled as he closed the door, and she opened it to let air inside.

"All right, let me lock up the house and we'll be ready to go."

"Malcolm, can you please give Lindsay the keys so we can turn on the A/C? We're cooking in here."

Malcolm tossed the keys in Kennedy's lap, who handed them to Lindsay, who turned on the engine and the air conditioner.

"All right, son, we're going to head on out now. Call your mother to let her know y'all got back safely."

"Sure thing, Dad."

Lionel opened the car door of the garnet metallic Cadillac CT4 Malcolm and Kennedy had given them as their wedding anniversary gift. He took his wife by the hand and helped her into the car. Smiling down at her, he closed the door, puckered up, blew her a kiss, and rounded the car to the driver's side. He waved to his son. "Drive safe, son."

"I will, Dad. You, too."

Before securing the house, Malcolm observed his father getting into the driver's seat, closing the door, leaning toward his wife, and planting a lingering kiss on her lips. Their gazes met, exchanging smiles before sharing another kiss. This time, the embrace seemed more intimate, and Malcolm saw his father caressing his mother's face, which brought a smile to his handsome face. Standing in the driveway, Malcolm watched his parents drive away, filled with pride as he admired his father's love for his mother. Their marriage served as a model for his relationship with Kennedy.

As the only child of Lionel, a retired electrical engineer from the Department of Defense, and Helen, a retired elementary school principal, Malcolm grew up in a home brimming with love, chivalry, affection, and excitement. Having lived through wars and economic hardships, and witnessing countless changes in the world, Helen kept her sense of wonder and love for learning and teaching.

Lionel was just as active as his wife, maintaining his fitness through regular walks with Helen around their Montgomery County neighborhood and light exercise routines. He possessed a profound appreciation for nature, spending his afternoons tending to his garden, filled with vibrant flowers and lush greenery. His attire mirrored his timeless style, with tailored suits and classic dress shirts, evoking an era of sophistication and elegance. With quiet confidence, he carried himself in a manner that commanded respect and admiration from those around him.

Malcolm's upbringing was far from ordinary, thanks to his adventurous parents. They were avid travelers, whisking him away to different states and countries every summer. However, Malcolm cherished his fondest childhood memories of Christmas. Annually, the day after Thanksgiving filled him with anticipation as his mother ventured into the attic to retrieve the ornaments for the tree. Malcolm's love for Christmas didn't stem from the multitude of toys his parents gave him from his extensive wish list from the JCPenney, Sears, and Montgomery Ward catalogs. Instead, it revolved around the quality of time he spent bonding with his father. Each year, they embarked on a quest to find the perfect Christmas tree, exploring various tree farms throughout Maryland. Their father-son moments held great significance for Malcolm. They would then return home to indulge in hot cocoa, popcorn, and boxes of decorations, including his favorite: tinsel icicles that glittered their house well into the new year.

Apart from Christmas traditions, Malcolm and Lionel would spend countless hours fishing on the Chesapeake Bay, which they still did, and collaborating on various woodworking projects, ranging from wooden planters to dining room tables. Lionel was a master craftsman, who passed down his skills and knowledge to his son. Although Malcolm didn't follow in his father's professional footsteps, Lionel took immense pride and joy in his son's achievements.

Helen was a lively woman, much like Kennedy. She never accepted Malcolm's misbehavior as a child, firmly believing that sparing the rod would spoil the child. Despite her sternness, she showered her son with love and support. She actively took part in the Parent-Teacher Association's bake sales, and passionately cheered for Malcolm during his sports activities, whether it was basketball, football, baseball, or anything in between. The bond between mother and son was profound, and Malcolm adored his mother as much as she adored him.

As Malcolm tended to the house and Kennedy and Lindsay sat in the SUV, Kennedy peered at her daughter's reflection in the rearview mirror. Tears of admiration formed. She was so proud of her offspring. Her only daughter was starting her freshman year in college, and she was a ball of mixed emotions in the back seat. Lindsay was academically astute, with the sharpest mind Kennedy had come across for someone so young. Throughout her schooling, Lindsay maintained a 4.0 GPA, was the president of the Student Government Association in her junior and senior years of high school, was captain of the debate team, and wrote for the school newspaper. She had become quite good at chess, too. Her baby was flourishing into a beautiful young woman who was now moving out on her own.

Excited for the chance to drive her father's SUV that not even her mother drove, Lindsay turned the stereo system to 95.5 WPGC as Beyoncé's "Love on Top" blared through the twenty-speaker Revel Ultima audio system. The entire block of Lansing Drive heard Beyoncé belting, *"Baby, it's you!"*

Kennedy's mouth dropped and her head shook, as if uncontrollably. "No, ma'am. No, ma'am. No, ma'am. You will not blast that in my ear."

With her arms up and shoulders bouncing, Lindsay snapped her fingers. "It's Beyoncé, Mom. *Baby, you're the one I need!*"

"Girl, if you don't turn that shit down, I swear—turn it down!"

With the typical roll of the eyes and teeth-sucking, she turned off the radio. Lindsay leaned back, rested her head against the headrest, and looked into the rearview mirror.

With a tilted head, Kennedy peered at her daughter in the rearview mirror. "What?"

"Nothing."

Kennedy looked out the window at the front door, wondering what was taking Malcolm so long.

Sitting comfortably in her seat, Lindsay gazed through the windshield. A multitude of thoughts ricocheted through her mind. Since her first day of senior year in high school, she couldn't wait to become an adult. Despite their wealth, Kennedy emphasized the value of hard work and understanding the significance of earning a living, which included pursuing scholarships. While her parents hoped she would attend their beloved alma mater, Columbia University, Lindsay didn't feel prepared to tackle the vastness of New York City. Instead, she chose Hampton University.

"I'm scared, Mom."

Kennedy leaned forward and caressed her daughter's shoulder. "Why, honey?"

She shrugged. "It's a new adventure for me, and without you and Dad."

"You'll be all right. Remember, you won't be the only one feeling this way. You'll blend right in, navigating your way through that expansive campus just like everyone else. It's going to be an incredible experience, trust me."

Malcolm opened the passenger door, climbed in, and kissed Lindsay on the cheek. "No heavy foot, please."

"Got it."

"I love you."

"I love you, too, Dad."

Kennedy strapped on the seat belt. "Okay, let's rock and roll."

Malcolm turned in his seat and winked at Kennedy. "Move over behind Lindsay, babe."

"Why?"

"So, I can look at your beautiful face when I want to."

"Boy, bye!" She chuckled.

Lindsay rolled her eyes and blew the horn, startling her parents.

Kennedy closed her eyes and pursed her lips. "I will beat her ass before she gets to Hampton. Can we go, please?"

As Lindsay shifted the SUV into drive, she extended her arm out the window, waving goodbye to the house. "I'll miss you." With determination, she maneuvered the vehicle around the circular driveway and merged onto the street, without a moment's hesitation or consideration for yielding.

Kennedy's eyes widened. "Girl! You're supposed to stop and look both ways!"

Lindsay shrugged and looked in the rearview mirror at her mother. "I didn't see any cars coming, so I didn't stop."

"Eyes on the road! If you can't follow the rules of the road, then pull over."

"Yes, sir."

Before reaching the end of the street, Lindsay engaged the turn signal, stopped, looked both ways, a few more times for good measure, and turned right into traffic, heading for Interstate 495 South.

Malcolm turned on Praise 104.1 FM. Erica Campbell's powerful voice enveloped the vehicle with her song, "Help."

Kennedy closed her eyes and settled into the seat, humming. "I love that song."

"Sounds sad to me."

Kennedy pondered Lindsay's words. "Yes, I suppose."

They rode in silence for fifteen minutes until Lindsay verbalized her thoughts. "Y'all are nasty." Lindsay drove across the Woodrow Wilson Bridge toward Northern Virginia, glancing at National Harbor, and regretting the words that had effortlessly left her mouth. "I'm going to miss that place."

"What was that?"

"I said I'm going to miss the National Harbor, Mom."

"No, before that."

"Nothing."

"What are you talking about, 'y'all are nasty'?"

"Nothing, Mom."

"Why would you say that?"

Lindsay huffed. "Y'all are the most sexually active old people I've ever seen in my life."

Malcolm realized this was a mother-daughter conversation, although he had to clarify one thing. "Who are you calling old?"

Kennedy chuckled. "Yes, well, I love me some him and there's nothing 'nasty' about it. I hope we are good role models for you, honey."

"You are."

"Honey, you're a woman now, and—"

"Mom, don't go there, please."

"I'm serious, Lindsay. Your dad and I waited to have sex until we got married. We waited until we both graduated college and got married before we even thought about sex."

"Y'all never did the foreplay thing?"

"Oh, yeah." Malcolm nodded, and Kennedy's jaw fell into her lap.

"Oh my God, Dad!"

"I love nice jazz. Your mom and I saw Fourplay in concert at Constitution Hall. Remember, babe?"

"Yes, I do, Malcolm, but she's not talking about music. She's talking about kissing, fondling, and everything else you do before sex."

"Yeah, Dad, I've seen you feel up Mom and stuff." She cringed at the thought, although she knew they were lovingly intimate nightly. She had gotten immune to her mother's nightly cries of ecstasy.

Embarrassment masked Malcolm's face. "Keep your eyes on the road." Having such a conversation with his daughter left him without words. However, his wife's ringing cell phone saved him.

Sifting through her bag, Kennedy welcomed the interruption as she retrieved her cell phone. "Hi, Dad. You're on speaker."

"Hey, baby. Just thought I'd call to see if y'all left yet."

"Yeah, Daddy, we're on the road now."

"Is my grandbaby with ya?"

Kennedy twisted up her face. "Of course. She's driving."

"Oh yeah? Can she hear me good?"

"Yes, Grandpa, I can hear you."

"Hey, Dad."

"Hey there, Malcolm. Ya take care of my girls now."

Nodding, Malcolm smiled. "No doubt."

"Lindsay?"

"Yes, Grandpa?"

"I love ya, ya hear me?"

"Yes, I hear you."

"Good. I want ya to get ya a good education from that school. Don't be down there messing around and whatnot."

"Yes, sir."

"Now, ya have my number, don't ya?"

"Yes, sir, I have it."

"Good. Now ya call me if you need anything at all. Ya hear?"

"Yes, sir."

"I love ya, baby, and I'm so proud of ya. Ya grandmother would be so proud of ya, ya know?"

"Yes, I know. I miss her."

"Yeah, we all do, baby. Ya go get good grades now, ya hear?"

"Yes, I will, Grandpa. I love you."

"I love ya more. Now, put ya mama on the phone."

"I'm here, Dad. You're on speaker."

"Okay, honey, ya gon' stop to see ya aunt while ya there?"

"Yes. We're going to stop on the way back."

"All right. Hug her for me and tell her I said hello."

"I will."

"All right, Malcolm, my man, take it easy."

"You, too, Dad."

Kennedy ended the call, inhaled deeply, and dropped the cell phone back into her bag. She enjoyed conversations with her father, Parker Rhodes, a retired sanitation worker. Kennedy was the apple of his eye. From the moment she came out of the womb, he was madly in love. Her mother, Delilah Rhodes, a former paralegal, died from heart disease one year before seeing her granddaughter, Lindsay, enter high school. Kennedy's relationship with her mother was close, as her mother became the sister she always wanted. She treasured her mother and, although she missed her terribly, she felt blessed to have had many years with her and that she had gotten to know her granddaughter.

Kennedy peered at the side of Lindsay's face. Her daughter's profile was so much like her mother's: bone-straight shoulder-length hair, with a café au lait complexion inherited from her paternal great-grandmother's Native American heritage.

"But seriously, Mom, how were you able to do all that kissing and stuff and not want to have sex?"

Kennedy closed her eyes. Clearly, Lindsay would not let this topic rest, so she realized the only way to deal with it was head-on and with honesty.

Goodness, this is going to be a long ride, Kennedy thought, as she chose her words carefully. "Yes, we kissed and…well, yes, Dad felt me up and stuff, as you so eloquently put it, but we love each other and—" Kennedy moved around in her seat and cleared her throat. "Malcolm, feel free to jump in."

"I believe in you, babe. You've got this."

Kennedy rolled her eyes at the back of his head. "Lindsay, have you ever kissed a boy?" She inhaled deeply for her daughter's response, the color draining from her face.

"No."

Kennedy released her breath and perked up. "So, that means you haven't had sex. Is that right?"

"Mom, I'm still a virgin."

Malcolm looked out the passenger window, smiled, and thanked the Almighty that, if he had to be present for this conversation, he didn't have to learn the opposite.

"That's good to hear." Kennedy looked at her daughter, who had a death grip on the steering wheel. Lindsay had always been the cautious type, and she knew she didn't have to worry about her. As her mother, though, it was her responsibility to reiterate, "Don't have sex until you're ready," as often as possible.

"I won't, Mom."

"There will be temptations, and I understand that, so make sure you use protection."

Lindsay realized she had three to four hours to listen to her mother's lecture, so she turned off her listening ears and focused on the road.

"Promise me you will call me before you do anything?"

Lindsay nodded.

"Yes, call your mother. Call me only when I have to lay hands on a dude for laying hands on my daughter."

Lindsay nodded, and with her mind on the nearing excitement of college life, drove in silence.

CHAPTER 6

Standing amid the bustling testosterone and estrogen in the lobby of the freshmen dormitory, Lindsay was ecstatic. Bright, cheerful colors adorned the walls, while the sound of chatter and laughter was almost deafening. A friendly student worker manned the front desk. Doors on either side lined the hallway, each marked with a name tag and decorated with posters and pictures. Years of use had caused the carpet to become worn, and the walls had scuff marks. The scent of microwave popcorn wafted through the air, hinting at the forthcoming late-night study sessions and impromptu movie nights.

With a smile wider than a Cheshire cat, Lindsay was in paradise. She loved everything about the atmosphere and the people—the different shades of beautiful people. *This sure isn't high school*, she thought, as young adults whisked past her, some with their parents on their heels, others excitedly adapting to their new environment. Here, she would meet her new family, with whom she would spend years learning. From various walks of life, she would gain brothers and sisters. She would become part of a community unlike anything she had ever experienced. She would begin her journey of growing into the fine young woman she would become.

Kennedy nudged Malcolm. "Is this a co-ed dorm?" She was concerned Lindsay might not be ready to commingle with young men who were at their sexual peaks.

Malcolm leaned into her. "I don't know, but it sure looks like it." He, too, was concerned, as he remembered being a young man in college, trying to sniff every panty within walking distance before laying eyes on Kennedy.

Kennedy faced her daughter with pursed lips. "This is not acceptable. A co-ed dorm?"

"Mom, it is not co-ed, geesh! These are just guys, that's all."

"Babe, it's fine. Listen, we raised her right. We trust her, don't we?"

Lindsay inched closer to her father and looked at her mother. "Yeah, don't you?"

"I do, but if I find out this is a co-ed—"

"It's not, Mom!" Lindsay sighed with a slight eye roll.

A young woman hurried past Kennedy. "Excuse me, honey, is this a co-ed dorm?"

The young woman stopped in her tracks, pivoted, and faced Kennedy with a smile. "No, ma'am, it's not."

Smiling, Kennedy tilted her head toward the young woman. "Thank you."

"No problem." Smiling, the young woman continued on her way.

"I told you it wasn't, Mom. So much for trusting me."

Inside Lindsay's dorm room, she chose the twin-sized bed, small desk, and single closet on the right side of the room, next to the window.

Kennedy peered out the window and onto the court. "You're going to love it here, honey."

Lindsay shrugged. "I guess so."

Turning around, she glanced at Malcolm and then at her daughter. "Let's get you settled. We're going to head back tonight."

Lindsay folded her arms across her flat chest and kicked out her leg. "I thought you and Dad were staying the night?"

Kennedy diverted her attention to the pile of luggage on the floor. "We changed our minds."

Lindsay propped her hands on her hips and pouted. "I thought we were going out to dinner. I wanted to try that seafood restaurant on the river. You promised."

Kennedy peered at her. "Who are you talking to like that? You are too old for the whining"

Being the pushover dad and feeling the need to comfort his daughter, Malcolm sighed and looked at his watch. "Tell you what, we'll have an early dinner. Your mom wants to see Aunt Caroline before heading back."

Kennedy shrugged. "Dad has spoken."

"Great! Thanks, Dad."

"Spoiled brat," Kennedy mumbled under her breath.

"I heard that, Mom!"

The room erupted in laughter.

For an hour, Kennedy lectured Lindsay about the young men on campus, the importance of her schoolwork and maintaining her academic grade point average, and other topics that weren't holding Lindsay's attention.

"As you settle in, you will realize this dormitory is more than just a place to sleep and study. It's a community of young adults, each with their own stories and aspirations, brought together by a shared experience of college life, honey, and—"

A knock at the door provided the perfect interruption for Lindsay to dash to open it.

The young woman stood with bags sitting at her feet and hung over her shoulders.

"Hi there."

"Hi, I'm Dorrie Arthur. I think we're roommates."

Lindsay stepped back and welcomed Dorrie inside. "I'm Lindsay Ellis, and this is my mom, Kennedy, and my dad, Malcolm."

Kennedy gasped at the introduction. After playfully popping Lindsay upside the head, she extended her hand with a warm smile. "Hello, Dorrie. We are *Mr. and Mrs. Ellis*. It's nice to meet you." She looked over Dorrie's shoulder, only seeing students moving about the hallway. "Are your parents with you?"

"It's nice to meet you both, Mr. and Mrs. Ellis." Dorrie walked into the room and set her satchels on the empty bed, leaving the suitcases in the doorway. "No, ma'am. They had to work today."

"That's too bad." Malcolm frowned, with Kennedy by his side.

"Not really. I live in Newport News, so it's no problem."

Malcolm moved toward the door to bring her luggage inside the room. "Oh, I see. Well, you're welcome to join us for dinner."

"I would love to, but my funds are limited. Maybe some other time."

Kennedy smiled. "Dinner is our treat. So, let's finish getting you girls situated and then head for a good seafood meal."

***

"I enjoyed dinner, Mr. and Mrs. Ellis. Thank you so much for inviting me."

In Lindsay and Dorrie's dorm room, Kennedy sat on Lindsay's bed and watched Dorrie as she finished unpacking.

"It was our pleasure, Dorrie. I would have loved to have met your parents. Hopefully, some other time."

Shrugging, she propped her hands up on her hips. "Yes, well, they both had to work. I'm not on a scholarship. They have to pay for this somehow."

Kennedy smiled at Dorrie and thought of how beautiful she was and quite mature. A little too mature for Lindsay, maybe. Compared to her roommate, Lindsay was still in a training bra and took after Malcolm's side of the family—no hips or ass—flat as a board, front and back. However, there was something about Dorrie she could not put her finger on. For one, she thought it odd for not one of her parents to have accompanied her on her first day of college and to have helped get her settled in. She appeared older, too. Had Kennedy thinking about Dawnn Lewis's character, Jaleesa Vinson from *A Different World*. Already, she wasn't too anxious about Lindsay growing up. To have her share a dorm room with someone who could show her the ropes—her child might come home on spring break unrecognizable. Kennedy shuddered at the thought.

Dorrie closed the bottom drawer of her dresser and sat on her bed. She crossed one leg over the other and crossed her arms over her knee. "So, Lindsay, what's your major?"

Lindsay looked at her parents. "I'm following Mom and Dad. Majoring in engineering and minoring in literature."

"You must be proud, Mr. and Mrs. Ellis."

"Yes, we are very proud of Lindsay, so long as she remembers she's here to work and not play."

Lindsay slouched and sucked her teeth. "Mom. Not again! Dad, please tell Mom to chill."

Sitting in the chair at Lindsay's desk, Malcolm peered over the *Forbes* magazine he was reading. "Mom, chill." He smiled at his daughter. "Is that better, honey?"

Lindsay stood akimbo.

"All right, all right." Kennedy looked at her watch. "Well, it's getting late, and I want to stop by to see Aunt Caroline before we head back." Kennedy stood with the Lorra Rivers bag hung over her shoulder and looked around the room, assessing Lindsay's sleeping space. "You're going to be okay, Lindsay?"

"Yes, Mom, I'm going to be fine."

Dorrie stood and pulled up beside Lindsay, draping her arm around her shoulders. "She'll be just fine. I won't let anything happen to her."

While Dorrie's words should have been comforting to Kennedy, she felt less at ease. She forced a smile at Dorrie and embraced her daughter.

"Call me if you need anything at all. I'm only four hours away. I'll be here faster than you can shake your tail feather."

"I know, Mom."

Kennedy kissed her daughter's cheek and hugged her again, this time a little longer and with a few tears.

Malcolm rolled the magazine and stuffed it in his jacket pocket. He pulled Lindsay into an embrace. "If you need anything at all, call me or your mom. Okay?"

Smiling up at her dad, he hugged her again.

Even Malcolm got choked up. "I'm going to miss you, pumpkin."

"I'll miss you, too, Dad."

Opening the door, Kennedy looked over her shoulder. "Dorrie, I'll see you again soon." She blew a kiss at Lindsay. "I love you, missy poo-poo."

Lindsay looked at her mother with tears. She hadn't called her by that name in a long time. "I love you, too." She watched the door close behind her parents, her protectors, and the ones who loved her the most. She was truly excited about being on her own, being an adult for the first time in her life and experiencing all it offered. Yet, overwhelmed with sadness, she imagined her parents walking down the hall, hand-in-hand. It felt like they were walking out of her life forever, though she knew better.

"All right, shake it off 'missy poo-poo.' You're a big girl now."

Smiling, Lindsay sat on her bed, crossed her leg at the knee, sighed, and wiped away her tears. "Yep. I'm a big girl now."

"That's right. Time to put on your big girl panties."

CHAPTER 7

South Acorn Road seemed like a stone's throw from the university. Kennedy spent many youthful years in Hampton, visiting her mother's sister, Caroline. As a child, many summers she rode her bicycle up and down South Acorn Road, sneaking to Roses Department Store and Giant to buy honey-dipped donuts and slices of cheese and pepperoni pizza.

When the Ellis' Navigator pulled into the driveway, it was like old times as Aunt Caroline stood at the front door, waiting for them. It was moments like this when the feeling of missing her mother gnawed at her heart. Aunt Caroline was truly her mother's sister— from appearance to the sound of her voice to the way she spoke Kennedy's name.

While Kennedy's smile was as wide as the ocean, her eyes were forming tiny puddles. She loved her aunt dearly, but each time she visited, memories of her mother moved to the forefront, creating an intense longing for her. She wanted to break down crying, but she suppressed that feeling. This was a happy moment, and she would not ruin it with tears.

As was the norm, Kennedy waited for Malcolm to open her door. As she put her hand in his, she stepped down out of the SUV and moved toward the steps leading to the front door, with Malcolm on her heels.

"Hi, Aunt Caroline! How are you?"

"Oh, I'm doing all right." Aunt Caroline wrapped her arms tightly around Kennedy's neck, planting a loving kiss on her cheek.

"Hi, Aunt Caroline." Malcolm kissed her on the cheek.

"Hey there, uh-huh. Come on in."

Walking inside the house, that familiar aroma intoxicated Kennedy. "I smell hot rolls."

Aunt Caroline laughed, an infectious laugh that only she possessed. It was one of those *ha-has*, with the last *ha* drawn out, dangling on her beautiful smile.

"Uh-huh, I baked rolls, and I have a few ham slices for you, too. Are you hungry?"

Kennedy smiled at Malcolm. Although stuffed after dining on lobster, shrimp, and crab, she would never turn down her aunt's hot, homemade rolls and Smithfield country ham.

"I'm starved! Did you, by any chance, bake a sweet potato pie, too?"

"You know I did."

As Kennedy and Malcolm walked through the living room, she stopped in the dining room and looked down the short hallway leading to a bathroom and two front bedrooms that belonged to Aunt Caroline's daughters—Faith, Patricia, and Wendy, who were all older than Kennedy by ten years or more. She closed her eyes, deeply inhaled the scent of Caress soap, and reminisced about the harmonious sounds of Wendy playing The Jackson 5 albums. Wendy would sing her heart out in her bedroom. Kennedy would give anything to hear Wendy singing "Stop, The Love You Save May Be Your Own" once more. She recalled, it seemed, every time her family visited, Wendy was off to a concert at the Hampton Coliseum, Patricia was heading to the beach with friends, and Faith was embarking on a shopping adventure in her yellow Volkswagen Beetle, circa 1970.

Oh, how she wished she could invent a time machine that would take her back to her childhood years. Aunt Caroline's house was in constant chaos, but in a good way. There was always something going on and family visiting, and Kennedy loved every minute.

Don't yuck it, yew it, Patricia! That was what Kennedy said when Patricia shared her bag of jellybeans with her. Kennedy smiled at the memory.

Faith, the oldest daughter, had that same infectious laughter as her mother, but it was louder and came straight from her heart. Affectionately called Rosebud, she was every bit of a rose, too— gentle, kind—with the whitest, polar-icecap melting smile.

Kennedy looked through the dining room and into the family room and saw that same recliner Uncle Cyrus, Aunt Caroline's husband, loved to lounge in. Kennedy smiled at the fond memory of listening to him play the guitar.

She proceeded through the dining room and into the kitchen, where Aunt Caroline prepared a plate of ham, rolls, collard greens with smoked pork neck bones, and potato salad.

Aunt Caroline had her head buried inside the refrigerator, retrieving a huge pitcher of homemade iced tea with mint leaves. "I have a bedroom fixed up for y'all."

"We're heading back tonight."

Aunt Caroline closed the fridge and placed the pitcher on the table. "Are you sure? You can get some rest and leave first thing in the morning."

"Yes. We really need to get back." She looked around the table. "May I have a fork, please?"

Obliging, Aunt Caroline pulled utensils from the drawer and took a seat at the table. She handed Kennedy and Malcolm forks. "It's good to see you. I haven't seen you since your mother's funeral."

Just when Kennedy had fought the urge to tear up, one fell down her cheek. "I know. I've been busy…"

Aunt Caroline poured two glasses of iced tea and moved a glass each in front of Kennedy and Malcolm. "You should never be too busy for your family. Everybody is so busy. Busy doing nothing."

Kennedy stuffed half a roll into her mouth. Her aunt was right, but how was she supposed to respond? She took a gulp of iced tea and swallowed.

Malcolm sensed his wife's uneasiness and stepped in. "Well, Lindsay is all settled in at Hampton."

"That's good. We'll keep an eye on her, and she can stay here as much as she wants to." Aunt Caroline paused, summoning composure, as her eyes welled. "It's not the same without Cyrus. I sure miss him. The house feels cold and lonely."

Kennedy reached out and caressed Aunt Caroline's hand. "I miss him, too."

Aunt Caroline nodded appreciatively at Kennedy's gesture, her eyes expressing gratitude for the shared sentiment. "He was such a warm presence in this house," she continued, a hint of nostalgia in her voice. "I never realized how much it would change without him. Every corner seems to echo his absence."

Kennedy squeezed her hand gently, offering comfort. "It's okay to miss him, Aunt Caroline. He left a lasting impact on all of us. If you ever want to share memories or talk about him, I'm here for you."

Aunt Caroline managed a small smile through her emotions. "Thank you, dear. Sometimes, it just hits me, you know? But having family around helps. I'm grateful for that."

Kennedy nodded understandingly. "We'll navigate through it together, Aunt Caroline. And whenever you need to talk or reminisce, I'll be here to listen."

Aunt Caroline sighed, appreciating the support. "You're a good soul, Kennedy, like your mother. Cyrus would be proud of the person you've become."

Kennedy smiled warmly, feeling a mix of emotions. "I hope so. I'm grateful for the memories we shared with him. They keep him close in our hearts." The dam holding back her tears finally opened, washing over her face. "Oh, Aunt Caroline, I miss Mama so much and now I've lost my baby."

That was Malcolm's cue to exit stage right. He stood with a plate and drink in hand. "Aunt Caroline, if you don't mind, I think I'll relax in the family room and watch a little television while I eat. Besides, I have to make a call."

"Sure, make yourself at home." Aunt Caroline smiled at Malcolm before turning her attention to Kennedy. "I know you do. I miss her, too. Delilah and I were close."

Smiling through her tears, Kennedy wiped her nose with her napkin. "I know. Two peas in a pod." She scanned the kitchen. "There are so many wonderful memories in this kitchen. I'll never forget the summer we visited and you,.Mama, and a host of family sat around this same table eating crabs and fried fish."

Aunt Caroline chuckled. "You remember that? That was a long time ago."

"How can I forget? It seems like yesterday to me."

"Yes, and you and Lynn were little then."

Kennedy nodded. "Yes, we were; both of us running around, sucking our thumbs."

Kennedy laughed at the visual. Lynn, Aunt Caroline's granddaughter and Patricia's daughter, and Kennedy were like two peas in a pod, too. With Kennedy being four years older, Lynn was like her little sister. Now she was a beautiful woman married to a prominent pastor with two beautiful children and living in Chicago. Kennedy was proud of her cousin and boasted about her and her family as frequently as she could to anyone who stood still long enough to listen.

"How's Lynn and the family doing?"

"They all are doing just fine. I'm going to Chicago in January."

"Dress warm. I hear Chicago's winters are brutal."

"You're looking good."

Uh-oh, here it comes. Kennedy lowered her head and settled in for what she knew was coming next.

"You're a little wide around the backside."

"Aunt Caroline, I have not gotten wide around the backside."

"No? Sure, looks like it to me."

"I love you, too, Aunt Caroline." Some things never changed, and Kennedy wouldn't have wanted it any other way. What she would have given to have heard her mother speak those same words to her today. It seemed to have been a family tradition to point out the wideness of one's backside or hips or how much weight one had gained.

Once again, Aunt Caroline's infectious laughter filled the house, and despite how wide her backside had grown, Kennedy fixed a second plate and settled in for an hour of reminiscing with her mother's sister and shedding more tears of laughter and love.

CHAPTER 8

Except for the stench of cigarette smoke and stale sex, Room 54 of the Moonlight Motel held no ambiance except for a queen-sized bed, one lamp, a nightstand, and a small, round table with two, orange-tattered, stained chairs tucked neatly under it. A single light shone from a bathroom big enough for one occupant.

It was their regular rendezvous, and Zora sat tailor-style on the bed. She looked at the silver, diamond-faced Badgley Mischka watch, a birthday gift from her best friend, Kennedy, and rolled her eyes. He was already thirty minutes late. Since they only had a limited amount of time, his consistent tardiness upset her.

"He's always late. He is an hour later than the last time. I'm so sick of this shit!"

She massaged her temples, trying to fight back one of those massive headaches that showed up when things simply did not go her way. Zora was a spoiled brat, and he intensified it by giving her what she wanted, but it was not always when she wanted, which only pissed her off.

As she flipped through the limited, local channels on the dated television set, automobiles traveling faster than the posted fifty-mile-per-hour zipped up and down Route 301, which was blanketed by darkness.

A car's headlights flooded the scant room through faded drapes.

Zora stiffened. The beat of her heart quickened.

The engine stopped running.

Suddenly, Zora's headache disappeared, and a smile graced her lips.

The car door closed.

She unfurled her legs, stretched them out in front of her, and wiggled her toes. She was now feeling giddy.

There was a knock at the door.

"It's open!"

The door opened and there he stood. As handsome as ever.

"Why are you sitting in here with the door open? That's not safe."

"I just unlocked it when I heard you pull up." That was a bald-faced lie. She quickly undressed and tossed her clothes over the arm of the stained, tattered chair. "You're late, honey."

"I know. Had other plans."

"You could have called."

"Why? You knew I was coming. I'll only call you *if* I'm not coming."

Resuming her warm spot on the bed, she crossed her legs at the ankles and pouted. "Your *other plans* are trespassing on our time."

He leaned down and kissed her on the lips. "How was your day?"

"Filled with missing you." She scooted up toward the headboard, eager for him to make up for lost time, but he was moving too slowly for her taste.

He pulled his iPhone from his pocket, engaged Pandora, and sat it on the nightstand.

With her back against the headboard, she folded her arms over her chest and tilted her head. "Baby, do you love me?"

Loosening his tie, he stood at the foot of the bed, as Chrisette Michele crooned, "A Couple of Forevers." Avoiding eye contact, he looked up at the ceiling as he pulled his tie from around his neck and tossed it on the tattered orange chair in the corner under the window.

"Well, do you?"

Still silent, the smirk on his face said, *Fuck no,* but he would not dare utter words he knew would crush her. From the collar, he unbuttoned his shirt, exposing a broad, hairy chest.

"Baby?"

"Yes." He stared at her naked beauty as he pulled off his shirt, exposing muscular shoulders and bulging biceps and triceps, a clear sign of a gym rat.

"I asked you a question."

Tossing the shirt in the chair and covering the tie, he obliged her with a response. "Yes, you did, and you ask me the same question every time, just before I dive between your tasty thighs." He raised a brow; the corners of his mouth turned up into a flirtatious smile that always melted her heart.

Smirking and rolling her eyes, she sighed heavily. "Yes, and each time you never respond."

He unbuckled the belt and removed it from the loops of a pair of antique rivet relaxed straight-leg jeans, pleasingly hugging his tight ass. He sat on the bed, bent over, and removed his shoes. Standing, he heavily sighed. "You know I care about you a lot." He unzipped his jeans and allowed them to fall around his strong calves.

She folded her arms over her breasts. "Yes, I care about you, too, but I want more."

Stepping out of the denim pile on the floor, he picked them up and tossed them in the chair on top of the rest of his clothing, except for underwear. He was a true-blue free-baller. Standing before her, his stiff penis, surrounded by a speckled-gray nest of pubic hair, beckoned for the warmth of her mouth. "Do you love me?" He knew the answer. He knew Zora was head over heels in love with him. Though, the feeling was not mutual. He adored Zora, but was he in love with her? No.

Nodding, she grinned like a child in a candy store, about to taste the sweetest candy in the world. She could not wait to suck the tip of his lollipop.

Looking down at the extended rod below his abdomen, he smiled. "Do you love him?"

"You know I do."

"I can't tell."

She crawled toward the edge of the bed, her ass up, with an arch in her back like a pussycat ready for a good stroking.

Palming the back of her head, he nudged her toward his pleasure stick. "Suck me off."

Opening her mouth wide, she devoured him and seductively wrapped her lips around the shaft.

Watching his tool disappear, feeling the head of his penis tap the back of her throat, he finger-stroked the sides of her neck, sending chills throughout her, setting her forest on fire.

Moaning, his head fell back, eyes closed, and mouth gaped open, listening to Zora suckle, swallow, and taste. The sounds she made with her mouth stoked an already blazing fire, causing his balls to tighten. "Shit, goddamn! You gon' make me come."

That was all she needed to hear, as she scooted back toward the headboard, spreading those thighs wide. "I wanna feel you come inside me, lover boy."

That was not happening. He moved toward his pants, pulled out his wallet, and eased out a gold foil package.

Her eyes widened. "Baby, no, not tonight."

"Nah, you know I can't go up in you raw."

"I'm good. I'm clean. I ain't got nothing, you know that!"

"That's not the point." He ripped open the package with his teeth.

"The point is, you don't trust me." Her whining wasn't working.

Shaking his head, he rolled the condom from head to shaft, careful not to cause any tears or holes. The last thing he needed was to shoot his seeds inside Zora for her to give birth to his kid nine months later. Climbing on the bed and crawling between her legs, he kissed her inner thigh.

Zora was still pouting. Her body stiffened at the kiss.

Now she was frustrating him. Time after time, he had to deal with her pre-school behavior, and it was working on his last nerve. "Come on, Zora. We've been over this. Don't spoil this evening." He stroked himself, trying to keep his erection. She was spoiling his mood, and there was no way he was going to let that sweetness go to waste. "Taste your pussy for me."

The look on his face made her realize the spoiled brat routine wasn't working. She slipped her middle finger inside her wetness and moved it around before pulling it out and holding it against his lips. "You taste it."

He deeply inhaled the sweetness on her finger. That did it. He was hard as concrete. With her finger deep inside his mouth, he climbed on top of her. Sucking on her finger, he aimed at his target. Bull's eye! Deep inside her, he pushed deep down until the thickness of her vaginal lips connected with his hairy flesh.

Zora moaned as she wrapped her arms tight around his neck, pulling him down on her.

Their lips met. His tongue parted her lips, and their tongues tangoed to a rhythm of their own. The kiss was passionate, yet fierce.

A deep push caused Zora to yelp, breaking their kiss.

He gazed into her eyes. "Are you okay?"

She nodded. "How do you want it? Wide open or tight as a glove?"

"A bit of both."

Zora's muscles contracted—tightening and widening—on her mental demand.

"Damn, Zora, *shit!*" That woman had complete control, making her muscles do whatever she wanted them to do, and he loved it! "Open up that hole. I wanna get deep in it."

In complete compliance, she raised her legs, pulling them back, her toes touching the headboard, her knees grazing her cheeks. Zora closed her eyes, concentrating on what she needed to do to please him, and, in a swift motion, she released her muscles, opening wide for him, just the way he liked it.

His thrusts became more powerful and deeper.

"Is that all you got? Shit, you ain't fuckin' nobody. I don't know what in the fuck you're doing." She knew taunting him would turn him into a wild beast. Since he wouldn't admit to loving her, she was going to make sure he banged her good, leaving that pissy-ass hotel room too exhausted for anything, or anyone else.

"Oh, you wanna be fucked, huh?"

"I don't think you can." She smirked as if his strokes were boring her. "Shit, fuck me, motherfucker! What the fuck's wrong with you?"

Quickly, he plastered his hand over her mouth and went to work, trying his best to knock a hole in her back as he stroked her hard. Drilling so deep inside her, the head of his penis bounced off the tip of her cervix. Each time he hit it, she damn near lost her mind. The pain was excruciating, and it showed on her face as his firm hand stifled her screams.

Something in him snapped. Did he love her? He loved how she loved it—forceful. He loved that he could release his beast to beat up on her vagina until it dried up twice a week, or as often as he called for it.

The urge was mounting as he stroked faster and harder, determined to screw her into a coma.

"Stroke your clit!"

She gazed into his eyes.

"Stroke it!"

Easing her finger between their abdomens, him pounding into her flesh; she reached her clitoris, amazed at how engorged it felt.

His eyes looked demonic. "Stroke!"

Watching her freaking herself, and her legs shaking uncontrollably, turned him on more than anything, and he pumped harder and faster, damn near about to injure himself. He could have cared less. As the last thrust hit her cervix, he exploded and stiffened. The veins in his neck protruded. After two more powerful thrusts and several animalistic grunts, exhausted, he rolled off her and onto his back, panting.

Zora was still rubbing her clitoris. "Babe, I've got to come."

He released a deep breath and assumed his position between her thighs. He had never been a selfish lover, and he would not start now.

"Spread those fat lips for me."

As she exposed her engorged knot, he tongue-stroked it with gentle, feathery licks.

"Yeah, that's it, baby." She cooed, followed by a deep-throated moan. Her back and head arched. He gave her the best head she had ever had.

With her juices flowing like crazy, wetting his chin, he wrapped his succulent lips around her knot, and sucked with fierce passion. As she panted heavily, he slid his middle finger inside her wetness and curled it up toward the roof of her vagina, locating her G-spot. That man stroked that spot until her head was about to pop. The more she moaned, the more he stroked, and the more her legs shook. When her toes pointed like a ballerina's, he knew she was nearing that wonderful place called euphoria. With a finger still inside her, he used his thumb to pull back the hood of her clitoris and sucked underneath.

That did it!

Zora's moans raised several octaves as she squirted inside his mouth. Not wanting to waste an ounce of her nectar, he opened wide, taking it all inside, holding it.

Once Zora lowered her legs, he knew she was done. He moved up to her mouth and pressed his lips against hers. She opened her mouth, tasting her juice, as their tongues frolicked.

"I love you, babe." She gazed into his beautiful, piercing brown eyes.

His response was a soft kiss on her lips and a roll onto his back.

An awkward silence hovered.

"I—"

"Hush and come here." He turned on his side and pulled her into him.

"But—"

Spooning her, he buried his face in her neck. "No." He softly kissed her neck. He massaged her breasts as she nuzzled against him.

An hour later, as she awakened, their limbs intertwined, she felt his hardened muscle against her thigh. She imagined it had a life of its own because, although he appeared to be fast asleep, his member was wide awake and ready.

He sighed, opened his eyes, and kissed her earlobe, running his tongue around the inside of her ear.

He was driving her mad. It tickled. She snickered.

He rolled over, sat up on the side of the bed, and looked at his iPhone. It was getting late.

He stared down at the stained carpet. "We have to find a new spot."

Rolling over, she rose on her elbow with a questionable look. "Why?"

"It's ratchet." He got up and strode toward the bathroom, his butt tight and round. She wanted to sink her teeth into it. He entered the bathroom and closed the door.

She looked around the small, dank hotel room. "It's not so bad. Besides, we're not here for the décor."

Minutes later, he exited the bathroom, smelling like cheap hotel soap, and moved toward the chair that held his clothes.

He started dressing. "Yeah, well, we should try someplace else for a change."

She forced a smile, feeling some kind of way. Could it have been guilt? No, she was feeling the same way she felt every time he dressed to leave her.

He patted his pockets for his keys. Grabbing his iPhone off the nightstand and ending the serenade of slow jams, he headed for the door and opened it. "I'm out."

Closing the door, Keith disappeared into the night, leaving a brisk stream of cool night air hostage in the room. She was alone after committing the ultimate betrayal and one of many indiscretions.

CHAPTER 9

Malcolm merged the Lincoln Navigator onto Interstate 64 East from Mercury Boulevard. Reaching inside her purse, Kennedy dug around for the pack of Winston Salem. She'd never smoked a day in her life until her mother died four years earlier. When she watched her mother take her last breath, she got a hankering for tobacco.

Lighting the cigarette, she told herself not to cry, but she couldn't help it. She couldn't believe it was humanly possible for a person to cry so much.

After taking five long drags, she rolled down the window and flicked the cigarette out onto the interstate. Wiping away her tears, she took a deep breath, leaving the window down to air out the smoke. The smell of it was making her nauseous. *I need to give this shit up*, she thought, as she dug in her purse for a stick of chewing gum.

Her mind now racing, she wondered what Lindsay was up to; she missed her already. The house would be empty without her, but it would give her and Malcolm serious alone time.

She looked at Malcolm as he focused on the road. "What associate did you call?"

Malcolm turned up his lips and bit the inside of his mouth in thought. He glanced at Kennedy. "Nobody. I just used it as an excuse to leave the kitchen. To give you some alone time with your aunt."

"I appreciate that, babe. Speaking of business, what's going on with the expansion?"

"Well, nothing is concrete, but…"

She pursed her lips and stared at the side of his handsome face. After a pregnant pause, Kennedy cleared her throat.

Malcolm reached across the console and caressed her knee. "It's nothing for you to worry your beautiful head over."

His touch sent chills throughout her, but her mind was on the current topic.

"Am I not a partner in this the business, Malcolm? You don't think I should know what's going on?"

With his eyes straight ahead, he nodded. "Yes, you are. Yes, you should."

"All right then." She repositioned herself in her seat, kicked off her shoes, and reclined the seat a smidgen.

"Look, Sam Jeffries and I are tossing around ideas about buying properties in Los Angeles. Specifically, in Black communities."

Kennedy looked at the side of his lips, watching him tongue-stroke his bottom lip. That sexy movement always turned her on.

"Malcolm, Los Angeles? Does that mean we would have to move?"

"No, but we would have to open an office there."

"Which means we would have to at least get an apartment there. California is at least a three-day drive and five-hour direct flight."

"Right, but we're not at that point yet."

"Good, because we're not making such a big move with our daughter in college."

"We're just tossing around the idea and planning to fly out to check out a few properties."

She raised her seat upright, faced him, and leaned her elbow on the middle console. "Malcolm Ellis, when were you going to tell me, your wife and business partner, that you and Sam are going to Los Angeles?"

Malcolm slouched and sighed. "It is not etched in stone." He squeezed her knee. "Babe, let's talk about this later. Right now, all I want to do is enjoy the ride with the love of my life."

"But, Malcolm, why Los Angeles? Why not here, where we live? Anywhere on the East Coast? I'm sure there are a shitload of properties you can buy and flip."

"It's time for Ellis Enterprises to expand."

"When is enough money going to be enough, Malcolm?"

Malcolm glimpsed her, looked in the rearview mirror, and looked back at the road. The moon lit up the night sky. "You can never have enough money."

Kennedy looked out the passenger window.

"Listen, nothing is going to change. We'll still live in Maryland. We don't have to buy a place in Los Angeles unless you want to. Honey, we can run several offices in several states from our headquarters in Maryland. It's that simple and easy."

"All right, Malcolm. I trust you know what you're doing."

"We haven't gotten this far without my not knowing what I'm doing."

"Yes, that's right."

Malcolm and Kennedy dated throughout their college years at Columbia University and eloped shortly after graduating. Malcolm was her one and only. She loved him more today than she did when he savored her for the first time, after they stood before a preacher on Valentine's Day, and recited their vows at The Little Chapel in Las Vegas, Nevada, in the spur of the moment, without loved ones by their side.

They were giddy with excitement and full of love. They were twenty-two years old and eager to start their honeymoon at the Wynn Las Vegas.

Initially, Malcolm wanted them to explore the Moonlight Bunny Ranch, but Kennedy wouldn't hear of it. It was an odd notion to spend a honeymoon at a whorehouse, but it wouldn't have been so odd for Malcolm, a sexually driven being. Now that they were married, Kennedy felt the key to a successful marriage was to be spontaneous, never denying her husband, giving in to him when and wherever he wanted—except for a brothel. That was where she drew the line. There was no way in hell she would watch her man screw another woman. Malcolm, however, fulfilled Kennedy's needs because he loved her beyond measure. She was his soulmate, his best friend, his confidant, and she had his back through thick and thin. They had spent three glorious days and nights in their marital hotel bed, only relying on room service for their meals.

Occasionally nodding, the neon sign of McDonald's golden arches towering over I-95 North caught Kennedy's attention. A hot cup of coffee was exactly what she needed. "Honey, let's stop at McDonald's and get some coffee and an apple fritter."

"Coffee and an apple fritter it is." Malcolm took the off-ramp. Fortunately, the hamburger haven was at the top of the exit, so they wouldn't have to drive too far from the interstate. Pulling into the parking lot, Malcolm found a parking space, and Kennedy retrieved the cell phone from her purse.

Lindsay's cell phone lit up with *Mom* across the display. She answered on the second ring. "Hi, Mom!"

"Hi, sweetheart. What's going on?"

"Nada, just getting used to my new digs."

"I bet you are. What time are you going to bed?"

"Mom, what kind of question is that?"

"Pardon me. I forgot you are a grown-up now." Kennedy paused, feeling sad. Her baby was no longer a baby. She was a woman now. "Lindsay, do you have condoms?"

Malcolm's head snapped around like Regan, the possessed child from *The Exorcist*.

"Do I have what? Mom!"

"Baby, there are lots of temptations in college. I want you to protect yourself, that's all. If you need me to send you a case of condoms, I will."

"Mom, a case? Are you serious?"

"Listen, just be careful. Okay?"

"Okay… Hey, Dorrie and I are going to a party tonight, welcoming the new students."

"Sounds like fun, sweetie. Please be careful and call me tomorrow. Okay?"

"I will."

"All right." Kennedy sniffled, overwhelmed with emotion. The reality that Lindsay was on her own had sunk in. The evolution was almost complete. She would soon be in the *girlfriend* stage. It was now time for Kennedy to stop being the mother and become Lindsay's best friend.

"Mom, you're not crying, are you? Geesh, Mom, I haven't moved to Iraq."

"I know, I know." Kennedy wiped her nose with the back of her hand. "I'm just being a big baby, that's all."

"I'll see you in a few weeks, anyway."

Hearing that really cheered her up. "Yes, that's right. For homecoming. Well, have a good time. I love you, sweetie."

"Love you, too, Mom. Bye!"

Tossing the cell phone back into her purse, Kennedy looked at Malcolm. From his expression, to say he was beyond shocked would be an understatement.

"What?"

"Babe, really? Condoms? A case? For our daughter?"

"Yes. *Your* daughter is a woman with a bleeding vagina."

Malcolm cringed at the thought, thinking back to the day Lindsay was born.

Lindsay was unplanned. Malcolm and Kennedy were young newlyweds and had their whole lives ahead of them. They wanted to wait at least five to ten years before starting a family. However, one heated night at a Holiday Inn in Orlando, Florida, while vacationing, they threw caution to the wind. The lovemaking was passionate, as usual, minus birth control.

When the happy couple learned they were expecting a bouncing baby in nine months, Malcolm was overjoyed, but Kennedy was terrified. While pregnancy was beautiful, it was also the miracle of life, the wonder of making a new person. The idea of their baby growing in her womb was a beautiful, overwhelming feeling, but what did she know about being a mother? Kennedy's upbringing was without sacrifices. Parker and Delilah Rhodes bathed her in all she needed and sent her to the best private schools on the East Coast. She knew she would do the same for her baby. After all, it was all she knew. However, she'd heard horror stories about the body changes and nine months of discomfort that came with pregnancy, and the excruciating pain brought on by pushing out an eight-pound human through what her husband's tool could barely penetrate without some discomfort.

All her fears and apprehensions dissipated on September 20 when her baby girl, Lindsay Grace Ellis, was born. Although she was in labor for nearly eighteen hours, and it was no easy feat to push out a seven-pound, eleven-inch baby girl, Malcolm took a back seat to being the love of Kennedy's life. As she held their newborn daughter to her chest, emotions overwhelmed the proud papa. It was love he felt, looking at the two most important, beautiful people in his life. Then, he determined he would put nothing or no one above the loves of his life.

Seeing the line inside McDonald's was longer than the drive-thru, Malcolm backed out of the parking space and drove through the drive-thru before resuming the remaining two-hour drive.

Enjoying the beautiful August night, she had to bask in the peaceful late-summer mode for a tick.

It was a perfect moment within an imperfect world.

Happiness and serenity oozed from her, so much so that she eased Jaheim into the CD player and pressed track five. "Put That Woman First" filled the vehicle.

Looking at her husband, she sighed with affection, thinking about how he put his family before everything. She had read many stories from abandoned women; tales of horror. Although she empathized with those women, it was good that she couldn't comprehend their despair. She had a good man.

And every good man deserves a surprise, she mused, slipping out of her shoes and wiggling her toes. She pulled up in the seat, leaned over to Malcolm, and stuck her tongue in his ear. "Either we do it right here, in the drive-thru, or you hurry and find a spot for us to fuck."

Without placing the order, Malcolm drove out of the drive-thru lane in search of a dark, secluded area.

CHAPTER 10

Lindsay stepped out of the communal shower room, wrapped in her bathrobe, and headed down the hallway toward her dorm room. Passing through the student lounge, young girls reclined on sofas and oversized chairs, talking on cell phones, and watching television. This was her newfound freedom, and she had fallen in love with it.

When Lindsay entered the room, Dorrie stood behind the door, admiring her outfit in the full-length mirror double-tacked to the back of the door.

Lindsay tapped Dorrie with the door. "Oh, I'm sorry."

"It's okay."

Lindsay looked at Dorrie from head to toe. "Wow, you look great." Actually, she thought she looked more like a stripper ready to hit the stage at the club than someone going to a campus party.

"Thanks!" Dorrie smiled, her glossy red lips exposing pretty white teeth. "Girl, you better hurry up. What are you going to wear?"

"Just jeans and a shirt."

"Jeans and a—" Dorrie laughed. "Girl, spice it up a bit. There's going to be men there. Don't you wanna look good?" She continued to admire her thick, curvy, busty frame in the mirror.

"Well, I guess…"

Dorrie faced Lindsay. "Let me guess. Is this your first party with guys?" Dorrie was as sarcastic as one could be, and Lindsay didn't appreciate it one bit, but she held her tongue and twisted up her mouth. She was no fighter, and Dorrie looked like she could tussle pretty well. "We're about the same size." Dorrie sorted through her tiny dorm room closet. "Let me see what I can find you to wear."

Lindsay found Dorrie amusing, as she was clearly smaller than Dorrie in size. Especially in the chest area. While Dorrie was a 38-F, Lindsay had barely graduated from a training bra. Compared to

Dorrie's curvaceous hips and thighs, Lindsay's were almost non-existent.

Yes, Lindsay was stepping into adulthood, but her body appeared to still be in junior high school.

"Ah!" Dorrie held up a sexy, deep purple skimpy dress that exposed the mid-section through a diamond cut-out. "This would be perfect for you."

"It looks a little too big for me."

"That's what safety pins are for, honey. What size shoe do you wear?"

"Eight."

"Me, too. You can wear these." She tossed a pair of gold shoes at Lindsay.

Lindsay quickly lifted her feet; the platform pumps barely missed her toes. She looked down at the shoes and distorted her mouth. "Uh, I don't think so. Look, I can wear my jeans and I'll be fine. Maybe I'll do the dress for another party, but I appreciate the offer. Thank you."

"All right then, but at least let me do your hair and makeup."

"What's wrong with my hair? And I don't wear makeup."

"For one, you look like you're one grade from getting out of elementary school with that ponytail."

"I do not!"

"*I do not!*" Dorrie shook her head. "You sound like one, too. Look, sis, we are in college. We're adults now, so we have to look and act the part."

Lindsay folded her arms across her chest in defiance. "I don't know about this, Dorrie."

Dorrie threw up her hands in exasperation. "Okay, suit yourself, but I'm telling you right now that you're not going to get anyone interested in you if you're going to be walking around here looking like you walked off the set of *Saved by the Bell*."

"Saved by the what?"

"It was before your time, never mind."

This was all too much for Lindsay. She'd never worn more than lip-gloss and a ponytail. She wanted to fit in, and all the young women she'd seen moving about campus wore eye shadow, lipstick, short skirts, and tight jeans, something her mother adamantly opposed.

Mom wasn't there to oversee, so Lindsay threw caution to the wind.

"Fine, but not too much!"

Dorrie perked up and released a giggle. She pulled out the chair from her small desk and positioned it to face Lindsay. "Sit here." She turned her back to Lindsay and plugged in her flat iron.

Lindsay moved slowly toward the chair and sat down with caution. She said a quick prayer and folded her hands in her lap. "My mama is going to kill me."

Dorrie grabbed Lindsay's ponytail, snatched off the rainbow-colored scrunchy, and threw it across the room, landing it in the trashcan. "Girl, yo mama ain't here, so relax."

Lindsay fidgeted. "You know, I'm not used to this kind of stuff."

Dorrie tapped her on the shoulder. "Keep still, and what are you talking about?"

"Girlie stuff. My friends…we never did each other's hair. In fact, Mom wouldn't allow anyone to do my hair except Ms. Siggy, who has been doing my hair since I was five years old."

Dorrie held hairpins between her teeth as she parted Lindsay's hair in sections. "When was the last time you greased your scalp?"

"I don't put grease in my hair."

"Your scalp looks mighty dry."

"No grease, Dorrie. If Ms. Siggy doesn't grease my scalp then you won't either."

"Fine." Surrendering, she used a flat iron to press a small section of hair between two hot plates.

Lindsay twitched her nose. "What's that smell?"

"Nothing. It's supposed to smell like that."

"My hair doesn't smell like that when Ms. Siggy does it."

"Ms. Siggy." Dorrie sucked her teeth. "I'm tired of hearing about Ms. Siggy. Ms. Dorrie is doing this head today."

"Dorrie—"

"Will you just relax, and think about that fine man you gonna give it up to tonight?" She chuckled, tickling herself pink with her off-handed, colorful comment.

However, Lindsay didn't find it the least bit funny. She rolled her eyes.

Fifteen minutes later, Lindsay stood before the mirror. She didn't recognize the beautiful young woman looking back at her. What used to be in a ponytail was now flowing down her back and around her face in a sophisticated feathered bob. Looking like a Black Farrah Fawcett, mocha glossy lips and smoky eyes accentuated her café au lait complexion. Lindsay was beyond speechless as her mouth hung open.

Still primping and fluffing Lindsay's hair, Dorrie beamed at her. "Well, what do you think?"

"I hardly recognize myself."

"I bet you don't. Gone is Mama's baby, and here to stay is Big Daddy's Girl."

Lindsay looked at Dorrie with a raised brow. "Uh, 'Big Daddy?'"

Dorrie nodded and smiled. The pair fell out with hearty laughter. Lindsay felt as if she were home with her girlfriends, and it felt good. Catching her breath, she looked at Dorrie and knew she would become her friend for life.

"Okay, now…since you insist on wearing those jeans, at least put on another top."

"What's wrong with my top?"

"It's plaid. It looks like something straight out of the hills of West Virginia. Look like you need to be saying, 'Night, John Boy.'"

"Being a little stereotypical, aren't you, and who is John Boy?"

"You don't watch much TV, I see." Dorrie sifted through her drawer. "Here, put this on." She handed Lindsay a sheer black sheath with a black camisole. "It hangs off the shoulder and will look good with your hair."

Shrugging, Lindsay surrendered and followed Dorrie's instructions. What could it hurt? She took off her plaid button-down shirt and slipped into the black sexy top. Looking in the mirror, she smiled, liking what she saw. She liked it very much. She could get used to the new Lindsay.

Dorrie handed her a pair of huge silver hoops. "Ears pierced, right?"

Lindsay nodded and reached for the earrings. Sighing, she put them on.

"Damn, sister, you look *hot!*" Dorrie shook her head. "If I were into women…"

Lindsay side-eyed Dorrie, smiled, and stared at her reflection in the mirror. Yes, she looked hot.

Dorrie wrapped her hand around the doorknob and took one last glance in the mirror. "Let's roll!" She opened the door, leaving Lindsay behind. "Come on, Lindsay!"

"I'm coming!" She rushed out the door, closing it behind her. "Who is John Boy?"

"Google it."

It was like nothing Lindsay had ever seen: wall-to-wall testosterone and half-naked young women bumping, grinding, and twerking, and dropping it as low as it could go. While she didn't partake in the typical partying activities of people her age, she bopped her head in fascination, observing the captivating scene unfolding before her. It was like watching a TikTok video. There was so much going on—kissing, gyrating, and groping body parts. She was a conservative fish in a liberal pond. She was beyond uncomfortable, but she was determined to go with the flow and experience this new life she'd embarked upon.

Bent at the knees, Dorrie gyrated her hips to Chuck Brown's "Chuck Baby." Grooving to the infectious rhythm of the go-go beat, a funky subgenre of music known for its distinctive rhythmic patterns and interactive call-and-response with the lively audience, she found herself immersed in a rich musical tradition originating from African-

American musicians in Washington, DC, from the mid-sixties to current day. She was grooving as though she were a native who grew up on the city's homegrown sound.

"Girl, isn't this hot?" Dorrie yelled over the loud music, but Lindsay didn't hear her, and she wasn't a lip reader.

Lindsay leaned in closer. "What did you say?"

"I said, isn't this hot?"

"Oh, yeah…I guess so."

"Come on, let's get us a drink!" Dorrie grabbed her by the hand, singing, "Chuck baby don't give a—" and pulling her to the makeshift bar. "I'll have a Moscato, please." Dorrie looked over her shoulder at Lindsay. "And my friend will have—" She faced Lindsay. "What do you want?"

"I don't drink."

Dorrie rolled her eyes and turned her attention to the young man distributing drinks. "She'll have the same."

"No! I won't have the same! I'm not twenty-one and neither are you or anyone else in here." She peered at the young man tending the bar, but he couldn't hear her. His back was to her, and the loud music and chatter surrounding him drowned her out.

"Girl, stop trippin'. We are off-campus." Dorrie took the red plastic cups from the bartender and handed one to Lindsay. "It's time for you to pull up your panties and roll with the big girls now, honey." She smiled widely. "Cheers!"

Lindsay forced a smile and reluctantly took her first sip of alcohol. She closed her eyes and allowed the sweet taste to swish around her mouth and ooze down her throat.

Not bad, she thought, opening her eyes and looking directly at Dorrie.

Dorrie smiled and nodded. "Good, isn't it?"

Lindsay nodded. "Very." She took a gulp. As she swallowed, she heard her mother's voice in her head: *Slow your roll, honey, that is not Kool-Aid. It'll sneak up on you.* Her mother could have been a seer, as far as she was concerned. She always seemed to creep into her mind when she was doing something she knew she had no business doing.

One hour and three cups of Moscato later, Lindsay felt no pain. She transformed into an off-beat, gyrating young woman, dancing alone in the corner. Each cup of wine eased her into a comfort zone she knew nothing about yet liked very much.

The conservative fish liked the liberal pond.

Dorrie never moved from Lindsay's side the entire evening. Knowing Lindsay lacked experience, she felt responsible for her new roommate. Besides, Lindsay was growing on her.

"You all right, girlie?"

"Yep, I'm good." Lindsay's speech was slurring, her tongue thick as a marshmallow.

"Yeah, I bet you are." She took Lindsay's cup. "Last call for you, honey bunny."

Zoned out, Lindsay smiled and looked around the quaint club—torn down from the floor down—fucked up and completely unaware of the cutie pie across the room that had been eying her for a while.

A junior at Hampton University, Maxwell Dawson was a premed student and an integral member of the university's football team. Throughout his college years, he showcased his athleticism and dedication to the sport, embodying the spirit of teamwork and perseverance. Excelling on the football field, he had earned the respect and admiration of both his teammates and coaches. Everyone young woman on campus adored him. Not because he was easy on the eyes, but because he had a bright, promising future.

Off the field, Maxwell possessed a warm and charismatic personality that drew people to him. His genuine interest in others and willingness to lend a helping hand made him an approachable and supportive friend.

Beyond his passion for football, Maxwell held ambitious aspirations for his future. He had a deep desire to pursue a career in medicine. His fascination with the human body and the opportunity to make a positive impact on people's lives fueled his determination. Maxwell demonstrated the same level of dedication and commitment to his academic pursuits as he did to football, constantly striving to excel in his studies and gain the knowledge and skills for his future profession.

Standing six feet tall, Maxwell's physical presence radiated a captivating aura of strength and athleticism. His well-built, muscular frame was a testament to his dedication to maintaining peak physical condition. His confident swagger was that of an accomplished athlete, and his broad shoulders gave him a commanding presence on and off the field. Maxwell's deep brown eyes, full of determination and focus, revealed a glimpse of his unwavering dedication to becoming Lindsay's first love. With a mocha complexion, with a warm undertone, Maxwell sported a short, well-groomed haircut that complemented his chiseled jawline, adding to his rugged charm.

Maxwell's style reflected a balance of athletic comfort and effortless coolness, often donning sport hoodies, well-fitted jeans, and trendy sneakers.

Standing on the sideline, Maxwell watched her awkwardly grind and pulsate her hips, clearly inexperienced, a sign of a fresh-off-the-boat virgin. Finally, it was time to make his move. He patted his friend, Charles "Chucky" Wilson, on the chest. "I'll be back." He maneuvered through the crowd toward Lindsay.

Her eyes were tightly closed, her body swaying to Frankie Beverly & Maze's "Before I Let Go."

"Hi."

She didn't see him. However, Dorrie spotted him before he made his move across the floor. Seasoned with young men, Dorrie never missed a beat. She noticed the dude checking out Lindsay when they walked through the door.

Dorrie nudged her roommate, startling her. "You have a visitor, girl. Open your eyes!"

Lindsay stopped moving. When she opened her eyes, her mouth hung open.

With a gentle touch, he lifted her chin with his finger, a smile playing at the corners of his mouth. Chuckling to himself, he felt flattered by her reaction to his mere presence.

"Hi." He flashed the prettiest smile she'd ever seen. He looked nothing like the boys from her high school.

"Hi. Umm, hello. I mean—" She sighed, her tongue feeling three sizes too large. She felt like a bumbling idiot, and she was beyond embarrassed. She wanted to kick herself, but she was too afraid to move. Her feet felt like they were deep in concrete.

Smiling, he extended his hand. "I'm Max."

Lindsay didn't move and stared at his hand like it was contagious.

He peered into her beautiful hazel-brown eyes. "Do you want my arm to fall off?"

Dorrie smacked Maxwell's arm and fell out with laughter. "Cute. I saw that movie, too."

Aware that Dorrie's personality was more outgoing compared to Lindsay's, Maxwell overlooked Dorrie and kept his focus on Lindsay. "Well, what's your name?"

"Lindsay. Her name is Lindsay. I'm her roommate, Dorrie." She nudged her roommate again.

"Yes, what she said." Lindsay lowered her head and fell back against the wall, grabbing her head.

"Are you okay?" Maxwell reached out for Lindsay's hand, offering support as he helped her regain her balance.

Sensing her unsteady equilibrium, Lindsay felt disoriented. This feeling was new to her. "Why is everything spinning? I don't feel well."

"Maybe we should step outside and get some fresh air."

Taking hold of Lindsay's arm, Dorrie agreed. "Yes, let's go outside."

However, Maxwell swiftly pulled Lindsay closer to him, asserting his protective presence. Looking directly at Dorrie, it was clear Maxwell held no affection for her.

Dorrie protested. "No way, I don't know you. I won't just let you take my girl and—"

Maxwell raised his hand, silencing her. "I'm Maxwell Dawson. I live off-campus at 222 Brinkley Road, Apartment 212." He then glanced across the room, pointing out his roommate. "That guy in the red shirt over there is Chucky Wilson, my roommate. Lindsay is safe with me, trust me. I won't let anything happen to her."

Lindsay's face flushed with nausea, causing her to stammer. "I think I'm going to—" She bent over and emptied her stomach.

Dorrie, startled by the scene, quickly distanced herself from Lindsay, much to Maxwell's irritation.

Remaining faithfully by Lindsay's side, Maxwell cast a scornful gaze at Dorrie. "Your girl, huh?"

It was definitely time for Lindsay to call it a night. All eyes were on her as if the entire student body had formed a circle around her. Embarrassed, Lindsay nestled into Maxwell's embrace while he escorted her outside. The waterworks started and Lindsay cried uncontrollably. It took all she had not to cry out, "I want my mama," but she knew she would've been the butt of every joke on campus if she had.

Once in the fresh night air, Lindsay regained her composure. She looked around, but Dorrie was nowhere to be found. *Figures*, Lindsay thought, as she thanked Maxwell for helping her. "I really appreciate it."

Maxwell shrugged. "Drinking isn't your thing, huh?"

Bashfully, she shook her head. "I don't drink."

"Then why start tonight?"

Aside from being abashed, she was speechless. She had never spoken to a college man before.

Motioning toward a park bench for them to sit on, he took her by the arm. "You know, a drunken woman looks awful."

"It doesn't feel too good, either."

"So, then why—"

"Is this your first year at Hampton?" Interrupting his inquisition, she simply was not in the mood to justify her actions.

"I'm a junior, you?"

"My first year."

"Oh, a newbie." He chuckled, resting his elbows on his thighs. "So, Lindsay, where are you from?"

"National Harbor, Maryland."

"Yeah? I'm from Bowie."

"Yeah? That's cool." She immediately regretted that she used that word. It sounded so immature. *Who says 'cool' anymore?*

Maxwell erupted in an outburst of laughter. "Yeah, you are a freshman."

Lindsay's relaxed posture stiffened. "What do you mean by that?"

Unknowingly, he had crossed the line, and she wasn't letting him get away with it, drunk or sober. One thing she learned from her mother was to demand respect and damn it, she was about to get it, as her body language suggested, regardless of the nausea.

Surrendering, Maxwell shook his head. "Whoa, whoa, baby. Don't get—"

She jumped to her feet. "Baby? Do I look like a baby to you?"

"Look, I'm sorry, all right? I didn't mean to offend you."

"Well, you did. Have a good night!" Pivoting, Lindsay walked away with tears welling in her ears, a spinning head, a nauseous stomach, and with no clue where she was.

"Wait! Lindsay! Wait!"

A mixture of emotions overwhelmed her, and regret flooded her thoughts as she felt she had made a colossal mistake. Instead of confronting the issue head-on, like the strong woman she aspired to be, she ran away, like a mere child.

As the first rays of morning sunlight filtered through the blinds, Lindsay retreated further under the covers.

Across the room, Dorrie occupied a spot on her twin bed, observing Lindsay.

Lindsay pulled back the covers to see Dorrie staring at her, which struck her as peculiar. "I feel awful." She flipped over onto her stomach. "I am never drinking again."

Dorrie leaned back on her bed. "Oh, you'll be fine. You just have to learn how to hold your liquor, that's all."

"I can't believe I threw up on him."

Dorrie's hyena-like laughter engulfed the small room. "Well, you didn't throw up on *him*, but you were close enough."

"I guess he thinks I'm a child, I'm sure."

"No, he doesn't."

Lindsay flipped onto her back. "Are you kidding me? I can't believe how childish I acted last night. My mother would have a fit if she knew."

"Will you leave *Mommy* in Maryland where she belongs? Besides, I won't tell her. Will you?"

Lindsay sat up, swung her legs over the edge of the bed, and slipped her feet inside faux leopard print slippers. Before she could respond to Dorrie's question, there was a knock at the door.

"Yes?" Dorrie called out.

A tiny female voice came from the other side of the door. "There's a call for Lindsay on the payphone, in the lounge."

"Thank you."

Lindsay frowned at Dorrie. "I wonder who that can be."

"Maybe it's your Mr. Wonderful." Dorrie slapped her thigh in laughter.

"You're chock full of jokes this morning." Lindsay put on her robe and left the room.

Approaching the payphone, she passed a circle of young women at a table, playing a game of spades. For it to be so early in the morning, they were jovial and full of high-volume chatter. Lindsay wasn't an early morning riser, and right now, she felt like crap. Her body ached, and with each step she took, she felt like her foot would break off at the ankle.

She grabbed the dangling receiver. "Hello?"

"Hi, honey!"

"Mom? Hey! Why didn't you call my cell phone?"

"I tried, but it went directly to voicemail. Did you forget to charge it?"

"Yeah, I guess so."

"How was the party?"

Though Lindsay desired to evade the entire subject, she was well aware of her mother's unwavering nature. Kennedy Ellis had an uncanny ability to address and delve into any matter, leaving nothing untouched or avoidable.

"It was okay."

"Just okay? What did you wear?"

"Mom."

"Oh, come on, Lindsay, I want to know. Your college years are going to be the most exciting years of your life, and I want to share them with you." She waited for Lindsay to respond. When she didn't, Kennedy started a trip down memory lane. "I remember when I was in college—"

"I wore jeans and Dorrie did my hair and makeup." Cringing, she regretted it as soon as she said it. *Here it comes…one, two—*

"Makeup? Lindsay, what did I tell you about wearing makeup?"

"I'm eighteen—"

"No, you won't be eighteen until September 20, young lady!"

"I'm sorry I told you, Ms. I-Want-To-Share-Them-With-You."

Kennedy surrendered. "Okay, okay. I raised you into a beautiful young woman. I trust you know what's best."

Lindsay's attention diverted to the game of spades across from her. They were having so much fun. She wished she knew how to play spades.

"How's Dad?"

"He's fine. You need to charge your phone."

"Okay, I've got to go, Mom. I need to shower and dress."

"What are you and Dorrie doing today?"

"Oh, I don't know. I'll let you know if we do anything interesting. I'll call you later."

"Do you know what her parents do for a living?"

Eyebrows bunching, Lindsay rolled her eyes. "I didn't ask."

"Well, does she have sisters, brothers—"

"I didn't ask."

"How old is she?"

"I didn't ask."

Now frustrated with the lack of answers, Kennedy sighed. "What did you ask?"

"Nothing. It's not my business, Mom."

"Sweetheart, you should know something about the person who is sharing your space."

"Mom, in due time. Okay?"

"And you'll tell me everything?"

A deep, resounding sigh left Lindsay's throat and into Kennedy's ear.

"All right! I'm done with the twenty questions, but will you do me a favor, please?"

"What's that?"

"Take your time when drinking liquor."

Stunned, Lindsay's back was ramrod straight. She looked around and up and down the corridor for a secret camera. *How does she know?*

"Don't mix your liquors. Lord, I can't believe I'm telling you this, but you have to know, or else you're going to spend your freshmen year with hangovers. If you start with drinking white liquor, don't mix it with dark. And, for goodness's sake, Lindsay, leave those mixed, sweet drinks alone. They are full of sugar and won't do anything but have you throwing up all over the place, and spreading those hips of yours…"

Kennedy's chatter seemed to have faded as Lindsay was speechless and dumbfounded. This conversation shocked her more than the birds and bees conversation she had with her mother when she was twelve years old.

"…and don't forget condoms, although you shouldn't have sex until you get married." Kennedy paused and sighed heavily. "Well, I guess that's it."

"Are you sure that's it?" Lindsay's sarcasm was as thick as molasses.

"Don't get smart! Oh, here's what I do. I drink Hennessey. Drink it straight, don't mix it with Coke, ginger ale, or any kind of soda or syrup. Sip on it. Or, better yet, stick to white wine, and sip it. I like Moscato. It's sweet. You may like it, too. Red wine isn't so bad either can be on the dry side, though. Don't let the guys see you drinking up booze like a fish. They'll take you for being a lush and easy. Plus, no man wants to take a lush or easy woman home to his mama. I remember when I was your age and came into the house drunk. Your grandfather said, 'I swear, ain't nothing worse than a drunk-ass woman.' So, you remember that. A drunk woman is ugly. Plain old ugly. You hear me, Lindsay? There's nothing cute about being drunk. Plus, a drunkard has no control of her faculties. Always maintain one hundred percent control over your actions and thoughts. Know what you're doing when you're doing it. Better yet, know what you're going to do before you do it. Oh, and for God's sake, please don't put a cigar in your mouth. I don't know why a woman wants to puff on a—"

"Mom!" Lindsay wanted to end the call so badly.

"You'll be all right if you just do what I tell you to do."

"Okay, Mom. I will. I love you."

"I love you, too, sweetheart. Tell Dorrie I said hello."

"I will. Bye."

"Bye-bye."

What on Earth? Convinced her mother had some kind of telepathy, that whole phone call was strange, but not unusual. She knew she couldn't put anything past her mother because she was truly old school. She had "been there, done that," her mother always told her. "You aren't doing anything that I haven't done," Kennedy had told her when she felt Lindsay was scheming. "In fact, I did it better, so don't even think about it! I played the game and played it well."

Lindsay chuckled at the thought and returned to her room.

She left the door ajar and plopped down on her bed. "I can't believe it."

Dorrie was flipping through *Vibe* magazine.

"Is everything okay?"

"Yeah, it was just my mom. My phone is off, so she tracked me down."

"At least your mom cares."

"What does that mean?"

"It means I haven't spoken to my mother since I've been here. Not even a call to see if I made it safely. So, stop complaining."

At the tender age of eighteen, Dorrie grappled with a strained relationship with her parents, which weighed heavily on her heart. Her mother, a dedicated home health aide, and her father, a hardworking laborer, existed as distant figures in her life, their presence often overshadowed by the challenges they faced within their marriage and their demanding work schedules.

Growing up, Dorrie had to figure things out on her own. A little independent warrior, she faced the world with little help. She really wanted the love and support that a caring family should give, but most of the time, she had to find her own way through life.

The absence of parental involvement left Dorrie feeling bitter toward her parents, harboring deep resentment. Despite these challenges, and knowing education was her ticket to a brighter future, Dorrie worked hard and researched all kinds of scholarships. She leaned on her high school counselors and teachers for advice, and they showed her how to write scholarship essays and highlight her achievements and community involvement to stand out from the crowd, but it didn't stop there. Dorrie didn't just sit around waiting for opportunities to fall into her lap. She got involved in extracurriculars and volunteered like crazy. Not only did it make her feel good, but it also impressed the scholarship committees.

She went into full-on detective mode and dug up many local organizations and foundations that offered scholarships. Dorrie wasn't about to miss any chance, so she applied for as many as she could. It wasn't always easy, but she kept her head up and stayed optimistic.

In the end, her hard work paid off. Not only did Dorrie receive a full ride to Hampton University, but her dreams were also coming true.

Speechless, Lindsay looked down at her slippers. "Sorry. I didn't mean to offend."

Dorrie shook her head. "You didn't offend me, roomie. I just don't have the best relationship with my folks, but my brother and sister—" Dorrie settled onto her bed, feeling the need to open up about her relationship with her siblings. She smiled, feeling a mix of nostalgia and fondness. "You know, Lindsay, I got two amazing siblings: Rachel and Marcus. They've been my rock, especially with all the family drama."

Her curiosity piqued, Lindsay crossed one leg over the other, and leaned in, resting her elbow on her knee. "Tell me more about them. I'm an only child, so I don't know what it's like to have siblings. What's your relationship like?"

Dorrie grinned. "Rachel's my little sis, a sophomore at Hampton High School. I feel responsible for her, you know? I wanna be there for her when our parents can't. We spill secrets, dream together, and have endless laughs."

Lindsay was hooked, captivated by their bond. "And what about Marcus, your brother? How's your relationship with him?"

Dorrie's expression softened. "Marcus is five years older, and he's like my college guide. He already did the whole first-gen college thing. We share experiences and he gives me solid advice, helping me navigate this new college world. We support each other, celebrate wins, and lend an ear when things get tough."

Lindsay's eyes sparkled with interest. "Sounds like you guys are super tight. How's it feel being away from them now that you're in college?"

"It's bittersweet, you know? I'll miss them like crazy, but being away gives me space to grow on my own. The bond's unbreakable, though. We'll still support each other through texts and calls. Plus, I'm here in Hampton, so they might drop by sometime."

Moved by Dorrie's story, Lindsay smiled warmly. "You really love your siblings, huh? Family is everything, right? They're a huge part of who we are."

"Absolutely. Even with all the stuff I've been through, they've been my strength. We've had to figure things out on our own, but those shared experiences make us who we are."

The room fell into a moment of contemplative silence as Dorrie's reflections lingered.

"So, Dorrie, what's your relationship like with your parents?"

The atmosphere in the room turned somber. Dorrie took a deep breath, contemplating how to convey her complicated relationship with her parents.

Dorrie's expression turned serious as she thought about it. "It's a bit complicated, to be honest. They both have demanding jobs—my mom's a home health aide, and my dad's a construction worker. They work crazy hours to provide for us, and I get that. But it also means they're not always emotionally or physically there for us."

Lindsay listened closely, feeling the weight of Dorrie's words. "That must've been tough. Did you have to fend for yourself a lot?"

Dorrie nodded, a mix of emotions surfacing. "Yeah, you can say that. I was a latchkey kid, so I had to take care of myself and my sister, Rachel, most of the time. It wasn't easy, figuring things out on my own without much guidance or support from my parents. It made me independent, but I also craved that emotional connection and guidance from them."

Lindsay extended Dorrie a warm smile and a head nod in support. "I can't even imagine how challenging that must've been. But girl, you've come so far! Your strength and resilience are shining through."

Dorrie managed a small smile, grateful for Lindsay's understanding. "Thanks. College will definitely be a game-changer for me. I'll be able to pursue my dreams and break free from some of that past stuff. Scholarships and hard work will really help me build a life."

Lindsay pointed at Dorrie, smiled, and nodded. "You should be super proud of yourself. Your determination is inspiring, seriously. You are proof that you can make a better future, even when life throws shit your way."

Dorrie's eyes glistened with gratitude and strength as she took in Lindsay's kind words. "Thanks, sis. Your support means the world to me. I'm still figuring things out but having you as a new friend and roommate makes it all easier." Then Dorrie chuckled. "You said 'shit.'"

"My mom's favorite word, among others."

In that moment, Lindsay and Dorrie shared a deep understanding and connection, as their conversation unveiled the complex dynamics of family and the strength it would take to maneuver this thing called life.

Dorrie's focus turned to her growling stomach. "I'm hungry, you?"

"Yeah, I suppose I could eat something."

"Great! I know a place off-campus where everyone hangs out. Let's get dressed and go!"

"Sure, let's go." Lindsay pulled herself up off the bed and sauntered to her closet, where she retrieved her toiletries, towel, and robe for the shower, with Dorrie on her heels, bubbling over with excitement. Smiling and shaking her head at her roommate, Lindsay was liking this independent part of life—coming and going as she pleased, without having to get permission from Mom and Dad.

The Diner was a hole in the wall off the beaten path and frequented by the entire student body. More like The Pit from *A Different World*, except no Mr. Gaines or Whitley Gilbert running amuck or jukebox playing, just what seemed like one hundred conversations going on at once. The loud chatter was deafening to Lindsay's hangover.

They slid into the only vacant booth near the back of the diner.

"I'll be right with you," the young waitress belted, as she flew past their table.

"Sure is crowded in here today."

Dorrie nodded, looking around. "Yeah, it's always like this after a party."

"You've been here before?"

"Nope."

"Then how do you know it's always crowded after a party?"

Dorrie shrugged and smacked her lips. "I don't know, just guessing."

"Oh…"

The young waitress returned with two glasses of water and two menus. "Welcome to The Diner. Other than water, would you like orange juice, apple juice?" She hastily looked from Dorrie to Lindsay.

"Apple juice sounds good."

Lindsay smiled. "Water's fine." She was still feeling a little sour in the stomach.

"I'll be back with your apple juice and to take your orders."

"Thank you." Dorrie's head swiveled on her neck. "This campus is full of fine brothers!"

Speaking of fine brothers, before Lindsay could fix her mouth to comment, Maxwell approached their table.

"Hi, Lindsay." He looked at Dorrie and smirked. "Hello." He smiled at Lindsay. "How are you feeling this morning?"

Should she smile now? Maxwell was so close she could see the pores on his smooth, hairless face.

Bashfully, she breathed, inched her chest forward, tilted her head, and looked up. "I'm feeling…fine."

He shoved his hands in his pockets, a sign of nervousness. "That's good. I was worried about you."

Ashamed of her behavior from the previous night, she still hadn't forgotten about him calling her a baby. That grudge she refused to relinquish. Her chest deflated. "Really?"

Feeling like it was time for her to flee and give them time to talk, Dorrie nodded across the diner. "I see someone over there I want to catch up with. Max, take my seat."

"Wait, what? I thought we were going to have breakfast. I thought you were hungry."

"I am and we are, except you're going to have breakfast with Max, and I'm going to mosey on over and talk to that fine boo sitting over there all by his lonesome. I'll see you later."

Dorrie hurried off as Maxwell took her seat and she darted toward Chucky, Maxwell's roommate, and took the seat Maxwell had vacated.

It was awkward, and Maxwell knew he had to make things right between them or else he would look at a sourpuss during breakfast.

"Look, Lindsay, I'm sorry. I didn't mean to offend you last night. I put my foot in my mouth, and I'm really sorry. Let me make it up to you. Whatever you want to do, we'll do; I just don't want you mad at me."

She smiled, feeling extremely flattered. If this was part of growing into a woman, she liked it. Plus, she liked him…a lot.

"It's okay, Max. I'm sorry, too. I overreacted."

He smiled, daring not to comment. He didn't want to fall out of her good graces…again.

CHAPTER 12

Zora paced the living room floor of her tenth-floor condominium at Maryland's National Harbor she shared with Maceo Hicks. She stopped in front of the floor-to-ceiling, wall-to-wall window and looked out at the Potomac River. The moon reflecting off it made it look like dancing glass. She loved the view.

Even though she loved him and was in a ten-year relationship with Maceo, she was *in love* with Keith. It was different with Keith.

Zora's bare feet slapped against the deep oak hardwood floor as she walked to the white Italian leather sofa. Riddled with guilt, she was so torn. On one hand, LaTonya was her friend, but they were not close like she and Kennedy. She had met her through her husband, Keith, who was Maceo's homeboy from New Orleans, Louisiana, who moved to Maryland one year after Maceo relocated for the woman he loved. After Maceo got a business loan to open Hicks European Automotive Shop, he invited Keith to move to Maryland to manage his new business. Excited to leave New Orleans for a better life, Keith accepted, and within six months, he was working for Maceo. One year later, Keith met LaTonya, who brought her Mercedes Benz into the shop for repairs. Eight months later, Maceo and Zora witnessed Keith and LaTonya on their wedding day.

Despite his marital status and her significant other status, Keith was the love of Zora's life from the moment she laid eyes on him. He was her soulmate. She had never felt this way about any other man, not even Maceo. Sure, she loved Maceo, but her love for Keith was deep-seated. Loving Keith was like opening a book and finding a language she had never read before. His love was beautiful and stimulating, although he never admitted to loving her or being in love with her. It was an enigma. She did not want to live without him in her life, even though she knew she could never openly have him.

As she closed her eyes, it rushed back to her—the day LaTonya hosted a party for Erika, her Jamaican-born girlfriend who was testing the waters with her new business venture, Erogenous Pleasures. It was a night of sex talk, vibrators, dildos, licking flavored body gels, eating edible panties, trying on sexy lingerie, and drinking an abundance of wine and Patrón shots. Needless to say, all the women were smashed and had released all inhibitions.

"A vibrator is all I need," one guest had said, who had licked the tip of her finger and stroked the crotch of her pants. "It's better than a dick, as far as I'm concerned."

Erika looked at her wide-eyed. "What?" Her Jamaican accent was thick like molasses. "Yuh crazy, gyal. There nutin' betta dan a hood."

"A hood? What in the hell is a hood?"

"Dats whuh wi call a penis inna Jamaica."

"Amen to that," added LaTonya, flipping through the catalog of fantasy. "With my husband, I don't need no goddamn dildo or vibrator, so I'll just stick with the slutty lingerie. Keith just loves that shit." She looked up from the catalog and smiled as all the women staring at her fell out with laughter.

However, Zora felt using a contraption to get an orgasm was out of the question. She excused herself from the group of cackling, overly sexed hens and stumbled into the kitchen, where Keith sat on the stool at the island, wearing a Polo shirt and shorts.

"I hear you gals in there talking about sex." He chuckled, shaking his head. "I guess it rules the world, huh?"

"Yes, well, I'm not really into that kind of talk." With a thick tongue, and already ten sheets to the wind, Zora opened the kitchen cabinet and pulled down a wine goblet. She looked over her shoulder and glanced at Keith, who looked rather tempting. "I prefer the real thing. You know what I mean?" She held up the goblet. "Care to join me?" She had already had enough libations for four people, so another glass of wine was the last thing she needed, but a hot cup of coffee instead. However, right then, the only thing brewing was between her thighs. Every time she would be around Keith, her oven would ignite and the only person on the receiving end was Maceo, who had no clue his woman pined after his best friend.

"Sure, but won't you be missed?" Keith felt Zora was extremely attractive and sexy, just like his wife, LaTonya. However, there was something about Zora that aroused his curiosity whenever she was around. The way she sashayed around him or gently caressed his arm, or her sweet fragrance—the same scent his wife wore—whenever she would lean in and seductively chuckle in his ear. Once, during one of her "innocent" chuckles, she stroked the side of his bare knee. Regardless, it never crossed his mind to satisfy that arousal. She was his best friend's woman. That was a line in the sand he refused to cross.

Zora shrugged, popped the cork on the bottle of Riesling and filled their goblets. She leaned across the island, her ample cleavage about to make for a nipple gate and handed Keith his goblet. Every move was intentional, including tongue-stroking her bottom lip and peering into his gorgeous brown eyes, which he diverted to her heaving bosom.

Her eyes followed his stare; she looked down and chuckled, stroking her cleavage. "My girls have a mind of their own." Then she licked her lips and caressed the rim of the goblet before delicately sipping the sweet wine.

What was she doing? Taking trifling to a whole new level, perhaps? She was crossing the proverbial line of friendship, and she could have cared less.

She was definitely beyond inebriated when she licked her finger and stuck it inside her blouse, stroking her nipple.

Keith did not have to sense, feel, or realize she was drunk. He knew it. He had seen this on numerous occasions. Although he was used to this type of behavior from her, he was not used to the erection growing in his pants for another woman.

He cleared his throat and diverted his eyes across the room. "So, how's Maceo doing?"

"He's not doing."

"What do you mean?" He took a sip of wine.

Peering him dead in the eyes, she fixed her mouth to say, "He doesn't fuck me good, like you be fuckin' LaTonya."

He spat out his wine.

"My pussy is throbbing right now. Don't you want to fuck me, Keith?" Zora was blunt and horny. Zora had spent endless hours listening to LaTonya describe Keith's exceptional oral skills and his deep strokes. She was now in the mood for some action herself.

Why should LaTonya keep that good dick to herself? After all, she was the one who told another woman how good her man was between the sheets, so why not? What was a good screw between two friends, as long as they both kept their mouths shut?

Leaning forward, this time closer, she parted her lips, stuck out her tongue, and wagged it. "I hear you've got skills, boo. I give good head, too." Her sexy whisper wrapped around thick, slurred words.

"Boo, huh?" He nodded, shocking himself, as he contemplated possibly crossing that line. No, he was not drunk like his best friend's woman, but as he tilted his head in thought, he was curious.

The uproar of laughter in the other room was a distraction from his building curiosity, for which he was thankful. He knew bedding her would be the death of his marriage if his wife were to find out. Not to mention what it would do to his friendship with Maceo, his brother from another mother he had known since the sandbox.

Zora wasn't letting up. Clearly, she gave two fucks about that proverbial line or her friendship with LaTonya.

"You know, I see how you look at me when you think I'm not looking."

Keith chuckled. "You're tripping right now."

"Am I?" She moved around the kitchen island and stood by his side. She caressed his thigh with a tight squeeze. "Do you want me to stop?" She squeezed his thigh again, moving her hand an inch up toward his growing member, which caused a chill to shoot up his back, making him sit ramrod straight.

He looked over his shoulder and, without hesitation, moved off the stool, took Zora by the hand, and hurried her to the guest bathroom off the kitchen. Locking the door behind them, he threw all caution to the wind and propped her up on the vanity.

Zora's ass was on fire, and he was panting like a dog in heat.

Placing her palms flat against the walls to brace herself, she spread her thighs, and he kneeled before her. He raised her dress and pushed the crotch of her panty to the side.

Inhaling, then exhaling, he looked up at her. "No. This is wrong." He stood, propped his hands on his hips, and vigorously shook his head. "This is wrong, wrong, wrong. What the fuck am I doing?"

As Keith turned to open the door, Zora hopped off the vanity and grabbed him around the waist, pressing him against the door.

"No one has to know, Keith. Please. Fuck me. Put out this fire you started."

He sighed heavily, dropping his hands to his side. Battling the flesh was becoming awfully hard to do.

"This will be our secret. Ours. I promise. No one will ever know. You have my word. Please. I need this, Keith. Please."

Swiftly, he faced her, cupped her face in his palms, and kissed her with heated passion. He propped her on the vanity, tore off her panty, pushed her thighs wide, unzipped his shorts, allowing them fall down around this feet. He released his sword, and pierced her opening, appeasing her with quick, purposeful strokes.

With no shame, Zora's hips met Keith's strokes as they gazed into each other's eyes. She tongue-stroked her top lip, making him pump harder.

LaTonya was right. This is some good dick. I can get used to this.

It was too late.

Zora was beyond hooked. She was in a fucked-up situation with no intention of turning back. Not only was she having a lapse in judgment, but she was also having an indiscretion with Keith—a married man, her best friend's husband, and her man's best friend. Damn!

The insertion of the key in the door interrupted her trip down memory lane. When Maceo Hicks walked through the door, he flicked a row of switches, turning on the lights. He walked into the living room and saw her curled up on the sofa, covered by a plush white velour throw.

"Hey, beautiful." Maceo tossed his keys on the sofa table, and picked up the mail and sorted through it.

"Hi, babe." She spoke barely above a whisper.

Sensing she was in a melancholy mood, he looked at her. "Are you okay?"

She responded with a nod, which was outside the norm of her perky personality. Whenever Maceo entered the room, she was all over him like starch on rice.

Something was not right. It was undeniable to him. He tilted his head. "Why are you sitting in the dark, love?"

"Enjoying the lights from the Harbor." She pulled her knees closer to her chest, resting her chin on her knee. "There's something peaceful about those lights."

He escaped to the kitchen and returned with two glasses of wine, placing them on the marble-topped table in front of her.

"Thank you." She smiled at him before he excused himself to the bathroom. He always knew what she needed without her having to ask for it.

After taking a few sips, Zora tossed the throw to the side. Standing, she stretched her arms above her head and walked over to the large picture window to admire the view, which was the prime reason she purchased the condominium. From where she stood, the state of Virginia was a stone's throw across the Woodrow Wilson Bridge spanning over the Potomac River that separated Maryland from Virginia and Virginia from Washington, DC.

She moistened her lips and hugged herself. "It's like another world up here."

She heard the toilet flush and waited at the window. She pictured him walking up behind her, draping his muscular arm over her shoulder, kissing the top of her head, and asking how her day went. Then, with the tips of his fingers, he would caress her chin, turning it toward him and they would kiss, soft and passionate, but that was what she wanted from Keith. She was not in the mood to settle anymore. When she didn't hear any movement behind her, she turned around.

Maceo stood at the entrance to the living room. "I'd like to make love to you."

Tilting her head, the corner of her lip turned up into a slight smirk. She wasn't expecting to hear that. Usually, when he came home from work, he'd be too tired.

He moved toward the table in front of the sofa and picked up the glass of wine. With the swift movement of a black cat, he walked toward her and handed her the glass. "Is that all right with you?"

There was no music or television, just the hundreds of headlights and taillights crossing the Woodrow Wilson Bridge, covered by the dark of night and a blanket of stars. However, it was so silent; she was afraid to speak.

She never spoke when they made love, for fear she would call out Keith's name.

Smiling, she took the glass and sipped the wine.

He shifted his gaze from her beautiful face and out the window.

She glanced out the window, too. "Yes, that would be all right." She wanted to be loved, so Maceo would have to do. She would close her eyes and think about Keith, but she had to take extra care that the only word she spoke was *baby*.

"Why don't you take off your robe?"

Obliging, she handed him her glass, slipped her robe off her shoulders and held it in front of her. She was braless. He pointed to a chair off to the side. She tossed the robe over it.

He smiled, admiring her beauty. Turning, he set the glass on the table. He grabbed his crotch and adjusted his bulge, which was ready to break through the confines of the denim overalls.

"Turn around…"

She slowly turned around and faced the window.

"…and pull down your thong…slowly. Poke out that sweet ass real good for me." He moaned deeply, still caressing his throbbing crotch.

She stepped out of the red satin panty. As she was pulling herself upright, he stopped her, pressing his palm into the small of her back.

"Don't. I want you bent over. I love the view from here."

He stared at her. From where he stood, she wondered if he could see that she needed a bikini wax. His foreplay had ignited her fire. She wanted to kiss him; he didn't even kiss her on the forehead as he usually did when he came home.

"Baby—"

He shushed her, admiring the roundness of her heart-shaped ass. "Beautiful, beautiful, just beautiful."

She shivered when the palm of his hand caressed her buttock.

Falling to his knees, he hungrily worshipped her vagina; his nose stroking the slit of her behind, his tongue dancing, delightfully darting in and out of her opening. He inhaled deeply, taking in the sweet essence of the woman he madly loved.

She released a deep-throated moan, desperately trying to steady herself. It was too much of a good thing, and she was ready to explode.

Wanting to yell out in pleasure, she kept her mouth shut for fear of calling out Keith's name as tears welled in her eyes. They weren't tears of pleasure, though. They were tears of guilt, of regret. The one man who loved her more than his own life was pleasuring her, but her heart belonged to someone else. She felt horrible. Her mind should have been with Maceo, but it was with another woman's husband. In her mind's eye, it was Keith's tongue stroking her, not Maceo's. It was the palms of Keith's hands caressing her ass, not Maceo's. It was Keith mumbling about how much he loved her, not Maceo.

CHAPTER 13

Nestled in a quaint community in Brandywine, Maryland, sat a charming two-story colonial home with a timeless design and a symmetrical look. The white clapboard siding and black shutters added a touch of grace and tradition. With dormer windows under the pitched roof and surrounded by lush greenery on one acre of land, the home had a warm and elegant feel, a peaceful oasis amid the busy world.

The front porch was lovely, with a swing and potted plants. It was the perfect spot to look at the stars or enjoy a cup of tea. Lanterns along the walkway lit the path through the green landscape, guiding visitors to the front door.

The backyard was like a magical haven, with lush and well-kept grass. Tall trees stood like guards, their branches reaching toward the night sky, creating beautiful shadows on the ground. The rhythmic chirping of crickets and other sounds of nature created a calming melody.

A pathway made of stones guided Zora to a cozy patio, an excellent spot for evening gatherings. Zora had visited this place countless times, so it wasn't unfamiliar to her. However, this time felt unlike any other.

Zora inhaled deeply and looked through the double French doors.

Suddenly having second thoughts, she shook her head and pivoted when the door opened.

"Going somewhere?"

The man behind the baritone, seductive voice stepped back and opened the door wider. Keith's mere presence caused her to stumble over her feet, as she stepped up on the porch, and even more so now, as he stood before her wearing only a black muscle shirt, accentuating every muscle on his gorgeous, chiseled frame. His uncovered penis aimed at her like a heat-seeking missile.

Damn, was the only thought that occupied her mind. "Are you serious now? And why come through the back?"

He chuckled. "Come on in. Nosey neighbors."

She glanced over her shoulder in search of prying eyes. "Where are your pants?"

He looked down. "What?" He smirked at her. "You don't like my outfit?"

"You are a fool!" She entered the house and stood with her back to him. She shuddered as he closed the door.

He caressed her shoulder. "I figured I'd save you the time of having to take them off." He covered a small portion of her neck with soft kisses, causing her to shiver.

He moved closer, pressing his erection against her.

He moaned in her ear. "Relax."

Her mind was foggy. She couldn't think straight, being poked by his poker. She cleared her throat. "How long has she been gone? Suppose she returns?"

"She's long gone. She left this morning." He kissed her neck again. "We are wasting time with all this talking." He pressed himself against her. "Can't you *feel* what I want to stick inside you?"

"I don't know, Keith."

"Would you feel better if I called her?"

Facing him, she inhaled deeply and held her breath. His scent was intoxicating, stirring emotions deep in her core.

"I would feel better if I weren't here." The last time she was with her friend's husband in her friend's home, she was drunk. This time, however, standing in her friend's house made her feel uncomfortable. "Couldn't we go to a hotel for the weekend?"

"Why spend that money if we don't have to?" He extended his hand. "Let me borrow your cell phone."

"Why?"

"To make the call."

She peered at him. "You have lost your goddamn mind!"

Chuckling, he took her by the hand and led her into the living room. "I was just kidding. Lighten up."

Removing the landline handset from its base, he dialed the number he'd committed to memory and placed it against his ear.

"Keith, are you sure we—"

He raised his index finger, as he spoke into the mouthpiece. "Hey, sweet thang, just checking on you."

She cringed at his words. *Sweet thang. That's what he calls me.* A wave of nausea washed over her. She sat down on the sofa. *Zora, girl, you are going to hell with gasoline thongs on.* Shaking her head, she leaned forward, resting her elbows on her knees, with her head hung low.

"Excellent." He flashed a smile toward Zora. "I'm glad you've made it there safely. Give your mother a kiss for me."

Zora peered at him, folding her arms across her chest, and rolling her eyes. She was feeling some kind of way about him talking to another woman—his wife—in her presence.

"Yeah, enjoy yourself, baby. I'll see you in a few days." He blew a kiss into the mouthpiece. "I love you, too." He chuckled out a seductive moan. "Yeah, I'm missing you, too, sweetness." Ending his call, he returned his attention to his mistress.

His conversation with his wife bothered her. She knew she had no business being there, but he was her addiction. No matter how bad she truly felt about screwing her best friend's hubby *and* her boyfriend's best friend, rehab was not an option for something that was more than an addiction. She was in love with Keith, down to the bone.

On cue, and like a corny, romantic movie, he extended his hand. Looking up into his eyes, she placed her hand in his. He pulled her up and wrapped her in an embrace. Their lips met and their tongues tangoed. His kiss erased all the guilt she harbored for the time being, as she refused to waste another second of being with him.

She rolled up his shirt, peeled it over his head, and licked his nipples, following the scented trail of Gucci Guilty cologne to his armpits, discovering a musty sharpness like the smell of cloves. Taking his nipple in her mouth, she suckled as she finger-pinched the other.

He gazed down at her, his eyes twinkling like slices of lime in a Corona beer. He had the body of a laborer. Brawny, like the back of a crocodile in swampy water. Hard. Strong.

"Tell me—" he kneeled before her "—how do you want me to love you?"

Caressing the top of his, she massaged his scalp. With each rendezvous, Keith surprised her with unique experiences.

"Do anything you want to me. Explore me…teach me about myself."

Inserting his finger inside the waistband, he eased the cotton yoga pants over her curvaceous hips and down around her feet. She never wore undergarments around him, so he always had easy access.

She released a sigh when his hand touched her inner thigh, gliding up to the thin flesh, hiding behind the labia. He gently finger-stroked as he peered into her eyes.

"When you touch yourself, what do you imagine?"

With her head hung low, she closed her eyes and pondered his question. "I don't know."

"You play with yourself, don't you?"

She nodded.

"Then tell me."

"Well, I'm a three-hundred-year-old mahogany table…and I'm being polished, and the slightest scratch would ruin my value." Pulling up her shirt, she licked her finger and stroked around her belly button.

"Okay," he whispered in her navel, "I will be gentle, careful not to scratch or devalue what I treasure."

His words wrapped tightly around her heart. He pulled her down to her knees and peeled off her blouse, exposing her breasts. There was that beautiful smile again that sent chills throughout her.

"You are so beautiful." He cupped her left breast. "So sexy." He pinched her nipple. He peered into her eyes. "I can't get enough of you or your sweet pussy."

She caressed his shoulders, kneading and massaging, before moving down between his thighs. There was an urgency to her grip on his erection. She wanted him—now!

Turning his head, he said, "Alexa, play 'Lady' by The Whispers."

The Whispers crooned "Lady" through the Bose Surround Sound System.

He smiled. "That's better."

Laying on his back, Zora straddled him and lowered herself onto his hardened shaft.

Shaking his head, he patted her on the hip. "Raise up for a minute."

Perplexed, her brows furrowed. "What?"

He reached between the sofa cushions and retrieved a gold foil packet.

"Oh, here we go with this shit, Keith."

Shaking his head, he tore open that packet, pulled out the condom, and rolled it down his shaft. "Okay, now where were we?"

Helping her, he eased his manhood inside her. Within a millisecond, her hips rotated on him, rising and falling, as her back arched with pleasure and her perky breasts jutted, slowly grinding in rhythm to The Whispers with each stroke.

Moaning, he sang along with The Whispers. "Your body's designed by the wisdom of time."

"I couldn't live without you," she sang, leaning in to kiss him passionately.

Aiding her ecstasy, he pinched her hardened nipples. Thrusting up to meet her ride, he repeatedly hit that deep spot within her, and each time she expelled a yelp followed by a satisfied moan.

Zora's breath grew short of the anticipation of something wonderful. Lowering more forcefully onto him, suddenly she stopped. Trembling, she grabbed his hands, intertwining fingers. Then she froze and released a shrill cry of ecstasy.

He joined her in a long, satisfying climax that left them both spent and damp with perspiration.

She tasted his mouth.

"Zora?"

"Keith?"

"This floor is killing my back."

With laughter, she rose to her feet and gathered her clothes.

Keith sat up, reclining on his hands. "How are you feeling?"

Sighing heavily, Zora stared at the floor. "We could go to my place, and I'd feel better."

"Woman, have you forgotten about Maceo? You want to get me shot?"

"How about a hotel?"

"Zora, relax. LaTonya is spending the weekend at her mother's on Maryland's Eastern Shore. She won't be back until late Monday night. We have the house to ourselves for a good two days." He paused for a moment. "Listen, I understand—"

"Do you, Keith? Do you really understand?"

He was silent as he felt her usual vent session coming on. So, he would allow her to do so.

She looked around the living room. "Keith, this is wrong, just wrong. We should not be here. Hell, I should not be here. What kind of friend am I?"

"So, what are you saying? You want to end this?"

Without hesitancy, she responded, "No." She paused, taking a deep breath. "That's not what I'm saying."

"Zora, how do you think I feel, fucking my best friend's woman and wife's friend? This ain't no emotional bed of roses for me either." Tilting his head, his brows furrowed. "What kind of friend am I, Zora? Hell, I'm wallowing with the scum of the earth by messing with you. If Maceo ever, and I mean *ever*, found out about us, I would lose a friend since childhood, and possibly my life, not to mention my wife. You know your dude goes from zero to one hundred in less than a millisecond." He shook his head. "Shit, maybe we should end this before it goes too far, before we both end up dead."

She dropped to the floor beside him. "No. I don't want to be without you."

He looked into her eyes. "There you go with your feelings, Zora. It is what it is."

"What is *it*, Keith?"

"*It* is two people who are satisfying each other's needs. That's it."

"Man, you do not *need* me. You and LaTonya, from what she tells me, fuck every night. It's a wonder your dick has enough energy for me."

Looking down, he chuckled. "Yeah, she has a high sexual appetite."

"See?" She jumped up and stomped off toward the kitchen.

Keith stood up and followed her.

"Zora, this has been going on for a good while. Why is it such a big deal suddenly?"

She faced him. "I don't want to hurt LaTonya."

"It's too late for that now, don't you think? Besides, she'll never find out. As long as we cover our tracks, we'll be fine."

"Good point, but you're still stank as fuck, too!"

As much as Keith tried to soothe her uneasiness, sour thoughts filled Zora's mind. She and LaTonya were more than acquaintances. They were friends. When Zora wasn't with Kennedy, she was shopping at some mall or at a restaurant, eating seafood with LaTonya. She stood by LaTonya's side when she and Keith married. Some kind of friend she turned out to be.

Keith stretched and grabbed the middle of his back. "I need to take a shower. My back is killing me, and I think I have a carpet burn." Keith chuckled, meeting her eye-to-eye.

She shivered.

He wrapped his arms around her. "You're cold? How about something to warm you up?"

A drink was exactly what she needed. However, she wasn't cold. That was the shiver of betrayal.

She sat at the round corner dinette set. "So, what are we going to do this weekend?"

Smiling, Keith faced her, grabbed his dick, and puckered his lips.

She sighed heavily. "Besides sex."

"I thought you enjoyed having sex with me."

"I love it, but can we at least see daylight and have dinner or something? Maybe go on a date for a change?"

Keith reached into the custom-designed cabinets, pulled out two glass snifters, and placed them on the table in front of her.

"Sure. Whatever you want. However, dating is for single folks." He unscrewed the top of the Courvoisier Cognac VSOP.

Zora rolled her eyes. "I am single."

"Yeah? I'm sure Maceo thinks otherwise."

Rolling her eyes, she stood up from the table. "I'm going to take a shower." She walked her naked, whorish ass toward her friend's bedroom. What a tramp!

"Do you need any company, and what about your drink?" Keith picked up his iPhone and aimed it directly at her.

"No, I can manage and save it for later." She pivoted and faced him, catching him snapping away, as if he were a professional photographer. "Don't do that!"

It was too late. Keith snapped several images of her naked beauty with her mouth wide open.

"You better delete them. I mean it!" She escaped up the staircase to the master bedroom.

Keith chuckled and ran behind her, still snapping images of Zora into his iPhone.

Zora tossed her clothes across the bed and faced Keith. "You play too goddamn much, you know that? I don't like you having naked pictures of me on your phone. Suppose LaTonya sees them? Suppose someone hacks your phone?" Her voice was now fragile and shaking. "That is so not cool. What the fuck, Keith?"

"She won't see them."

"Just delete them, please!"

"Okay, but on one condition."

She looked at him blankly. "A condition?"

He nodded. "Lay on the bed and spread your legs."

"What?"

He stood his stance, his once again erect penis aiming at its target, his arms folded across his chest. "Okay, then I will not delete them. I will keep them for my enjoyment."

"Giving Him Something He Can Feel" belted through the stereo system. *Perfect timing, Ms. Re*, she thought, as Aretha Franklin sang Zora's story.

"Why?"

"Just do it."

"Keith…"

"Zora…"

Sighing heavily, she complied.

Laying on the bed, with her legs open, Keith stuck out his tongue and slithered on the bed, like the sneaky snake he had become.

Within seconds, he was at it again, forgetting about the photographs on his phone and his wife.

CHAPTER 14

Unknowing what had come over her, she'd gotten too comfortable, as she reclined lazily in the chaise lounge across the massive bedroom, watching Keith sleep without a care in the world.

Scanning the massive bedroom, she admired LaTonya's interior design skills. It was truly something out of *Elle Décor*. The master bedroom's media center featured a motorized pop-up television at the foot of the bed and another video display at the far end of the bedroom by the fireplace. Seamless control of the audio, video, lighting, climate, and security was provided by a Crestron control system. Speakers were in the ceiling, with a subwoofer hidden in the wall. To say that LaTonya's taste was eclectic was putting it mildly. The huge, black lacquered, four-poster bed donned a gray silk canopy that draped down around a button-padded headboard. A silver-trimmed, fifteen-foot mirror stood against the wall next to the bed.

Keith and LaTonya were financially well-off, and it was clear in the way they lived. They had a beautiful home; both drove high-end vehicles and wore expensive designer clothes. They knew how to handle money and credit wisely to their advantage. Keith was the general manager of Hicks European Automotive Shop, Maceo's foreign car repair business, and LaTonya was an attorney at a prestigious law firm in Washington, DC, with ambitions to become a partner within a year. Alongside their successful careers, they also had a profitable stock portfolio that allowed them to live comfortably.

Standing, Zora tiptoed across the room, careful not to wake Keith, and entered the enormous his-and-her walk-in closet.

This is ridiculous, Zora thought. *No one should have so many damn shoes.*

Six custom-built, floor-to-ceiling, wall-to-wall shelving held at least two hundred pairs of shoes, as a matching marble-topped dressing island occupied the middle of the floor. It housed every piece of jewelry LaTonya owned, from pearls to diamonds. A hint of envy shot through Zora's veins, warming her. Why couldn't she have this life, too? She would appreciate it far more than LaTonya would.

Looking across the closet, she spotted a fur coat behind the door. She made a beeline for the silky black diamond mink and slipped into it. Closing it up around her neck, it felt so good. It was soft and warm. *Now, this is pure luxury. I could truly get used to this!* She made her way down the wall to the shoes. A silver pair of strappy heels caught her attention. She had never seen these before. Taking them in her grasp, she looked at the bottom of the shoe. *Red bottoms?* Huffing, she dropped the shoes to the floor and slipped her feet into them. She twirled around and stared at the jewelry and took it upon herself to slide a diamond ring on every finger.

Standing before the floor-to-ceiling mirror, she ogled at herself. She loved the image looking back at her. After twirling around the room, she came face-to-face with Keith.

He looked at her with astonishment, as if she had lost her mind.

"What are you doing in here?"

In a daze, she was speechless and dizzy.

"Answer me!"

"Well, I—"

"Take off that coat. It belonged to LaTonya's grandmother!"

Quickly, she slipped out of the coat, and before she could hang it up in its respectful place, Keith snatched it from her and hung it up.

"You don't belong in here." He looked down at her feet. "Take them off, now!" Irritation was causing the hair on his arms to rise as he got a glimpse of Zora's hands. "Goddamn it, Zora! What the fuck are you doing?"

"Keith, I wasn't doing anything. I was just—"

"You were just what? You're not my wife, so take off her shit and get the fuck out of her closet!" He stormed out of the room and down the steps.

Zora was beyond dumbfounded as tears streamed down her face. He made her feel like a thief in the night. Returning LaTonya's belongings, the way she found them, she pulled LaTonya's silk robe off the hook from behind the door, slipped into it, and followed Keith. When she reached the bottom step, jazz music wafted from the great room at the back of the house.

"Keith." She got no response. She moved toward Miles Davis's horn. "Keith." As she moved through the French double doors, she spotted him in the leather, high, wingback chair, with his leg draped over the armrest. "Honey, I'm sorry."

"Maybe you're right," he mumbled, taking a sip from the snifter of Remy he poured before her intrusion, which was exactly how it felt.

"What do you mean?" She moved toward him. When she stood in front of him, he got more infuriated.

He looked at the silk robe. He recognized it as the robe he'd given to LaTonya on her birthday the previous year. "Is that yours?"

"What? Oh, no, LaTonya's."

He angrily sighed.

"Damn, Keith, I can't very well walk around here naked."

He looked away from her. "You clearly didn't have a problem rolling around in my wife's bed naked."

Ouch! "Look, I'm sorry, okay? But please don't treat me like I'm shit on the bottom of your goddamn shoe. I don't deserve this treatment." She kneeled before him. "Keith, please don't do this to me. I love you so much. You're killing me, baby."

He looked at her just when the tear fell from her eye and rolled down her cheek.

"Babe, I'm sorry."

Keith's face relaxed as he wiped away her tears with his thumb. "We just have to be careful."

"I know, and I'm sorry."

"LaTonya is very particular about her things, and she's no fool."

He pressed the rim of the snifter against her lips. "Take a sip and relax."

She sipped the potion and allowed it to roll down her throat.

"Feel better?"

She nodded.

Leaning forward, he kissed her on the lips. "Good." He took another sip.

"So, what are we going to do?"

"What would you like to do?"

"Well, I am hungry."

He nodded. "I worked up an appetite, too."

"I would love crab and avocado from Yellow Fin!"

"Yellow Fin it is."

"Besides, it'll be a nice ride, and it's away from everything and everyone."

"Let's shower and dress and maybe we can catch a movie afterward."

"Yes! I would love it!"

As Keith's BMW 430i xDrive convertible headed east on Route 50 toward Annapolis, Maryland, he caressed Zora's thigh. "Where exactly does Maceo think you are?"

"At the hospital, preparing for annual review." Zora caressed Keith's hand. "I love riding this road at night."

With a tight, sensual squeeze to her thigh, he nodded. "So do I." He paused, as if in deep thought. "He hasn't called to check on you?"

"Check on me for what?"

"Well, to see how you're doing. You are his woman, after all. I mean, I would call—"

"I'm a grown woman. He doesn't need to check on me. We don't do that. He trusts me and—" She caught herself.

Keith nodded and, for the first time, felt some kind of way about squeezing the thigh of his best friend's woman, let alone sexing her. "Yes, Maceo is a very trusting man." He was feeling like shit until Zora's fingers nestled in the warmth of his crotch.

"I'm feeling absolutely wonderful."

He felt a slight urge in his loins. "All right now. Don't start nothing you can't finish."

She d cupped his crotch. "Now you know I finish *everything* I start." Her fingers moved up to his waist and unbuckled his belt.

"You know I have no cut cards."

She unzipped his khakis.

"Zora…"

Wiggling her fingers inside his khakis, she searched for her target. *Got it!* She caressed the head of his penis.

He moaned, readjusting himself in the seat, trying to maintain his focus on the two-lane, winding road. He glanced at her. "Pull your pants down."

"Huh?"

"You want to play, right?"

She chuckled softly. "I always want to play."

"Then, pull your pants down."

Doing as she was told, Keith was flipping the script, taking control.

"Spread your legs."

Her thighs were sticking to the leather.

He inhaled deeply, the smell of her nectar permeating his nostrils. Without hesitation, he inserted his middle finger inside her wet box and simultaneously stroked her clitoris with his thumb.

Zora was losing her mind as she grabbed hold of the seat. "Ooh, *shit.*"

With less than ten minutes from their destination, Keith needed to speed things up. "Fuck my hand." His order was firm and quite brisk.

As her hips thrust forward, the palm of his hand smacked against her clitoris, causing even more stimulation. The connection sent her to a head spin as deep, throaty moans escaped her.

"Yeah, that's it. Let it go." The more he urged her, the more the intensity heightened, and the faster his palm smacked against her labia, sending enormous waves of sensations throughout her.

By the time Keith turned left onto Old Solomon's Island Road, Zora's screams were ear-piercing, as she squirted in the palm of his hand.

With a burst of deep, hearty laughter and a feeling of pride, he pressed his palm against her mouth. "Taste yourself."

She smacked his hand away. "Boy, get out of here. Do you have any tissue?"

"Nope."

"Nothing?"

"Nothing."

Ugh! Just great.

As Keith pulled into the parking lot of the Yellow Fin restaurant, he parked and faced Zora.

"You're a mess." He smiled, flashing cave-deep dimples.

"I can't go in there with a wet ass and smelling like twat."

"Well, now see… this happens when little girls play with grown-ass men."

She rolled her eyes. "You know you make me sick, right?"

"I'll be right back." He got out of the car and walked toward the back. He popped the trunk and looked around. "Well, I have towels I've used to wipe down the car."

"Are you kidding me? You expect me to wipe my ass with dirty towels?"

"You can always go inside to the restroom, Zora." Keith huffed, becoming irritated. While he enjoyed being with Zora, he did not enjoy that whiny, complaining side of her, which was something he never got from his wife, who was not a complainer. LaTonya moved with the flow.

"Can you go inside for me? Please, Keith!"

Annoyed, he went inside the restaurant and approached the host stand where a beautiful, shapely woman with flowing hair stood.

"Good evening, sir. Long time no see."

"Hi. Uh…" Dumbfounded, Keith was completely lost for words. "Uh…" He recognized her but could not place her. *Oh, hell.*

"It's been a long time." She looked around him. "Is LaTonya with you?"

For the first time in his life, Keith Jordan had lost the ability to do what he was good at doing—thinking on his feet. *Shit! Shit! Shit!*

His face had a blank expression, as if he were deep in thought.

"Wait…let me find out you don't remember me, Keith." She chuckled, moving from behind the stand. "The last I saw you was at the company's annual picnic last summer." She tapped him on the arm. "Valerie Holmes." She glowed with excitement. "It's good to see you!"

Admittedly, Valerie's face was familiar, but he simply could not place her. So, he faked it. "Yes, hi, Valerie. It is good to see you, too. Please forgive me. It has been a good while."

"How have you been? Is LaTonya with you?"

"Yes, well," he shoved his hands in his pockets, "LaTonya is not with me. She's visiting her mom this weekend."

"Well, table for one?"

"Uh, yes, but let me park. I came in to see if there was a wait. I'll be back." He tore out of the restaurant, hopped in the car, and sped off with no explanation.

Zora peered at him as he ran the red light, heading toward Route 214.

With one hand gripped to the wheel, Keith massaged his forehead with the other, in deep thought.

"Are you going to tell me what happened?"

Not wanting to speak, he turned on the radio. *We didn't think about the price we'd have to pay*, were Shirley Murdock's words as she crooned "As We Lay," a song that truly struck Keith at his core. *Fuck!* He turned off the radio.

"Keith!"

"What?"

"What's wrong? Why did you speed off like that?"

He pounded the steering wheel. "What am I doing?"

Zora removed her seatbelt and faced him, looking at the side of his face. "Keith, I don't know—"

"This is wrong on so many levels."

"What is?"

"This."

"What is this?"

"This!" He slammed his hand on the dashboard. "Us, goddamn it! Us. Us. Us!"

"Okay, calm down, baby, and talk to me. Something happened inside the restaurant to make you feel this way. What was it?"

Keith slowed the vehicle and pulled into the Sonic parking lot. "Are you hungry?"

Food was the last thing on her mind. Her man, the man she loved, just told her that "they" were wrong.

Keith pulled into a stall, rolled down the window, and aimed his attention at the menu.

"Keith?"

"What do you want to eat?"

"I don't know…"

"A Sonic burger?"

"I don't know…"

"A hot dog?"

"Keith, I—"

"Fuck, Zora, order something!"

Startled by his outburst, she repositioned herself in the seat, cupped her hands in her lap, and looked straight ahead. "I'll have what you have."

"Fine." He pressed the red button on the menu board to place the order.

"Hello and thank you for eating at Sonic. May I take your order?"

"Two Sonic burgers with fries and Cokes."

After the order was repeated and Keith slipped his credit card into the reader, he rolled up the window and reclined in his seat.

Zora remained silent.

"I pretended like I didn't remember her…"

Zora sat in her seat as straight and stern as a statue. She did not know where this conversation was about to go, but she didn't want her head chopped off again. So, she remained silent.

"Valerie Holmes. I remember her now. She and LaTonya work at the same law firm."

Zora cleared her throat. "It all makes sense now."

"She asked if LaTonya was with me."

"What did you tell her?"

"I told her no, of course. Then she asked me, 'Table for one?'" He inhaled and blew out an exhausting breath. "I told her I had to park, and I got the hell out of Dodge. I surely can't go in there with you." His sarcastic tone complemented his eye-roll.

Zora frowned. "Of course not." She felt some kind of way. "Keith, what do you want to do?"

"About what?"

"About us."

"I don't know."

CHAPTER 15

As Keith stepped out of the shower and wrapped a towel around his waist, steam exuded from his masculine pores, further stressing his sexiness as he moved around his bedroom.

Squeezing her lids shut and opening them with admiration, a soft moan devoid of any guilt escaped Zora.

She sat on the edge of the bed and watched him watch her in silence. She extended her hand. He took it. Pulling him toward her, she leaned back and opened her thighs. He fell into her embrace, trembling with need and expectation. The lights were on. They both wanted silence and darkness, but neither would move to pull away from the other's yielding flesh. They chafed against each other, finding crevices and surfaces to move over and under and in between.

Her ears, nose, chin, brows—he studied her, using his tongue like a blind man would a finger, gliding over them…pausing…retracing… moving forward only when he was sure he could sketch them from memory. She kissed him as he licked her, dabbing his face as if he'd been in a fight, and her lips were a pair of cotton balls soaked in healing oil.

She nuzzled his chin, licked his throat, and nibbled his ear before kissing him, consuming his lips hungrily, trailing her fingers at the back of his head. His tongue searched the sides of her mouth, of the soaked-in memories of another man, other kisses.

Licking his shoulders with love, Zora took his nipples in her mouth and traced extravagant flourishes on his skin.

He stood up and stared at her, his eyes glistening like a sugary candle apple.

"What's wrong? Don't you want to be inside me?"

He nodded. "Gotta get a condom."

"No, without the condom."

Keith shook his head.

"But I want to feel your flesh against mine. Just like our first time."

"You know I can't do that."

"But—"

"Don't ruin the moment."

"But I want to feel—"

"Listen, I won't do that."

"I won't get pregnant, if that's what you're worried about. I didn't the first time we fucked."

Keith sighed heavily because Zora was blowing his mood. He fixed his mouth to respond, and just then, her cell phone alerted her of a new voicemail message.

Zora looked at the phone sitting on the nightstand beside LaTonya's bed. Her initial thought was to ignore it but decided against it.

"I didn't hear my phone ring. Let me see who called."

"Really?"

"Give me a sec." Reaching overhead to retrieve the phone from the nightstand, she checked her missed calls. She shot ramrod straight up in the bed. "Oh, shit!" Without hesitancy, she listened to her voicemail message.

"Hey, girl, it's me. Call me back. I'm heading home early to surprise Keith, and I wanted to stop by your place to borrow something sexy! I want him to open the door to all this sexiness, girl. Call me back!"

Eyes wide with a new kind of fear, a terror that came when the clandestine world of an affair began crumbling, Zora was panic-stricken.

She hopped to her feet. "Woo shit! She's coming home tonight."

"Who is?"

"Your wifey!"

"No, she won't be back until—"

"That was her…the missed call…she left a message, saying she was on her way home early to surprise you."

Keith stood in silence, as if in a trance.

Zora stormed around the bed and snapped her fingers in front of his face. "Keith!"

"Call her back…see exactly where she is."

"Yes, yes…good idea." Zora called LaTonya's cell phone as she peeked out of the bedroom window. "Come on, pick up," she mumbled under her breath, scared as shit that this man's wife was about to catch her having one of her many indiscretions with her husband.

She exhaled when she heard LaTonya's voice.

"Hey, girlie. Where are you?"

"Uh…hey, LaTonya. Oh, I'm out and about…uh," she paused, having to think quickly, "I'm headed to the VFW."

"On a Saturday night? I thought you and Kennedy went during the week."

"Uh…yep. Sometimes we do Saturdays, too. You're on your way home? I thought you were visiting your mom for the weekend. Is everything okay?"

"Everything's fine. Just felt like coming home early to surprise my man. I was calling you because I wanted to show up wearing something sexy." Zora could hear that smile in her voice. "But since you're not home…oh well."

"Oh, wow…okay." Zora looked at Keith, who was on pins and needles.

"Where is she?" he whispered.

"LaTonya, where are you?"

"Just crossed the Chesapeake Bay Bridge. I'll be home in about forty minutes."

With the speed of lightning, Zora flashed around the room, gathering her clothes. "Just crossed the bridge, huh? I hate that bridge." She looked at Keith, who was now stripping off the bed. She looked at him like he was crazy and shrugged.

Get off the phone, he mouthed, rushing around the room, and grabbing fresh linen from the hall closet.

"Okay, girl, I've just pulled into the parking lot." She balled her clothes and tucked them under her arm. "Let's talk tomorrow, okay?"

"Okay—"

"Bye!" Zora ended the call before LaTonya could utter another word.

"Oh shit! She'll be here in about forty minutes, and you know she drives like a bat out of hell."

"Yep!" Zora darted toward the hallway. "I'm out of here!"

"Wait!"

She spun around and peered at him. "What?"

He looked at her naked ass up and down. "You're not going to get dressed?"

"I'll dress in the car. See ya!"

Like a bolt of lightning, Zora flashed down the staircase and out the front door. Within seconds, her car sped out of the driveway and down the street.

Keith quickly changed the bed linen and climbed into bed with a pounding heart. *Whew, this shit is way too close for comfort.*

CHAPTER 16

LaTonya pulled into the driveway. The house was dark, as if Pepco had turned the power off. She looked at the digital clock on the dashboard of her car: 10:15 p.m.

That's odd, she thought. *Keith never climbs into bed before one o'clock in the morning.* Shrugging off the thought, she pulled down the visor, and after looking herself over in the mirror, she refreshed her lipstick and fingered her bangs.

Once inside the foyer, she closed the front door behind her and looked around in the darkness. Music playing from the bedroom caught her attention. She smiled, and quickly disrobed and kicked off her shoes, wearing only a black lace bra and panty ensemble. Leaving her clothes in a heap, she sauntered up the staircase toward the master bedroom, stopping at the closed door.

Opening it, she struck a sexy pose in the doorway, her arm resting against the doorframe, watching Keith under the covers.

Walking with sensual intent, LaTonya's stride from the door to the bed was long, lean, and purposeful.

She climbed into bed and whispered into his ear. "Mama's home, lover."

Keith stirred about, rolling onto his back to face her. "Hey." He knuckled his eyes as if he'd been asleep for hours, acting pleasantly surprised. "What're you doing here? I thought—"

"I missed my man." She kissed him on the earlobe. "Are you not feeling well?"

"Yeah, why?"

"You're in the bed, and it's not even midnight."

"Just relaxing is all."

LaTonya rubbed against Keith and moaned. Whenever she spooned him, he knew she was in the mood.

Tonight, however, would be an exception: his ass was exhausted. Zora had seen to that.

"Sweet thang, I'm tired." He kissed her palm. "Maybe in the morning."

Wide-eyed in shock, LaTonya couldn't believe her ears. Keith, her smoldering sex machine, had turned her down. Disappointed, she moved to the bathroom to take a shower to douse the fire at her core. She kicked off her heels, slipped out of her bra and panty, and stepped her bare feet onto the damp bathroom floor.

Why is the floor wet? She looked around the bathroom.

Noticing two towels strewn on the floor, she looked over her shoulder at Keith and refocused on the towels. As she moved deeper into the bathroom and closed the door behind her, something didn't feel right.

Now on the commode urinating, out of habit, LaTonya looked down at the floor and around the sink.

LaTonya was a meticulous woman who prided herself on keeping her home clean and organized. She always took care of the housework, including scrubbing the bathroom. What happened next made her sit ramrod straight.

Spotting a strand of hair, she picked it up and held it up to the light. *That's not my hair color.* Questions swirled in LaTonya's mind, and she couldn't help but wonder who the mysterious owner of the hair could be. She placed the hair strand on the sink and stood without wiping herself. Urine trickled down her leg as she hovered over the sink, examining its contents. Her bottles of lotions and sprays looked out of order, too. Keith bothered nothing on her side of the vanity, and vice versa—she left his things alone. She wrapped the strand of hair in a piece of toilet paper and tucked it neatly in the back of her accessory drawer under the vanity.

Paralyzed and demoralized, uneasiness overcame her. Her heart palpitated. She loved Keith and trusted him but didn't put shit past him or any man. A two-legged dog was a two-legged dog, was her motto, and it appeared her husband could be a two-legged dog.

This wasn't the first sign, however. Two months ago, she spent the week in New York City, shopping, dining, and taking in Broadway plays with her sister-friend, Julia. Keith stayed behind. In fact, over the past five years, Keith rarely traveled with her anymore, but LaTonya thought nothing of it. She loved spending time with her girlfriends, doing girlie activities and bonding, but also appreciated being alone from time to time.

She stepped into the shower and reached for the faucet when she saw more strands of hair. Again, it wasn't her color.

Her hair was black.

The anonymous strands were auburn red.

She turned on the shower and stood under the running water. Finally thawing into an unpleasant reality, a flood of emotions poured from her when she realized another woman could have been in her house and, most likely, in her bed. *No, Keith*, she thought, crying into her palm.

Wearing a terrycloth robe, her hair wrapped in a turban towel, LaTonya sat on the edge of the bed, rubbing Dove lotion on her arms, and listening to Keith's silent snores. Looking at the clock on the nightstand that read 11:25 p.m., she sat in the dark. The streetlamp tossed a glow through the partially opened blinds. She scanned the bedroom, stopping at her pillow. She tilted her head and squinted, leaning in closer.

Before leaving earlier that morning, she changed the linens as she did every Saturday morning.

Why would he change the sheets? She looked around the room and down at the floor. *Maybe he spilled something.*

She didn't know but was curious. Keith never changed a sheet a day since they'd been married. She disrobed, pulled back the sheet, slid underneath it, and stared at the chair her friend, Zora, had sat in hours before she arrived home.

CHAPTER 17

Truluck's Ocean's Finest Seafood and Crab in downtown Washington, DC, exuded a comforting ambiance, with soft jazz music weaving its magic through the air. Laughing and sharing stories, Kennedy, Zora, and LaTonya sat at a corner table. Tonight, however, something weighed heavily on Zora's heart, and she knew she couldn't keep it from her two best friends any longer.

Kennedy raised her glass with a warm smile, breaking the chatter. "To the unbreakable trio—Kennedy, Zora, and LaTonya. Cheers, my beautiful sisters."

LaTonya and Kennedy clinked their glasses with Zora's, but their eyes held concern, sensing that something wasn't quite right with their friend. She seemed melancholy the whole evening.

With a deep breath, Zora shared her burden. "There's something I need to tell you both. A few days ago, I found a lump in my breast, and I'm really scared it might be cancer."

Instantly, a hush fell over the table, replaced by a shared sense of empathy and love.

LaTonya reached out to hold her friend's hand. "Oh, honey, I'm so sorry you're going through this." LaTonya's voice was heavy with compassion.

Kennedy nodded, her expression reflecting the strength she always emanated. "We're here for you, girl. You're not alone on this journey. Have you scheduled an appointment with the doctor yet?"

Zora nodded, tears welling in her eyes. "Yes, tomorrow. I'm so afraid to face it, to hear the worst news. But I couldn't keep it from you two any longer. Y'all are my girls."

With unwavering support, LaTonya encouraged Zora. " We love you, and we'll be by your side every step of the way."

Zora inwardly cringed at LaTonya's words. Would she still love her if she were to learn Zora was keeping company with her husband?

Kennedy leaned over and wiped the tears from Zora's cheek. "You know we won't let you face this alone. We'll be there for the doctor's appointment, for treatments, for whatever you need. We're family, sis."

Nodding, LaTonya added, "And trips to the dispensary."

With pursed lips, Kennedy side-eyed her. "The what?"

"Yeah, girl. You know that shit's legal in Maryland now, so we can all get high together."

Zora chuckled. "I work in a hospital, remember? I'm tested regularly like everyone else."

"Okay, but it's legal."

Zora shook her head. "Doesn't matter, honey."

"Well, I don't want none of that shit. Don't need it. I'm naturally high," Kennedy belted.

"Hush, girl." Zora looked around the restaurant.

"You're naturally crazy as shit, too."

Kennedy gave LaTonya a high-five and exclaimed, "That's the truth right there!"

Zora, feeling grateful for her friends, gently patted under her eyes with her fingertips and smiled. "Thank you, both of you. Your support means the world to me. I'm just so scared of what the future holds."

LaTonya caressed her hand reassuringly. "Fear is natural, but we'll face it together. No matter the outcome, we'll be strong together."

Kennedy nodded in agreement. "Exactly. We'll handle whatever comes our way as a team. We'll be here to celebrate the victories, big or small."

Zora's heart swelled with gratitude. "I don't know what I did to deserve you two, but I'm eternally grateful. Let's hope for the best and face whatever comes our way head-on."

LaTonya spoke with unwavering support. "That's the spirit, girlfriend! And remember, we'll be right here, holding your hand through it all."

"Exactly!" Kennedy raised her glass. "To our sis, Zora. We've got you, girl!"

The best friends clinked their glasses.

As their emotions settled, the waiter approached their table, offering a moment of respite. They composed themselves and decided on their orders, finding solace in each other's presence.

As Zora sat at the table, as her two best friends expressed their unwavering support and willingness to stand by her side, conflicting emotions swirled within her. She felt a mixture of gratitude and guilt, her heart torn between the immense love she had for her friends and the weight of her deep-seated betrayal.

While genuine care and compassion from LaTonya touched her deeply, it also intensified her feelings of regret. Zora was keeping a significant part of her life hidden from LaTonya—a secret that would not only crush her friend but would, most likely, ruin her marriage. She would lose both LaTonya and Keith. As her friend vowed to be with her through thick and thin, Zora couldn't help but feel the weight of her deception.

As the evening wore on, Zora grappled with her conscience. The love and support she received from LaTonya and Kennedy only magnified the conflict within her.

Zora couldn't shake the feeling she was undeserving of their love and support. Every genuine gesture of care from LaTonya felt like a knife to her conscience, a reminder of the betrayal she was perpetrating behind her friend's back.

At that moment, Zora understood the magnitude of her actions. If she truly valued her friendship with LaTonya, she knew she had to confront her secret, no matter how painful or uncomfortable it might be. She couldn't bear the thought of allowing this lie to continue, knowing the potential consequences it could bring.

With a heavy heart, Zora made a silent promise to herself that she would find the strength to end her affair with Keith, regardless of her love for him. She knew it wouldn't be easy, but she couldn't bear the guilt any longer.

CHAPTER 18

The green digital on the dash flashed 3:30. Zora glanced through the car's passenger window.

Fear gripped her when she read the sign: Medical Building.

She pulled the 1979 Mazda RX-7 Maceo had restored and gave to her one Christmas into the first available parking space. Procrastinating, she sat in the idling car, trying to shake off the anxiety. Eventually, she retreated from the car at the pace of a snail, with her head hung low.

Taking her time entering the building, her gait was slow, precise, and premeditated. What if she had cancer? What if it was nothing? She didn't want to die! Remembering Maceo's mother had breast cancer; it was the most horrific time of his life. It was a bad time for his mother—chemo treatments, radiation treatments, then death. Never had Zora encountered a situation as heart-wrenching as that. Maceo grappled with the devastating news of his mother's cancer diagnosis. The weight of helplessness settled heavily upon her shoulders as she watched him struggle to come to terms with the harsh reality that life had thrust upon him.

Trying to numb her fear with mental anesthesia, with a knot lodged in her throat, she turned the knob to enter the doctor's office. She shivered, though it was warm and inviting. The waiting area looked modern but cozy, with pictures on the walls, showing beautiful landscapes and colorful art. The chairs were comfy and came in earthy colors; arranged in a way that gave everyone some privacy. Live plants and small trees were all around the room, making the air fresher and giving the place a natural feel. The large windows let in the warm and inviting daylight.

She timidly approached the receptionist's desk and forced a smile.

"I'm Zora Vaughn. I have an appointment with Doctor Thompson."

"Good afternoon, Ms. Vaughn. It's good to see you again."

"Likewise, thank you." Zora smiled, but she was thinking something different—she didn't want to see that woman, not under current circumstances.

"Have a seat and you'll be called back shortly."

Already nervous as hell, the last thing Zora wanted to do was sit and wait. Forging a courageous smile, she took a seat beside an end table covered with outdated magazines. *Marie Claire*, with a half-naked celebrity exposing her pregnant belly on the front cover, caught her attention. *Damn, how old is this magazine? Chick had that baby a long time ago.* She picked it up and huffed at the image. She thought it appalling to expose something so private and delicate to the world for money and the press.

Zora's disgust turned to self-pity. Being a mother was always high on her bucket list, but not before marriage, of course. She sighed heavily and tossed the magazine back on the end table as if it had become a sudden nuisance. As she reached into her satchel for her cell phone, the door allowing entry into the back office opened.

"Zora? Hi, sweetie, come on back." Harriet, Doctor Thompson's physician's assistant, smiled.

Grabbing her bag, she followed Harriet down a long corridor to Exam Room 2. The lights in the hallway seemed dimmer than they actually were, or maybe it was Zora's imagination.

Out of the blue, "Dead woman walking," rolled off her tongue, loud enough for Harriet to hear.

"You'll be fine, sweetie." Harriet opened the door to a white, cold room that reeked of rubbing alcohol and could comfortably fit maybe four people. "Don't get yourself worked up before you know anything." Harriet caressed Zora's elbow. "How have you been?" She pulled a paper cover-up from a metal drawer.

"Good, until now." Zora dropped her belongings on the black plastic chair situated in the corner.

"Here you go, sweetie." Harriet handed Zora the cover-up. "Just need from the waist up today. Doctor Thompson will be in shortly."

"Thank you."

"No problem." Harriet warmly smiled, opening the door. She paused and faced Zora. "You look like you need a hug."

Zora nodded as tears streamed down her face.

Harriet stepped to her and embraced her lovingly. "You're going to be fine. You are in excellent hands."

Zora and Harriet were not strangers. Zora had been Doctor Thompson's patient for as long as Harriet had been his physician's assistant, which was about fifteen years.

"Thank you, Harriet. I really needed that."

"Sure thing. Now, strip down for Doctor Thompson." She chuckled at that little joke she used with all the patients before leaving the room.

Zora disrobed her blouse and bra and eased into the paper-thin cover-up. With a slight shiver, she laid her clothes over the back of the plastic chair and hopped up on the padded examination table, briskly rubbing her arms.

"It's cold as shit in here. You would think they would make this room a little more warmer."

Wound tightly, she needed to relax. She reclined on the table and placed her hands behind her head, supporting her neck. She took a deep sigh and closed her eyes. Prayer was all she needed. *God, my fate is in Your hands. It is Your will, God, but I do not want to die. Lord, I do not want to experience any of this. God, please, have mercy on me.*

A few moments later and, with a soft knock on the door, Doctor Thompson entered, looking as handsome as ever. Zora loved everything about him, especially his bedside manner. He carefully chose his words to put his patients at ease. Besides, looking like Larenz Tate's twin didn't hurt either—sexy from head to toe, but a few inches taller.

She sat up. *Lord, have mercy,* was all she could think when she saw him. Seeing him took her mind off the reason for her being there, if only for a hot minute.

"Ms. Vaughn, how are we doing today?" He looked her square in the eyes, with a smile that would melt away all fears.

"Well, *we* are not so good."

"No? What's the problem?"

"I felt a lump in my left breast."

"Okay, lay back for me, and let's take a look."

Zora lay back, resting her arms above her head, and closing her eyes, as his soft, warm hand slid under the cover-up, pressing gently on both breasts, focusing more on the left. Then he moved toward her underarms, feeling for swollen lymph nodes.

"Do you feel it?"

He nodded. He removed his hand and extended it toward her, helping her to sit up. "I felt something. Have you noticed any changes in the size, shape, or appearance of your breasts?"

"No."

"Are you experiencing any pain or discomfort in your breasts?"

"No."

He picked up the chart off the metal workstation and opened it. "Do you have any family history of breast cancer or other breast conditions?"

"No, I don't think so."

"Any nipple discharge or changes in nipple appearance?"

She shook her head. "No."

"I want to schedule you for a mammogram and then, based on the results, a biopsy."

A biopsy? More fear consumed her. *Jesus.*

"Harriet will be back in to schedule everything for you."

"Thank you, Doctor Thompson."

"You're welcome, and hey, try not to worry. Let's find out first and go from there. Okay?"

She smiled and inclined her head.

Even though his attempts to calm her nerves worked for thirty seconds, Zora was working toward a nervous breakdown.

CHAPTER 19

Anxiety enveloped her and yet despite it, or perhaps because of it, she found herself oddly detached, as she frantically rushed from the Medical Building to her car.

She climbed behind the steering wheel. "Why me?" Her chest heaved as tears clouded her vision. She was tired of crying.

When her scream came, at last, her heart leaped wildly in her chest.

"Oh, God!" She was hysterical, followed by a loud shrill, like a wounded animal, banging the steering wheel. "Why? Why? Why? Why?"

You are just wrong!

Zora sat ramrod straight. Sitting as still as a statue, she was afraid to move. Was that her imagination playing tricks on her?

"This shit is making me crazy."

Don't make no sense!

Then she heard it again. She silenced herself, her fingers now gripping the steering wheel, her nails piercing her flesh.

You are just wrong!

There it was again. The masculine voice was as clear as day, as if someone was in the car with her.

Karma is a bitch. You're getting what you deserve.

"What?"

See what happens when you canoodle with your man's best friend? You should be ashamed of yourself, Zora Marie Vaughn! The venom in its voice chilled her to the bones. *Keep doing what you're doing and you'll be with me soon enough.*

Her eyes widened, and she rubbed her forehead. Yes, she was now going crazy. There was no other reason. "That's it, I'm going batshit crazy! Jesus!"

Don't bring Jesus into your mess. What about Maceo? He loves you!

She covered her ears, gently rocked, humming—anything to block out this madness.

Nothing but a common slut! A canoodling slut! It laughed; psychotic and evil. *There's a place, especially for the likes of you, Zora, and you're going straight there!*

Her face distorted, as she yelled, "Shut up! Shut up! Shut up!"

Passersby looked confused and dumbfounded at the nutcase yelling and pulling at her hair.

Laughter engulfed her head; loud like thunder cracking across the skies.

"Dear God, please help me!"

Then, she heard, *That darn devil sure is busy. He needs to go on about his business. Just works my nerves.*

She hadn't heard that voice in years. It was soothing, comforting, and one she missed.

Make it right.

She opened the door, quickly got out of the car, then climbed back in, kneeling on the seat and facing the back. "Mama?"

Tears streamed down her face; her eyes were bloodshot. She listened intently. There was silence.

"Mama?"

You know we didn't raise you like that, baby girl.

Startled, her heart pounded profusely. "Oh, Lord…Daddy?"

That girl is your friend. How could you do that to her?

Fix it, honey. You have to do the right thing.

"What in the fuck is going on?" Zora slammed her fists on the steering wheel, followed by another outburst of tears. She grabbed her head. "What the hell is wrong with me? I'm losing my goddamn mind! I'm going fucking crazy! Goddamn it!"

I see your vocabulary is still limited. You always had a filthy mouth, Zora.

Yes, and you're using God's name in vain? For shame, Zora.

Now still, her eyes shifting from side to side, she was ready to be suited up.

Releasing the grip on her head, she gripped her knees. Without moving her head, she looked in the rearview mirror, and, boy, did her eyes bulge larger than a deer caught in the headlights, damn near twice their size. She couldn't believe it. Hastily, she turned around. What she saw took her words. She opened her mouth to speak, but nothing came out. She couldn't believe it.

Zora's complexion paled; she looked like she'd seen a ghost—two ghosts.

"What the…what?"

They smiled at her lovingly and warmly.

Reluctantly, she smiled back.

Uncertainty gnawed at Zora. Were her eyes deceiving her, or was she truly witnessing spirits? The figures of her beloved parents, Jeffery and Cora Vaughn, who had tragically died in a car accident when she was just a teenager, appeared seated comfortably in the back of the two-seater. A mix of emotions overwhelmed her heart as she grappled with the haunting sight.

For a moment, she drifted back to the past, recalling how the tragedy of losing them had left her feeling adrift, like a ship without a compass, navigating the turbulent seas of grief and loss at such a young age. The pain of their departure weighed heavily on her soul, leaving her feeling profoundly lost and alone. She struggled to come to terms with the stark reality that her loving parents were no longer part of her physical world, forever separated from her by the cruel hands of fate.

Zora's parents looked so real and alive, not like the ghostly figures or apparitions she would expect from the spiritual realm.

"Mama?" A lump formed in her throat. "I can't…I can't believe it's you."

You don't see anyone else?

Oh, hush up, Jeff. Of course, she sees you. Don't be silly.

Zora blinked several times. *What the fuck?* She wiped her eyes.

There's that nasty mouth of yours, again.

"I didn't say anything."

No, but you thought it.

Leave her alone, Jeff. Listen, Zora, I know you love Keith, but he is Maceo's best friend and his wife, LaTonya, is your friend, and—

"How do you know?"

Her mother pointed upward. *He sees everything.*

"Who, God? You're in heaven?" She smiled widely. Since their deaths, she'd worried so much about her parents. Though she never doubted where their souls would end up, confirming they were in heaven made her feel so much better.

Well, where did you think we were?

Yes, baby, we're with the Heavenly Father.

If you're not careful, you'll end up with that fool that God cast out of heaven and was just here.

Jeffery! Why must you be that way? You can see she's not doing well.

Zora slouched, broke down, and turned on the faucet, tears flowing profusely. "Oh, Mama, I miss you so much."

Well, I guess you don't miss anyone else.

"I miss you, too, Daddy." Her father's snappy comebacks were what she missed most about him. Coupled with her mother's soothing side, they kept her balanced when they were alive. Now, though, she felt out of sorts. "Thank you, God."

Why are you thanking Him?

Jeffrey, she should always thank Him.

"For giving me what I need, when I need it, Daddy. I need you two right now."

He's always right on time, isn't He?

"Yes, Mama, He sure is." Zora lowered her head and closed her eyes. "I may have cancer." She raised her head and looked into her mother's eyes. They were so calming and peaceful looking, never harsh or judgmental.

Zora, put it in God's hands, for He will never forsake you. Pray on it and give it to God. He'll take care of it and you. Believe me when I tell you He will. I am a witness to His work every single day.

Amen to that, Cora. He is phenomenal, for sure.

"Okay, Mama, that's what I'll do."

That will not end the fact that you are betraying people who love you.

"I know, Daddy."

Then if you know, why continue to do it? Zora, you've always been that way. You know what to do, but you insist on doing the opposite. You know wrong from right, but you are a glutton to always do wrong. I never could understand that to save my life.

Touché, honey. Cora chuckled. *Yes, Zora, you have that wonderful Maceo—*

"Yes, he is wonderful."

Didn't your mama tell you that He sees everything? I don't think He likes what He's seeing either.

"I don't want God to hate me, Daddy."

Oh, Zora, God doesn't hate, sweetheart. He does want you to do the right thing, though. Just because He died on the cross for our sins doesn't mean we have to sin all day, every day, 'til the cows come home, daughter.

"Yes, Mama."

Once you do the right thing—

Yes, like Spike Lee said—

Jeffrey, please. Zora, you will see how your life will change…for the better. Your father and I only want what is best for you.

"I don't know what to do."

You're a smart cookie. You'll figure it out.

She smiled at her father. "I love you, Daddy."

I love you, too, baby. We're keeping our eyes on you, too.

Yes, we're always with you, honey. He's a wonderful God, letting us visit you.

"I love you, too, Mama."

I love you, too, Zora.

"Hey, Mama…"

Yes, sweetheart?

"What's it like?"

What's what like, dear?

"Heaven."

Her mother smiled, leaned forward, and caressed Zora's face. *Darling, it is magical. Peaceful. Perfect. All your ancestors are there, too. I never knew we had so many folks in our family.*

"Really, Mama? Like whom?"

Honey, too many to tell…

"I miss you, Mama. I can't wait to be with you and Daddy again."

Oh, Zora, sweetheart, don't be in such a rush. God is not finished with you yet. You still have a lot to do, and a lot of life to live. You're doing good things at that hospital. Your father and I are very proud of you, daughter.

"Really? Like what?"

You must be patient and live your life right.

"Yes, Daddy."

Yes, Zora, your time will come and when it does, we'll be there waiting for you. We all will be waiting for you.

"'We all?'"

Oh, yes, Zora. All of your aunts, uncles, grandparents, great-grandparents…all of your ancestors, we're all there. Even folks you've encountered here on Earth. We're not going anywhere.

Her father smiled at his wife. *Let's hope they would want to see her, the way she's living down here.*

Jeffrey, hush. She'll right the wrong, won't you, Zora?

"Yes, I will!" She fished around inside her purse. "I just have to find my…here it is!" She held up her cell phone and looked in the back seat.

Her smile turned into a frown.

They were gone, but she knew what she had to do.

She turned around in her seat and dialed the number. Anxiety wasn't quite what she felt, but she was borderline scared shitless. It had to be done…before she lost her nerve.

"Hey, LaTonya. I need to talk to you." She leaned her head back against the headrest, trying her best to hold back the tears. She wanted to cry out because she knew deep down, she was going to lose a friend and the man she loved. "How about we meet up for drinks this evening? The VFW? You feel like dancing?" She laughed, listening to her friend's voice. "I was thinking about Stan's. Someplace a little quiet. And no, let's not include Kennedy. I have some things I need to get off my chest, and I'd rather not bring her into the mix."

As she listened to LaTonya speak on the other end, she looked in the rearview mirror, hoping to see them again.

"Okay, how about eight o'clock? Great, see you then. Oh, and LaTonya? Please, bring an open heart."

CHAPTER 20

*D*arn hiccups!
It never failed. Whenever Lindsay was nervous about anything at all, the hiccups would start, and she was nervous as hell. She wanted to call her mother but decided against it. She was a big girl now, a young woman, and she would simply have to handle this on her own. When things went wrong, she wouldn't be the grown woman who ran to her mommy.

However, things weren't going awry; she was going on her first date. Ever! Those damn hiccups simply would not go away, no matter how long she held her breath or how much water she drank.

Wrapped in a towel, she stood in front of the mirror and pressed her toes flat against the cold tile floor of the shower room. The coolness of the floor calmed her, and soon she was breathing regularly, the hiccups of hysteria receding. She knew what she had to do. Pull up her big girl undies and enjoy her first date.

Sighing heavily, she gathered her things and headed to her room, her bare feet slapping against the floor, afraid to put on any shoes or else the hiccups may return.

Lindsay walked through the door and plopped down on her bed.

Dorrie sat on the edge of her bed, flipping through the pages of *Essence* magazine. Observing her roommate's pouting lips, she closed the magazine and tossed it to the side. "What's wrong now?"

Lindsay rolled her eyes upward and fell back on her bed. "Life."

"What are you going to wear?"

Lindsay sat up and shrugged. "Jeans…I guess."

"Honey, you can't wear any jeans. Here, let me see what I have in my closet." Dorrie sprung up and rushed to her closet.

Lindsay briskly shook her head. "No, thank you. I'm good." While she knew Dorrie had good intentions, tonight she would not look like a two-bit hooker. "We're just going to a movie, so jeans will be fine."

Dorrie faced her, took three steps toward her, and flipped Lindsay's hair. "Alrighty then. Do you want me to do your makeup and hair?"

"Nope. Bare face and ponytail."

"But—"

"Dorrie, I want Max to get to know the real me." Standing and retrieving a pair of low-rise jeans off the chair in front of her desk, she slipped into them. "Without the makeup and fried hair." She pulled on a fitted hot pink V-neck knit ribbed top.

Dorrie waved in surrender. "Okay, okay. You're feeling real grown, huh?"

Lindsay smirked. "What do you mean?"

"Well, you done put on everything else except for your bra and drawers." The two looked at each other and burst into laughter.

Lindsay undressed, slid into her undergarments, and then dressed again. She slipped her feet into a pair of no-name tennis shoes.

Dorrie looked down at her shoes. "Wait, you're not going to wear those, are you?"

Lindsay rolled her eyes and hissed.

"Okay, okay, geesh! But you have to fill me in when you get back!"

Now dressed, Lindsay headed for the door and smiled. "I'll think about it. Night-night, roomie!"

Descending the steps, Lindsay looked through the glass-paned door and caught sight of Maxwell restlessly pacing in front of the building. The night was flat and moonless, casting an eerie darkness over the campus.

She smiled. He looked nervous, too, and that made her happy—she wasn't the only one.

Yes, he was very nervous. So nervous he hadn't realized she had walked out of the building and was standing behind him.

She tapped him on the shoulder. "Hi, Max."

He damn near jumped out of his skin as he spun around. "Oh, hi, Lindsay." He looked at her from head to shoes. "You look great!"

She blushed. "Thanks, so do you."

As they faced an awkward moment, a sense of uncertainty lingered, but an unspoken connection pulled them closer together. He gathered his courage, leaned in, and gently wrapped his arms around her. She hesitated for a tick but allowed herself to relax into the hug.

At that special moment, it felt like the world disappeared, leaving just the two of them wrapped in a sweet embrace, something she had never experienced. As he held her, she inhaled. He smelled good—a mix of clean clothes and subtle cologne. It sent a thrilling shiver down her spine.

His gentle touch made her feel safe and understood, as if he could sense her insecurities of a first date. In that hug, she felt a comforting warmth that made everything seem right.

They held the embrace for a while, their emotions swirling around them like a beautiful dance. It was just a simple hug, but it spoke volumes about their new connection. They didn't need words to understand each other; their hearts did all the talking.

When they finally let go, he smiled at her. "You ready to go?"

She nodded.

They locked hands and walked toward his car.

CHAPTER 21

Before heading home, Zora stopped by Triangle Liquors. She needed a drink, and she was apprehensive about meeting LaTonya this evening.

Inside the kitchen, she popped the cork on her favorite red wine from Linganore Winecellars in Mt. Airy, Maryland, and filled the wineglass to the rim. Zora was a huge patronage of local wineries. From the living room, her cell phone rang, alerting her: *Keith Mobile.* She sighed heavily and gulped the wine while the call went to voicemail.

Carrying the glass to the living room, she turned on the radio to MAJIC 102.3 FM, placed the glass on the end table, plopped down, and stared at the phone. Should she call him back? Maybe if she called him back and broke things off with him, she wouldn't have to tell LaTonya. She wasn't worried about Maceo. What he didn't know wouldn't hurt him and as long as she continued to take care of home and his needs, he had no reason to think her loyalty lay elsewhere. Then, she wouldn't lose her friend, because what she doesn't know wouldn't hurt her, either. Yes, of course, it would be a secret she would carry to the grave. Why hadn't she thought of that before? She was also confident Keith wouldn't tell a soul. After all, it wouldn't go well for him if he told.

She reached for her cell phone; her fingers gripped around it.

Keith picked up on the first ring. "Hey, sweet thang!"

Something about his voice—its warmth, its sanity—undid her, and she moaned, except this time softly, keening into the phone, before she could even get a word out. She didn't want to speak anymore. She just wanted to cry.

"Hey." Her voice trembled.

"What's wrong?"

"Um, well…"

"What's wrong? Are you all right? What's going on?"

At first, she could only whimper in response.

"Is this an emergency? Should I call nine-one-one?"

She eked out, "No."

"Stairway to Heaven" by the O'Jays enveloped the living room from the surround-sound stereo system, and memories of their sexual moments rushed back like wildfire. She didn't need an ambulance. She needed to be Mrs. Keith Jordan, but he already had a wife.

"Keith, I need to talk to you."

"I'm listening."

Searching for the right words, she closed her eyes and allowed Eddie Levert's deep falsetto to embrace her. Before she knew it, she was in a trance, singing in Keith's ear.

"That's my song."

She could hear the smile in his voice, which made her smile.

"Do you remember The Four Seasons?" He was now taking her down memory lane to Georgetown in the northwest quadrant of Washington, DC.

"Yes. I remember."

He moaned into the phone, igniting her fire. "Remember the rose petals from the door to the bed?"

Nodding, Zora remained silent. Pulling her knees into her chest, she pressed the phone snuggly between her shoulder and ear, and traveled with him.

"Zora, you were so beautiful that night…"

There was a minute-long silence, during which Zora involuntarily trembled. The memory of what transpired that night was making her moist.

How could she forget? It had been a magical night at The Four Seasons. She had moaned when he entered her, thrusting deeply, maintaining the slow stroke until he withdrew to the tip of his penis, then sliding inside her again. Wrapping her legs around his waist, arching up to meet him, wanting and needing to be filled, she draped her arms around his neck. Bringing his lips to meet hers, the look in her eyes was as articulate as any spoken word.

He slowed down long enough to raise her legs to rest on his shoulders. She took his weight—and the length of his shaft—as deep into her cave as he could dive, and she was not silent, crying out at his strong thrust, moaning and sighing.

He had felt himself nearing nirvana, so he slowed his pace a little to make it last.

Initially watching the contours of his healthy frame—his stomach, his hips pumping to please her, his muscular control, every part of his anatomy working in harmony like an athletic assembly line—the visual made her succumb to the pleasure as she screamed.

He didn't stop, and he was deep inside her when her muscles gripped tightly around his pumping steel. She was whimpering, clawing his shoulders, and he didn't slow, thrusting through her tight contractions, seeing her eyes register the pleasure of the first stroke after orgasm as she climaxed, gasping, legs uncontrollably trembling, and crying out.

He stroked her through three orgasms before he lost control, holding her tightly and feeling her throb around his tool like a tight, wet fist.

Like cold water splashing against her face, reality drowned her mental picture, returning Zora to her present anxiety. Rocking on the couch, still searching for the right words, she couldn't bring herself to say, "We can't see each other anymore," so instead she said, "I have cancer, Keith."

Just as fast as those words flew out, she plastered her hand over her mouth, jumped up, and turned down the radio.

"What did you say?"

She sat back down. "I detected a lump."

"You were diagnosed with cancer?"

"No…not exactly."

"What do you mean by 'not exactly'?"

"Well, there is definitely a lump in my breast, but he—Doctor Thompson—wants me to get a mammogram first and then possibly a biopsy."

"Oh, I see." Keith was at a loss for words now. "Well, maybe it's nothing."

"Maybe…" She didn't know what else to say. Well, she did, but could not bring herself to say it. If she had cancer, she wanted to die with a clean conscience. "We have to end this."

"Zora?"

"No, Keith, we have to; I can't keep doing this to LaTonya and Maceo. Soon, I won't be able to look her in the face, knowing what I've been doing to her for so long."

"That's mighty selfish of you, don't you think? You've been looking in her face for five years now, without apprehension or acting like you give two fucks!"

"Excuse me?"

"You don't give a damn about *my* wife while you are fucking *her* husband's brains out, now do you? Now that you *think* you *might* have cancer, you want a clean fucking conscience. So, what? Just fuck you, Keith, is that it? Fuck your motherfucking feelings, Keith!"

Zora was quiet for several moments, contemplating if she wanted to continue this conversation. Keith had never used this tone with her before. She didn't know what to make of it. Sure, she figured he would be upset, but she didn't care for this side of him.

"Oh, so what? I strapped you down and fucked you against your will for five years? You play a role in this, too. How the fuck do you look at your wife every fucking day, Keith? Huh? Answer me that, you self-righteous bastard!"

"Yeah, just like you fuck Maceo, without a goddamn conscience!"

Her mouth gaped. That stung. "Look! This is not right, Keith. You know it's not right. Maceo is your best friend and LaTonya loves you—"

"And I *love my wife*! How fucking dare you?"

Zora shivered, as his voice was as cold as ice, sending a chill coursing through her. His words felt like a nuclear bomb, dropping on her heart.

She cleared her throat. "I'm so sorry, Keith. It's over. It has to be. I love you, but—"

"Love me! Love me! How dare you speak those words to me? Fuck you, Zora! I don't need this shit!" He disconnected the call.

"Damn. Wow…"

She picked up her wineglass and guzzled it to the last drop.

Zora stood by the sink, her hands immersed in the soapy water, gently scrubbing away the remnants of their breakfast. It had become an evening ritual for her, a moment of solitude and reflection after a busy day. The clinking of plates and the gentle swish of water provided a comforting soundtrack to her thoughts.

As the warm water cascaded over her hands, her conversation with Kennedy bothered her. For as long as she had known her, Kennedy had never used such harsh language with her. Kennedy was seething mad with her. Zora knew she deserved such a backlash but wasn't expecting to receive it from Kennedy. Deep down, she knew that once LaTonya got wind of the affair, she would lose her friendship. A severed friendship with LaTonya, she could learn to live without, but Kennedy was another story. Kennedy was her best friend, her sister, her rock, her confidant, and, as of late, her scolder.

Her heart wrestled with conflicting emotions as she continued to scrub the dishes. The guilt of the affair weighed heavily on her conscience, but despite betraying Maceo, the entanglement had a hold on her that seemed impossible to break. She was in too deep in a web that she had spun.

With each passing day, the bond she shared with Keith grew stronger, yet Zora understood the feelings were one-sided. She was in love with him, but she couldn't deny that he didn't reciprocate those emotions in the same way. It was a painful realization, one that gnawed at her heart. She also felt, with time, his feelings would change. As with life, Zora felt that if she loved Keith enough, gave him what he wanted, when he wanted it, including herself, that he would change his mind about loving her. Did Keith love Zora? Of course, however that love didn't exceed past friendship. He would never love her like he loved his wife. Never.

Maceo had always been her rock, her true love, the foundation of her life. Deep down, she loved him to the core of her being, and they had shared a journey together filled with joy, understanding, and unconditional support. Yet, the allure of Keith, and the excitement and passion of their five-year-long intimacy, created an enticing but dangerous contrast that she struggled to resist.

Zora felt torn between the love she knew was right and the forbidden love that was an intoxicating secret. The feeling of being torn apart inside was tearing her apart emotionally. She wanted to be honest with Maceo and end the affair with Keith, but fear held her back. Fear of hurting him, fear of losing Keith, and fear of facing the consequences of her many years of indiscretion.

As she rinsed off the last dish and set it on the drying rack, the evening sun cast long shadows through the living room window, symbolizing the darkness she had allowed into her life.

Zora's thoughts turned to Maceo. Just then, the sound of the front door creaking open broke through her reverie, as she knew it was Maceo's unmistakable entrance. As he stepped into the condominium, a combination of exhaustion and satisfaction showed on his face. The scent of engine oil and gasoline clung to his clothes.

Their eyes met, and a tender smile spread across Zora's face, conveying a silent welcome. Maceo reciprocated the gesture, his eyes lighting up as he saw his longtime partner in the kitchen, a sight that brought him comfort and a sense of belonging. He carefully removed his work boots by the door, a habit they had developed over the years to keep their home clean.

"How was your day, love?"

"Busy, as always, but you know what? Seeing your face at the end of the day makes it all worth it."

Her heart swelled with affection at his words. Zora dried her hands and stepped toward him, enveloping him in a warm embrace.

A montage of precious memories from the years they had spent together flashed through her mind. They had experienced carefree days of doing nothing at all, as well as faced and conquered the challenges life had thrown their way. Throughout it all, they had grown together, supporting and encouraging each other through thick and thin. The mere thought of him discovering her infidelity would be utterly devastating—to them both.

Zora took Maceo's hand and led him to the dining table, where she had prepared a simple yet comforting meal.

Maceo kissed her on the neck. "Thank you. Looks good." Sitting down, he rested his elbows on the table. "When is the mammogram, beautiful?"

Zora took a deep breath, grateful for his support, but also feeling the weight of her own emotions.

"Next week."

"Cool, I'll take off and go with you."

Zora appreciated his willingness to be present during this challenging time. However, the strong and independent side of her urged her to assure him she could handle it alone. "No, no, don't do that." She placed her hand on his shoulder. "I want us to continue living a normal life. I'll be okay, and having you take time off might just make me more anxious. Besides, you have your work and responsibilities, and I don't want to burden you."

Maceo's eyes softened with understanding, and he squeezed her hand gently. "You know I'll do anything to support you through this, but I also respect your decision. Just promise me you'll let me know if you need anything, and I'll be there, no questions asked."

"Of course, and I know you'll be there when I need you most."

Maceo's eyes caught sight of the nearly empty wineglass resting on the end table, and he gestured toward it. "Any more left?"

Zora's lips curled into a playful smile. "Barely. Want some?"

"Only if you'll join me." He escaped to the kitchen and returned with two wine goblets and a bottle of wine, filling their glasses.

Maceo raised his goblet with a glint of excitement in his eyes. "To us."

"To us."

Unexpectedly, Maceo's next words caught Zora off guard. "Marry me." His smile was wider than she had ever seen before.

Her eyes widened in surprise as she absorbed his request. "What?" Her heart was racing.

"Marry me."

Zora gnawed her bottom lip, a nervous habit she couldn't control. She set her glass on the table and retreated to the floor-to-ceiling window, seeking a moment of solitude to process her emotions.

Observing her sudden escape, Maceo couldn't help but feel unsure of how to interpret her reaction. Undeterred, he followed her, standing beside her and taking her hand tenderly. "Baby, what's wrong?"

Her voice quivered as she tried to articulate her feelings. "Why did you ask me to marry you?"

Confused by her inquiry, Maceo peered at her intently. "Because I love you, and I want to spend the rest of my life with you. What kind of question is that?"

"Are you sure it's not because you're feeling sorry for me? I don't want anyone to feel sorry for me, Maceo."

"I can't believe you said that!"

"Don't go getting upset."

"I ask you to marry me, you turn me down, and then you tell me not to be upset?"

"I didn't turn you down."

"No? Then what do you call it?"

"I just…I don't know, Maceo—"

"Zora, don't you love me?"

Thoughts of Keith clouded her mind, making her hesitate. "Of course, I do. You know I love you."

Despite her reassurance, resignation settled in as Maceo released a heavy sigh. His excitement had shifted to feelings of rejection. "I don't know what to think anymore. I won't beg you to be my wife. I sure as hell won't beg you or anyone else to love me."

Tears welled in Zora's eyes. "I just need some time. Please, just give me some time."

"Time? Time for what? Zora, we've been together for ten years. If, after ten years, you don't know, then…" He firmly jammed his hands into his pockets as he gazed out of the window, captivated by the breathtaking beauty of the setting sun on the Potomac River, flowing under the Woodrow Wilson Bridge. The warm hues painted the sky in a mesmerizing display, yet questions that weighed heavily on his heart preoccupied his mind.

"It's been ten years, Zora. How much more time do you need?"

Zora's shoulders slumped under the weight of his words, and she strolled away from his side, seeking refuge in the comfort of a nearby chair. With a heavy sigh, she plopped down; her face revealing a myriad of emotions she struggled to articulate.

You're a complete mess. That man loves you and you're going to throw it all away because of a married man.

Despite her best efforts, Zora found it impossible to ignore her father's voice echoing in her head. The memories of his powerful presence seemed to linger in the air. Feeling a gentle breeze on the back of her neck, she turned around, and there he stood, just as she remembered him—his massive build and commanding presence sending shivers down her spine—with his beautiful wife by his side.

Zora, sweetheart, pay your father no mind.

"I can handle this."

Maceo looked over his shoulder. "You can handle what?"

"Nothing."

You'd better handle it, because God doesn't like what's going on with you. That much I know.

She lowered and tilted her head as if to speak secretively. "All right, Daddy."

"Daddy? Zora, what—"

Zora flew out of the chair to Maceo, grabbed him from behind, practically tackled him, and tightly embraced him. "Just give me some time, okay? I'm scared, Maceo. With all that's going on with me now, I just—please, bear with me."

With his hand gently pressed against the windowpane, he lowered his head, attempting to shield the single tear streaming down his cheek. The weight of the emotions he carried was in that solitary tear, a silent testament to the pain he couldn't express in words. "I'm not going anywhere."

Her father now stood by her side. *That's what he says now, but just as soon as a pretty little thing comes his way, he'll be gone and you'll be alone.*

Zora looked to her right for her father, but he wasn't there. She knew he was right. Maceo was the best thing that had happened to her, and she knew there was no future with Keith.

So, what was her holdup?

CHAPTER 22

LaTonya slipped into a red sleeveless dress and matching pumps. She took a last glance in the full-length mirror, smoothed her hands over her hips, and smiled. "I've still got it going on," she mumbled, turning on her heels and heading downstairs.

The Roku Smart TV was still tuned to Pandora from that morning. As she descended the stairs and turned the corner into the kitchen, Luther Vandross crooned, "*I promise to love faithfully*," and it took her back to her and Keith's wedding. "Here and Now" was the all-time favorite of all brides; a dream to enter through double doors, stepping on red carpeting, and being escorted to the love of her life. Sighing, if she had to do it over again, she would marry him in the middle of McDonald's, with Ronald McDonald officiating and the Burglar witnessing. She loved that man's dirty boxers.

Closing her eyes, she delved into the song, swaying with the melody. Oh, how she missed Luther Vandross, one of her favorite performers. She never missed a concert when he performed in the Washington, DC, area.

Wait… *Oh, shit,* she thought, as she sang, "Why must they try to tear down the house we built?" Shaking her head, she shrilled. "They are playing my songs this evening." As Anthony Hamilton sang to his woman, "I Can't Let Go," LaTonya stretched her arms above her head, moving her shoulders, followed by her hips. She was blissfully absorbed in her own world, relishing every single second of it—until the front door abruptly swung open and shut.

"Sweet thing, you home?"

She dropped her hands to her side and slouched. "Is my car in the driveway?"

"Yeah," he said, kicking off his shoes at the front door.

"Then I'm home!"

Like a whirlwind, Keith blew into the kitchen, dropped his keys and cell phone on the island, and made a beeline for his wife.

"You are a sight for sore eyes." He pulled her into him, kissing her with passion.

Pulling back, LaTonya turned up her lips in a seductive smirk. "Wow, what's that all about?"

"Can't a man miss his woman?"

"Absolutely, so long as the man continues to greet his woman this way." She patted him on the shoulder. "Gotta run."

"You're looking hot—should I be jealous?"

"Of?"

"Another man tapping *my* ass."

She chuckled. "Last I checked, it was still *my* ass."

He tapped her left butt cheek and opened the refrigerator. "Where are you going?"

"Meeting Zora for drinks."

He stopped searching for a snack. "Yeah?" His head was still inside the refrigerator. "With Kennedy, too?"

"Nope, just us."

Various thoughts raced through his mind, but he maintained his composure. "Okay. Well, have a good time."

She grabbed her clutch, cell phone, and keys off the island. "Wait up for me."

"Always."

As the front door closed, so did the refrigerator door. With bottled water in hand, Keith mounted the stool in front of the island and whispered her name. He missed Zora and wanted to see her, but she ended it. No longer wanting to see him, Keith felt betrayed. He gave her the best five years of his life, so he thought, but she no longer appreciated him. Just thinking about it made him angry. He craved her as much as he craved LaTonya. However, when he made love to LaTonya, he saw Zora. Yes, he was in love with LaTonya, but Zora was an obsession. Her smell intoxicated him, and every time they met for their rendezvous, she allowed him to take her any way he wanted. He did things to Zora he would never dream about doing with his wife.

"All my love is all I have," Debra Laws belted out, as he listened to the song, "Very Special," by Ronnie and Debra Laws. Yes, Zora was very special to him, but it wasn't love.

Twisting off the top of the bottle, he shook his head and took a gulp. There was no way he would leave LaTonya for Zora. He loved his cake and loved eating it, too.

He looked at the cell phone sitting on the countertop. Tempted to call her, he figured what was the use since Zora was not answering his calls. He'd called her five times today, each call going to voicemail.

Reaching for the phone, he stopped short of picking it up. Shaking his head, he would not beg for sex when he had it twenty-four-seven with his wife.

Yet, he could not get her out of his system. When he kissed LaTonya's lips, he pretended they were Zora's lips. Just one more time. That was all he needed, and he would never bother her again.

CHAPTER 23

The feeling was mutual. She missed him, too. Seated in the corner booth of Stan's Bar & Restaurant in downtown Northwest Washington, DC, Zora stared at a couple sitting across from her. She wondered what their story was, as they snuggled, him nibbling her neck, she was smiling, and enjoying every minute.

Zora felt a pit in her stomach, aching for Keith. That couple reminded her of the many nights she spent with Keith cuddled in the corner of a secluded bar somewhere deep in Northern Virginia, playing with each other under the table. A smile graced her lips, thinking about the time Keith fingered her into an orgasmic stratosphere at Cleo's, a quaint whole-in-the-wall.

"I want to feel you," he had said to her one evening as they huddled in a corner booth, partaking in libation straight with no chaser. Both were high as kites off of each other and threw caution to the wind. Moreover, there was no chance of encountering anyone familiar with them or their circle of friends.

"I want you to feel me."

"You naked down there?"

"You told me to be."

"Spread your thighs."

"Here?"

"Yes."

"Now?"

"Yes."

"Suppose someone sees us?"

"So?"

"I can't do that here."

"You can."

She opened them.

"Wider."

Parting her thighs wider, she looked around to make sure there were no eyes on them.

She looked into his eyes. "Satisfied?"

"Very." He kissed her lips as he finger-stroked her thighs, moving toward her warmth, nestling within her bush. "You're wet."

She gazed into his eyes, her lips parting. She nodded, caressing the back of his neck, pulling his face even closer, covering his mouth with hers. Slight moans escaped her with each feathery stroke against her tender flesh.

Her hips gyrated. Her moans got louder.

"Shhh, not so loud."

She nodded. "Right there. Right…ooh, there." Her body stiffened, and he held her tight.

"That's it. Let it go."

She let it go; squirting her juice in the palm of his hand, under the table, in a dark, crowded club.

She shivered. Just thinking about Keith wore her out. She loved that about him. He could screw for hours without busting one nut. He was the perfect lover, insisting she had multiple orgasms before he got his. Even with Maceo, she'd become numb to his touch that she no longer desired. He was not Keith.

She'd stopped taking Keith's calls because she felt it was the best thing to do. Yet deep down, it wasn't what she wanted to do. She wanted to talk to him. She wanted to hear his voice. Over the years, Keith had become more than her lover. He'd become her confidant. They talked about any and everything under the sun—politics, sports, business, love, relationships, why the sky was blue, the first man on the moon—whatever the topic, they discussed it. Maceo never watched the news. He had not a clue what was going on in the world—nor did he care—and that bothered her. Why couldn't he be more like Keith—more worldly and outgoing? Why couldn't Maceo know all of her spots and hit them at the right time, just like Keith?

That was the problem. Maceo was not Keith and never would be. She often wondered if she loved Maceo. Before her affair started with Keith, Maceo was the end-all-be-all to her everything. So what if he didn't watch the news? That didn't matter in the bedroom. Maceo loved Zora, and this she knew without a doubt, but did Zora *still* love Maceo? Yes, she loved him, but she was in love with Keith.

Reaching inside her purse, she retrieved her phone to send Keith a text. She couldn't put up the charade anymore. She needed to see him again; just one last time. She didn't have to scroll through the Contact List, as he'd called her five times that day. She fingered his name, pressed *message* and started typing.

I miss you. I want to see you. Our usual spot—The Bragg—at 10 tonight. Can you make it?

CHAPTER 24

As LaTonya turned into the Colonial Parking facility, the cell phone vibrated in the passenger seat. As she reached for the phone, the parking attendant approached the car. She dropped it back into the seat.

"How long will you be, miss?"

"Just a couple of hours."

"We close at ten o'clock."

LaTonya looked at her watch. "I'll be out long before then." She smiled, grabbed her clutch and cell phone, and exited the car.

"I just need your ignition key, ma'am."

"The extra key is in the ashtray." She smiled at him. *He's a cutie-patootie.* "Thank you." She walked up the ramp and onto Vermont Avenue.

She'd forgotten about the vibrating cell phone until it vibrated again as she dropped it into her clutch. Retrieving it, she looked at it. *This isn't my phone*, she thought, realizing she'd picked up Keith's phone instead. *Damn it!* Well, at least she had a phone with her, as she loathed being out and about with no phone in case of an emergency.

She would not have even considered peeking at Keith's phone, let alone picking it up or answering it, but her curiosity got the best of her. While walking, she used his password to open the message.

I miss you. I want to see you. Our usual spot—The Bragg—at 10 tonight. Can you make it?

"Oh my God," she blurted. Looking at the sender's name, she felt like falling to her knees.

Spotting the empty park bench at the bus stop, LaTonya needed to take a seat and gather her thoughts and feelings. In just a few paces away, she was going to sit face-to-face with her now *former* friend.

Tears flooded her eyes, blurring her vision, and flowing down her face like a river. *How could you do this to me, Keith? With my friend, of all people?* She felt light-headed, like she wanted to faint. The evening was mildly warm and not a breeze to be felt.

The parking attendant noticed her and felt something was wrong. He called out to her. "Ma'am, are you okay?"

She grabbed the bench and took deep breaths. She was hyperventilating.

He shouted out to her again.

She shook her head, and he ran toward her. "What's wrong? Do I need to call nine-one-one?"

"No. I just need to get myself together. I'll be fine."

"I will sit here with you until—"

"No, please. I'm fine. I don't want to cause any trouble for you." She straightened her shoulders. "See? I'm feeling much better. I just need to sit her for a few minutes and gather my thoughts."

The Latino specimen obliged her. "Okay, but if you need me…or *anything* at all, I'll be across the street until ten o'clock."

She looked up at him. *Is he flirting with me?* "Thank you. I appreciate your help."

Smiling, he nodded, turned, and swaggered across the street like Denzel Washington. "Damn," she mumbled, watching his ass. It was a marvelous view from where she sat, although it only diverted her attention from the inevitable for a hot minute.

What was she going to do? As clear as a sunny day, she had proof of betrayal.

There was no way in hell she would stand for this, but she also didn't know how she could sit across from a traitor, smiling in her face as if she were the golden child.

She looked at the time on the cell phone: 8:23 p.m.

After minutes of staring off into the distance, she replied to the text message.

I miss you, too. She paused, her hands trembling. Sighing, she erased what she typed, realizing she had to respond how Keith would respond. *I miss U 2. 2nite's good.* She pressed send.

Without actually being punched, she felt like someone had punched her in the gut. The knife in her back would not stop twisting. She felt like vomiting.

The cell phone vibrated, alerting her of a received text message. LaTonya read it.

*I'll see you at 10 pm. I can't wait to feel you inside me. I need you so badly. I love you! *kisses**

That was the upper cut that astounded her. Staring at the phone, wondering what she would do next, the feline in her wanted to scratch Zora's eyes out of her ugly face, but she was above that kind of retaliation.

"Is this why she wanted me to come with an open heart? How could she do this to me? She is supposed to be my fucking friend!" She hollered at the top of her lungs.

The foot traffic stopped, and all eyes were on LaTonya, but she could have given a rat's ass. She was in pain—emotionally and mentally. She was experiencing the ultimate betrayal by two people she loved. Devastation wrapped around her like an unwanted stranger. She felt like crawling into a corner to lick her wounds, but it was too late for that now. What was done in the dark had come to light.

LaTonya looked down at her hand, paying extra attention to her wedding band. *For better or worse, my ass*, she thought, yanking the tight ring from her finger. Standing, she threw the ring across Vermont Avenue. She wanted to yell, "Fuck you both," but she'd had enough of the looky-loos.

Erect with squared shoulders, LaTonya patted around her eyes, wiping away the tears, ran her fingers through her hair and smoothed her dress over her full hips. It was time to confront Keith's indiscretion.

When LaTonya pushed her way through the double doors, she saw her. Zora was wearing a cream-colored dress, her legs crossed at the ankles. She waved and held up a glass of wine.

LaTonya walked through the crowd of happy hour regulars with her head held high, trying to hold back the tears. She refused to cry. She wanted to face the bitch head-on.

Zora smiled when LaTonya reached the table. "Hi, sweetie! I ordered you a glass of Moscato."

Maintaining her composure, LaTonya forced a smile. "Thanks, but I'm going to need something stronger." She hung her purse on the back of the chair and took a seat.

Zora frowned, sensing that something was amiss. "Is everything all right, LaTonya?"

"Yes. Why do you ask?"

"You seem a little disturbed?"

"No, honey, I'm just fine." LaTonya took a sip of wine.

"So, what's been up with you lately?"

LaTonya lowered her glass and stared Zora in the eyes. "Same old stuff. Anything exciting in your life?"

"Same old stuff here, too."

"How's Maceo?

"He's fine."

"Great." LaTonya drank the last of the wine and summoned the waiter. "Courvoisier, double shot, please."

The waiter nodded.

"Ooh, girl, you're trying to grow hair on your chest or something?" Zora chuckled.

"What do you want to talk to me about, Zora?"

"Oh, well…"

LaTonya sighed, beyond annoyed.

"Just wanted a little girl time, that's it. All this cancer stuff is scary."

"Cancer? Your doctor diagnosed you with cancer?"

"Well, no, I have to have a mammogram—"

"Okay, but we've been through this before. Remember? At Truluck's—you, me, Kennedy—with your *friends*."

"Yeah, I know… What's with you, LaTonya?"

"Not a damn thing." She looked over her shoulder. "Where in the hell is my damn drink?"

"Whoa, are you sure everything's all right? This behavior is not you at all."

LaTonya sighed. "You're right. Tell me more about the lump in your breast...*again*. I suppose this is what I'm supposed to have an open heart about, your lump?"

Zora leaned back, squaring her shoulders. "Wow, okay..."

Zora was irritating her beyond words; she wanted to haul off and slap her across the face—hard enough for Keith to hear it in Brandywine, Maryland.

"I'm sure you'll be fine. Fuck the drink, I'm going home."

"Wait, what?"

"I'm not feeling this at all. I'm going home."

"But you just got here, and I have so much to talk to you about."

LaTonya stood up, grabbed her purse and swung it over her shoulders. "Call me in the morning." She turned on her heels, left Zora's presence, and pushed through the double doors.

Zora took a swig of her drink. "What in the world just happened?"

CHAPTER 25

Lindsay and Maxwell sat in the very back row of the movie theater, where they could see everything happening below. It was a popular spot for young couples to hold hands, cuddle, and make out.

They both felt a little self-conscious, not knowing exactly what to do with all the affection going on around them. However, they were also glad to be together, enjoying each other's company and the movie on the big screen.

Lindsay stole a quick glance at Maxwell, and he smiled at her as if sharing the same mix of amusement and slight awkwardness.

Whispers, giggles, and the occasional soft laughter from the couples below filled the atmosphere in the theater, but Lindsay and Maxwell found comfort in just being side by side, sharing the movie experience of *Top Gun: Maverick* together.

They whispered comments about the film to each other, laughing at the funny parts and enjoying the suspenseful moments. Despite the lovey-dovey ambiance, they felt a sense of contentment in their own little bubble.

Sitting there, they discovered that the best part of the night was simply being together. The movie was enjoyable, but the real show was the connection they were building.

At the end of the movie, they walked out, hand in hand, toward the car. Maxwell cleared his throat. "What would you like to do now?"

Lindsay looked at the time on her cell phone. "Well, it's still early."

"We can grab a pizza and go to my place."

She looked up at him, her brows furrowed. "Your place?"

"Yeah, Chucky went home for the weekend."

Lindsay felt a mix of excitement and nervousness. She liked him, and the idea of spending more time together was appealing but also frightening. She had a feeling the moment might lead to something more intimate—something she didn't think she was ready for—and there was something she needed to share with him.

Taking a deep breath, Lindsay looked into Maxwell's eyes. "Max, I want to be honest with you. I haven't been in a relationship before. I've never had a boyfriend. I've never dated. This is my first time being alone with a boy—I mean, man—who is not a family member, and I'm a virgin."

Maxwell's expression softened as he listened to her. He caressed her hand. "Thank you for telling me. I appreciate your honesty, and I want you to know that I respect your feelings and boundaries."

Lindsay felt a sense of relief wash over her, knowing Maxwell understood and didn't judge her for being honest about her lack of experience. "I really like you, Max, and I want us to take things slow. I'm glad you understand."

"Of course. Our relationship—"

Lindsay tilted her head. "Relationship?"

"Well, yeah."

"Oh, so you're my boyfriend?"

"I would like to be."

"But we just met and—"

"And I'd like to see where this goes…if you do."

Lindsay smiled. She had a boyfriend, and she was tickled pink. "Yes, I do."

"I don't want us to be just about physical intimacy. I want us to get to know each other and build a strong connection. I'm in no rush, and I'll always respect your pace."

A genuine smile spread across Lindsay's face. She felt he was someone special, who truly cared for her well-being and feelings.

As they got into the car and continued their conversation, Lindsay felt a sense of comfort in their openness with each other. They agreed to take their relationship step by step, focusing on building emotional intimacy and trust before considering anything more physical.

At that moment, Lindsay realized she had found someone who valued her for who she was, and that was a precious gift. She knew that with Maxwell, she could be her authentic self with no judgment or pressure.

She'd made one of her many adult decisions and she couldn't wait to call her mother to tell her all about it.

Lindsay looked around the two-bedroom apartment. "How can you afford to live off-campus, going to school all day? You don't work, do you?"

"As long as I maintain the Dean's List, and stay out of trouble, my parents pay my half of the rent and utilities."

"Oh, I see. Your place is nice."

"Thanks. Have a seat. Can I get you something to drink?"

"Yes."

"I have Pepsi, Coke—"

"Pepsi."

As he escaped into the tiny kitchen, Lindsay gingerly settled onto the navy-blue velour sofa, taking in the tasteful decor of Maxwell and Chuck's apartment, marking her first time alone in a man's place. Nervously, she fidgeted with her hands, unsure of how to act or what to do. She genuinely liked Maxwell, but she was terrified to so much as think about taking their newfound relationship to the next level. Kennedy's voice echoed in her head, advising her not to put herself in situations she couldn't control, but Lindsay believed she could handle it.

When Maxwell returned, carrying their drinks, she couldn't help but admire the sight before her. He exuded a captivating aura of handsomeness, with a confident swagger that made her heart flutter—a perfect blend of coolness, confidence, and undeniable sexiness. Maxwell was unlike any boys she knew from high school— hot masculinity from head to his Nike-covered feet.

Dorrie, had done her research and learned that others admired Maxwell for his authenticity, kindness, and genuine concern for the less fortunate. Now a junior at Hampton University, he excelled as a premed scholar, maintaining a remarkable 4.0 grade point average, and also showcased his talents as a wide receiver for the Hampton Pirates. As a natural leader, his calm empathy made him even more appealing, drawing people toward him effortlessly.

Contemplating what she should and should not do with Maxwell, he stood in front of her, extending the glass of soda. He cleared his throat. "Where are you, Lindsay?"

"Oh, huh?"

"You look like you're someplace else. What's on your mind?"

She shrugged, took the glass, and sipped the beverage. She watched stretch his arms high above his head and yawned.

"Are you sleepy?"

"Naw, I'm good. Hey, that movie was good, right?"

"Yeah, very much so."

Maxwell sat down beside her and patted his lap. "Put your feet up."

"Huh? Oh, no…that's okay."

"No, put your feet up."

She hesitated.

He gazed at her. "I won't bite you."

She slid back on the sofa and placed her legs across his lap. He took off her sneakers and socks. She was relieved she and Dorrie had gotten pedicures earlier that day.

"You have pretty feet."

"Thank you."

As he gently caressed her feet, she felt a rush of emotions she hadn't experienced before. Besides the occasional visit to the nail salon, nobody had ever touched her feet, and with such tender affection. The sensation was entirely new, leaving her feeling inexplicably delighted and cherished.

"I'm not rubbing too hard, am I?"

"No, it feels nice."

"How about some music?"

She nodded, and he reached for the remote control that sat on the table in front of the sofa. He pressed a button on the remote and Jeffrey Osborne belted, "We Both Deserve Each Other's Love."

"Yeah." He nodded, returning his attention to her feet. "That's my song. I love old school."

She smiled. "My mom and dad are old-school heads, too."

"Yeah, so are mine. I grew up on this stuff—The O'Jays, The Isley Brothers, The Whispers—"

"You, too?" A joyful laughter escaped her lips.

"Who's your favorite singer?"

"Beyoncé is my girl, but I'm feeling Rihanna, too. I love me some Raheem DeVaughn!"

"You do, huh?"

"Yes, indeed…whew! DMV all the way."

"Yeah, he is a smooth cat. What's your favorite Raheem song?"

She inclined her head slightly. "Hmmm, well, 'Guess Who Loves You More' but my favorite will always be, undoubtedly, 'Ridiculous.'"

Acknowledging with a nod, Maxwell raised her feet, stood up, and made his way to the sound system. He sifted through a stack of CDs until he found Raheem DeVaughn's *A Place Called Loveland*. Swiftly, he inserted the CD into the player and selected Track 8, setting the stage for the desired musical ambiance.

Noticing she'd finished her soda, he excused himself to the kitchen and returned with the two-liter bottle, refilling her glass.

Lindsay's radiant smile lit up the entire apartment, her charming dimples adding an extra touch of warmth to her presence, as she slow-bopped her head to Raheem DeVaughn's melodic voice, and sang along, "I never said that every choice I make everyone was gonna like."

Looking at her, Maxwell smiled, resuming his position beside her. He said nothing, just stared deeply at her.

Uneasiness enveloped her. Her panty felt damp. She moved about, slightly wiggling her hips.

He noticed and looked at her hips. "You okay?"

She nodded. "I guess. I think I peed on myself, but I don't remember feeling—" She pursed her lips. She panicked, and Maxwell could read it all over her face.

"You peed on yourself?"

"No. That's not what I meant."

"Girl, you better not be pissing on my sofa," he belted, followed by hearty laughter.

A blush spread across Lindsay's cheeks as she lowered her head, feeling a mix of embarrassment and frustration with herself. She couldn't help but feel like she was behaving more like a little girl than the strong woman she aspired to be. The urge to cry tugged at her heart, yet she held back the tears, determined to stay composed.

"Oh, no." Gently, he lifted her chin with his finger. "Sweet baby, you have no reason to lower your head around me. You hear me?"

Maxwell drew Lindsay closer to him, and she instinctively pressed her hand against his firm chest, feeling the heat radiating from his body and the rhythm of his pounding heart.

Looking up at him, Maxwell pressed his mouth against hers. He knew what to do, and he wanted to do it. To let Lindsay feel his attraction. Needing to get close to her, he held a strong desire to touch her in a way she would always remember. He wanted her and all that came with it—her heart, her soul, her love, and her naiveness. In a short time, he realized one thing: he wanted to be her first, her everything.

At the very core of his being, he was certain Lindsay Ellis, the shy and blossoming young woman from Maryland, was his destiny. In his heart, he fervently wished for her feelings to be mutual.

With a gentle gesture, he wrapped his arm around her waist, pulling her closer. Though a tiny voice in his head urged caution and to take things slowly, he ignored it. His instincts took over as his tongue slipped between her lips and tasted the sweetness of her breath. The touch of her lips felt pleasant and soft, reaffirming his belief that their connection was something truly special.

Likewise, when Lindsay parted her mouth, no longer was she feeling awkward. She teased at a deeper kiss, aware of inviting him to the warm cavern of her mouth but more aware of satisfaction at the contact than of any expectation of arousal. That was there, too. The garden between her thighs that no one had ever trespassed in was craving its first trespasser and it was a pleasant feeling.

Their tongues touched and teased, and it sent a chill through her that made her shiver.

Lindsay tunneled her arm under his shirt to circle his back. It felt natural for her to do so. Maxwell didn't move, didn't avoid what he wanted—the inevitable—when he moved her hand down and around his hips toward his crotch.

She didn't pull back. With her eyes closed tight, she blindly explored his erection. It was huge, and within the grasp of her hand, it felt like it wouldn't stop growing. She'd never felt an erection, and it scared her, yet it continued to stir up desire in her core.

Beyond aroused, Maxwell thought he would burst, but he had to slow his roll. He did not want to have sex with her. He wanted to love her. Pulling back from their heated connection, he caressed her face, exploring the contours of her brow.

Slowly, she opened her eyes to see him gazing at her. She gently touched his still-parted mouth with her fingertips. "I'm afraid."

"Why?"

"I'm a virgin."

"I know."

"Will it hurt?"

"I'll take it slow."

"I don't know."

"We don't have to."

"But I want to."

"Okay."

He gently took her hand in his and led her toward the back of the apartment. As they walked, she stole a glance inside the compact bathroom they passed before entering his bedroom. Despite its small size and lack of light, it was clean, infused with the scent of his cologne. Unlike many messy rooms, there were no clothes scattered on the floor, no cluttered dresser, and no open closet door, revealing a haphazard collection of shoes, hats, pants, socks, and miscellaneous items strewn about. Instead, his space reflected a tidy and organized mindset.

Still holding his hand, she sauntered around the room, not knowing what to do with herself. Masking her fear of the unknown with the poise she learned from her mother, she touched his elbow. "Max, before we, um…may I use your bathroom?"

"Sure." Before letting go of her hand, he pecked her lips, sending another rush through her.

Maxwell had ignited a fire in her that she had better douse quickly. With a smile, she excused herself into the bathroom, closing the door. Lindsay turned on the water so Max could not hear her. Sitting down on the edge of the tub, she made a silent request to God as she called her mother. *Please let Mom answer.*

"Hey, honey!"

Turning her head away from the door and over her shoulder, she spoke in a whisper. "Mom."

"Honey, what's wrong? And do I hear water running?"

"I'm not on campus. I—"

Kennedy's motherly instincts kicked in. "Do you have protection?"

Lindsay's eyes widened. "Mom, how did you know?"

"Mothers know their children. As I said, I've done everything you're about to do. I had one leg out the panty when I was your age, too."

"Mom, goodness. Did you ever call Grandma from a guy's bathroom?"

Kennedy chuckled. "Well, I never did that, and that was because I was always prepared. I'm glad you called me." After sharing a stifled chuckle with her daughter, Kennedy continued. "So, what's his name?"

"Max. I really like him, Mom."

"Is this your first date?"

"Yes."

Strike one, Kennedy thought. *Never on the first date.*

"Do you have protection?"

"No."

Strike two. Grateful for her daughter's transparency, she now could do her job—not as a mother, but as her best girlfriend.

"Lindsay, then you must say no."

"But—"

"Honey, there are a lot of feelings and emotions that come with sex, and you want to make sure you're not only equipped physically to deal with everything that comes with intercourse, but emotionally as well. Judging by this conversation, it's not time yet."

Lindsay seemed confused. "Just because I told you I don't have condoms means I'm not ready?"

"Yes. Right now, you might not understand what I'm saying, but you will once the night is over, and you've had time to think about it. You want him, or any man, to respect you. Him wanting to have unprotected sex with a virgin is not respect."

"What if he has condoms?"

"Make him wait. You should do nothing on the first date because men may think of you as easy."

"Times have changed, Mom."

"No, baby, the game is still the same. Your body is your temple, and if Max likes you as much as you like him, he'll wait. What's the rush? A young man with proper rearing won't do anything unless the young woman tells him it's okay."

"Proper rearing?"

"It means if his mama and daddy raised him right, he'll do right." Then, Kennedy asked the one question that knocked the wind out of her daughter. "You want to feel an orgasm, right?"

"What?"

"Do you want to know what it feels like to have an orgasm?"

"Dang, Mom. Are you drinking or something?"

"No. I'm being transparent. Just how I always want you to be with me. Never feel you cannot talk to me about anything. Got it?"

Lindsay nodded.

"Got it?"

"Yes. Yes, got it. What's an orgasm?"

Kennedy closed her eyes, searching for the right words to lead her daughter down the right path. "I cannot believe I'm going to say this, but… I wanted transparency, huh? Okay, so here's what you do. Tell Max *no* to sex. Tell him you're not ready. Be honest with him, honey. Tell him you like him, but you're not ready to have sex, but… are you ready for this?"

With furrowed brows, and knowing her mother, Lindsay feared what was coming next. "I'm not so sure."

"Let him finger you, but not penetrate you."

"Mom!"

"Oh, hush. Don't act like you've never fingered yourself, Lindsay."

"I'm just done. I cannot believe—who is the adult in this conversation?"

Kennedy smiled. "We both are. Anyway, I trust you will make the right decision, and whatever you choose, I've got your back. Okay?"

As much as she didn't want to admit this to her drenched core, Lindsay knew her mother was right, but she wouldn't say so just yet. "Look, Mom, I've been in here long enough. I've gotta go."

"So, what are you gonna do?"

"I heard every word, Mom. Don't worry, I'll be okay."

"I love you, honey, and *no* to sex, *yes* to the finger."

"Oh, God. Love you, too. Bye."

Lindsay flushed the toilet, then turned off the faucet. Going down the drain with the running water was the aroused feeling she owned a short time ago, including her mother's fingering suggestion.

Someday would not be tonight.

Entering Max's bedroom, wearing a look of disappointment, she knew she had to be soothing as she stood her ground.

"Are you okay?" He smiled and pulled her into his arms.

Feeling the hardened heat at his groin, Lindsay was again at war with herself. However, her mother's words prevailed.

"Max, I changed my mind. Please don't think you did anything wrong. I'm just not ready to have sex."

The journey of Maxwell's sadness traveled through his frame, wilting his erection. However, what he felt in his groin was not as important as what he felt for Lindsay in his heart.

"I understand." He spoke with such tenderness that it gently eased the tension between them as they sat on the edge of his bed.

Lindsay held his hand. "Max, please don't be mad at me. I wasn't trying to lead you on."

"I know. A real man will do nothing unless his lady tells him it's okay." Noticing that Lindsay raised her brow in amazement, he looked perplexed. "Did I say something wrong?"

"No, Max. You didn't." She gave him a soft peck on the lips.

Wrapping his arms around her, she melted into his embrace.

CHAPTER 26

Gazing out the window, watching the rain fall steadily outside, Kennedy sat on the couch, sipping a cup of Earl Grey black tea. The pitter-patter of droplets against the windowpane was soothing, almost meditative.

Relishing the warmth of the tea as it spread through her body was a simple pleasure that brought her comfort and one she enjoyed doing alone. She closed her eyes and basked in the peacefulness.

She opened her eyes to see the family cat, Serenity, perched on the arm of the couch, watching her intently. Kennedy smiled and stroked Serenity's soft fur. "Hey, girl." The cat purred contentedly under her touch, leaning in for Kennedy to scratch behind her ear.

Serenity jumped down to the floor and Kennedy turned her attention back out of the window, watching the rain intensify, the drops bouncing off the pavement. The sound was almost hypnotic, and she found herself lost in thought, wondering what Lindsay was up to in Hampton. She missed her daughter, but she was very proud of her. Then her thoughts turned to her mother, wishing she were there to see Lindsay blossom into a beautiful, intelligent young woman.

Kennedy set her tea aside and grabbed the novel, *No Gentle Rain* by Orv Cullen, from the side table. An avid reader, she loved reading books by new authors like CJ Carson and she reveled in Ann Jeffries' "Family Reunion—Wisdom of the Ancestors" series. Opening to Chapter One, she lost herself in another world entirely, until the phone rang.

As Kennedy sank into her plush couch, she sighed, contemplating whether to answer it. She looked at the phone. It was Zora, her bestie, disturbing her moment of peace.

"Hey, girlie."

"Hey, Ken. I need to talk."

"Is everything okay?"

Lounging cross-legged on the soft leather sofa, Zora sighed, tracing her fingers over the cushion beside her. "Not really. I'm just feeling overwhelmed lately, you know? Like everything is piling up and I can't keep up."

There was a pause before Kennedy spoke up with gentle reassurance. "I'm sorry to hear you're feeling that way. It's totally normal to feel overwhelmed sometimes but remember, you don't have to tackle everything alone. I'm here for you, whether you need someone to listen to or to help you figure out a plan to manage everything. You've got this, and I've got your back."

"Thank you, Ken. I really needed to hear that."

Kennedy's brows furrowed. She and Zora had spoken every morning, a cherished ritual between them. Sensing a shift in Zora's demeanor, Kennedy knew instinctively that something else was going on. After all, she'd known Zora for far too long to miss such cues.

"So, you gon' tell me what's going on?"

"I just don't know what to do, Ken."

"About what?"

"So much is going on right now, and I need my best friend."

"I'm here for you. You're making me nervous."

Zora pursed her lips, considering how to approach the topic to garner her sympathy. She knew she needed to soften the blow before revealing the true reason for her call. "I've fucked up and I don't know how to fix it." Her breath caught in her throat as her mouth moved faster than her thoughts.

"All right, are you going to tell me?"

"I can't."

"If you don't tell me, how can I possibly help you, Zee?"

"You can't help me."

"What did the doctor say?"

"Nothing yet. I'm scheduled for a mammogram and a possible biopsy."

"When? I'll go with you."

"I'll be fine."

"Hey, you've got this. I truly believe it's going to be nothing. We'll keep positive vibes and focus on it being benign. That's our mindset, okay?"

Zora chuckled. "What makes you so confident, *Doctor* Kennedy?"

"I had a talk with God. Enough said."

"Ken, can I ask you something?" Zora's voice barely rose above a whisper, sending a wave of concern through Kennedy.

"Of course."

Zora hesitated, her mind grappling with the weight of the question she was about to ask. She took a deep breath, trying to steady herself before finally mustering the courage to speak. "Have you ever thought about—you know, having an affair?" Her voice trembled, barely above a whisper.

Taken aback by Zora's question, Kennedy pondered for a bit. She could sense the gravity in her friend's voice. "Zora, that's unexpected." She chose her words carefully, trying to convey both understanding and concern. "Is there something specific that's prompted you to ask me such a question?"

"I mean, with someone who's not your husband."

"I know what an affair is, Zora, but why are you asking?"

"Well—"

"Damn, woman, will you spit it out? Is this something you're considering?"

"More than considered. I've been having an affair with Keith."

There was a prolonged silence.

"Ken?" She heard a heavy sigh on the other end of the phone line. "Yes, you're still there."

The line was still silent.

"Ken, please say something!"

Shaking her head in disbelief, Kennedy seethed with anger. The words that tumbled from Zora's lips were utterly incomprehensible to her. "What do you want me to say? How could you—why would you betray LaTonya? Hell, how could you betray Maceo? Shit, Zora!"

"I know and I feel awful about—"

"How long?"

"How long what?"

"How long have you been fucking Maceo's best friend and your girlfriend's husband?"

Zora winced, fully aware of her wrongdoing and lacking any justification for her actions. "Five years."

"Goddamn it, Zora!" Kennedy sprang from her seat, her movements sharp with disgust, and began to pace restlessly from room to room, unable to contain her revulsion. "You don't feel all that damn awful. I just can't believe this! Why, Zora? You want to fuck around on Maceo, fine? Do it outside the friend circle. Girl, Keith and Maceo are like brothers. So, you might as well be fucking your brother-in-law."

"They aren't brothers, and we aren't married."

Kennedy halted her pacing, her voice rising sharply. "No! You cannot be a smart-ass with me when you're wrong as shit right now."

"I don't know...I just feel so...unfulfilled, you know? Like something's missing. I can't help but think that maybe that's what I need."

Kennedy closed her eyes and bowed her head, taking a deep breath to quell her anger. "What in the hell are you saying? Listen, you feed that bullshit to someone who doesn't know you. You're selfish, Zora. You've always been selfish. You would probably make a move on Malcolm if I turned my back long enough."

"Really, Ken? Malcolm is like a brother to me. Besides, I would never do that to you."

"No? You did it to LaTonya. What's the difference? A friend is a friend, Zora."

"Ken, I love him."

"Whew, give me a motherfuckin' minute, girl." Now in the kitchen, Kennedy flopped onto the stool by the kitchen island, the weight of frustration evident in her posture.

Zora's sniffles escalated into quiet sobs. Hunching over, she drew her legs close, curling into herself as her chin sank onto her knees, overwhelmed with guilt.

Kennedy exhaled deeply, a sense of calm washing over her as she regained control. "Okay, listen. I guess you do love him after five years of intimacy. Did you not think about the consequences of your actions? Affairs are incredibly destructive to all parties involved."

"Kennedy, I need my best friend now, not a judge."

"No, ma'am, not for this one. I cannot and will not support you on this. The nerve of you to even suggest I do such a thing. Of all the dick in the state of Maryland, why, on God's green Earth, Keith? Shit, let alone your man's best friend. If either finds out—" As Kennedy heard the doorbell ring, she couldn't help but feel a sense of relief, grateful for the interruption. "Listen, somebody's at my door. The biopsy and anything you need as far as that is concerned, I've got your back one hundred percent, sis. You know that, but you're on your own with this here shit. I've got to go. We will talk later."

Before Zora could even speak, Kennedy terminated the call.

Appalled by her girlfriend's behavior, she stole a glance at the clock, puzzled by who might be visiting at such an untimely hour. As she neared the door and cracked it open, she gasped.

"May I help you?"

The young man stood on the porch, rain pouring down relentlessly around him. His heart pounded in his chest, a mix of nerves and excitement racing through him. He adjusted the collar of his light jacket, futilely attempting to shield himself from the rain that was starting to soak through the fabric, chilling him to the bone.

His gaze met hers. "Hello, ma'am. I'm looking for Malcolm Ellis. Is he here?"

Kennedy's brow furrowed in puzzlement. "No, he's not." She eyed the stranger cautiously. "We don't need a new roof or—"

"I'm not selling anything."

"May I ask who you are?"

He drew in a deep breath, bracing himself for the forthcoming admission. "My name is Eric. Eric Murphy. I…I'm his son."

The words lingered in the air, Kennedy's eyes widening in astonishment as she absorbed the revelation. Her mouth opened, but she found herself speechless, staring at Eric in disbelief.

Eric squirmed under her scrutiny. A sudden sense of vulnerability enveloped him. "I'm sorry to just show up like this, Ms—"

"*Mrs.* Ellis. Malcolm's wife."

He smiled. "So you're my stepmother."

Kennedy raised a brow and pursed her lips.

"Oh, okay. Well, I've been trying to find him for a while now."

Kennedy's thoughts raced all over the place. A young man stood before her, asserting himself as Malcolm's son.

"Why do you believe Malcolm is your father?"

"I don't believe, Mrs. Ellis. I know. I was born twenty-one years ago. My mother never disclosed my existence to my father, but I've always been aware of him."

Kennedy's mind buzzed with questions, but before she could articulate them, Eric made another request.

"May I come in?" His eyes beseeched her for acceptance.

Kennedy hesitated. She didn't know this man from a can of paint, and letting him into her home, while she was there alone, was the furthest from her mind. However, as she looked into his face, she saw her husband. Could he really be Malcolm's son? After a moment of contemplation, and since the sky had started to rumble, she nodded slowly. "All right, Eric." Her tone was cautious yet sympathetic. "Come in. Let's talk inside. You better not try anything. I'm armed and dangerous."

Eric cracked a smile, then suddenly realized it wasn't a joke when he glanced at the seriousness on Kennedy's face. *Okey dokey then,* he thought, stepping over the threshold.

She gently closed the door behind him, gesturing for him to follow as she led him into the family room. With each step, her mind raced with thoughts of what other secrets her husband might have kept hidden from her over the years.

Once Eric settled into the plush armchair, she took a seat on the sofa opposite him. For a moment, the room was enveloped in silence, punctuated only by the weight of unspoken questions hanging between them, thick with tension. Kennedy studied Eric's face intently, searching for any hint of the emotions swirling behind his eyes. She couldn't shake the uncanny resemblance between him and Malcolm—the strong jawline and piercing brown eyes, though Eric's complexion was notably lighter.

"I'm just trying to wrap my head around all of this."

Eric nodded understandingly. "I can imagine. It's a lot to take in, I'm sure."

"How are you so sure Malcolm is your father?"

Eric looked up, meeting Kennedy's gaze with a mixture of sadness and determination. "Other than my birth certificate, I don't have any concrete proof." His eyes flickering briefly to the floor before returning to meet hers. "My mother was an honest woman. She would have never lied to me. It wasn't in her nature to do so."

As their conversation drifted into silence once more, Kennedy stole a glimpse of Eric, who seemed to be lost in thought.

"But why now? Why after all these years?" she wondered aloud, her mind racing with questions.

"I have the right to know my father, Mrs. Ellis."

Before Kennedy could respond, the garage door opened. Her heart skipped a beat as she realized Malcolm had returned home. She exchanged a quick glance with Eric, uncertainty flickering in her eyes.

The side door opened and closed. "Babe, I'm home!"

Kennedy stood with her arms folded across her chest. "In here, Malcolm."

A wide smile grew on Eric's face, now overwhelmed with excitement. He was about to meet his father.

Malcolm entered the room, stopping in his tracks at the tall, handsome stranger standing next to his wife. "Uh, hello?" He looked at the man. There was a feeling of familiarity.

"Malcolm, this is Eric Murphy."

Malcolm extended his hand with a broad smile. "Hey, Eric, nice to meet you."

Kennedy sat down, crossed a leg over her knee, and looked up at the two men.

Eric took a deep breath and sighed out, "I'm your son."

A wave of disbelief crashed over Malcolm, sending a jolt of shock through his entire being. His eyes fixed on the young man before him, struggling to process the bombshell revelation. The words "I'm your son" echoed in the air, laden with implications that Malcolm found nearly impossible to grasp.

For a moment, silence engulfed the room, broken only by the sound of their shallow breaths. Malcolm's mind raced; his thoughts a whirlwind of confusion and skepticism. How could this young man standing before him claim to be his son?

Kennedy watched anxiously, her heart pounding in her chest as she waited for Malcolm's response.

Finally, Malcolm found his voice, though it emerged as little more than a hoarse whisper. "My son?" He looked at Kennedy. "Is this some kind of joke, babe?"

Kennedy shook her head.

Eric nodded slowly. "Yes, I am your son."

"I don't understand. How—how is this possible?"

"I know this is hard to believe, but it's true. I have proof." Eric retrieved a folder from the backpack he'd brought into the house with him and handed the folder to Malcolm. "This is my birth certificate and some photos of me and my mom."

Kennedy sprang to her feet and was at Malcolm's side, looking at what Eric presented.

Malcolm saw the birth certificate with his name listed as the father, and Giselle Murphy as the mother. He saw photos of Eric as a baby, a toddler, a child, and a teenager. He couldn't deny the resemblance. Upon seeing Giselle's photograph, Malcolm's stomach sank as vivid memories flooded back. It transported him to a night two decades ago, where he found himself seated at a bar, engaged in a conversation with a beautiful, irresistible woman. As the evening unfolded, one thing led to another, and now he was confronted with the realization that he had a son from that encounter twenty-one years ago. He looked at his wife.

"Sweet Jesus!" Malcolm felt his head spinning. He looked at Eric again and saw the resemblance—same nose, same chin, same eyes, and same smile. Malcolm's genes were strong—Eric favored his daughter, Lindsay, so much. There was no longer doubt in Malcolm's mind. Eric was his son. "My God." Malcolm shook his head and gnawed at the inside of his mouth. "Where is your mom?"

"She passed away two years ago."

"I'm sorry to hear that."

"Thank you. She was the best mom. She was my best friend. She raised me by herself. She never told me who my dad was until she was stricken with ovarian cancer."

"Why didn't she tell you before?"

Eric shrugged. "She said she didn't want to bother you. She said you were young when she met you, and, although she was embarrassed to say it, it was a one-night stand. She was attending a convention in New York City, and she met you at the bar of the Hyatt Regency. She knew you were younger—much younger, about my age—but she couldn't resist. She was being—in her words—'a cougar.'" Eric's almond complexion blushed at having to repeat this story. "She said you didn't even know she was pregnant, let alone her name. She mentioned something about you had left your wallet," pausing, he crossed eyes with Kennedy, "in her hotel room. That's how she knew your name and address. In fact, a year ago, I went to that address, but—"

"My parents sold that house at least ten years ago." Standing akimbo, Malcolm gazed at Eric. A chill shot through him. "What do you want from me?"

Eric held a hopeful expression. "I don't want anything from you. I just want to get to know my father."

"Malcolm, I think we should have a DNA test. He's agreed to one."

Pondering her suggestion, though it was a good one, Malcolm chose honesty as his approach. "Babe, he's my son—your stepson."

As Malcolm's words hung in the air, Kennedy's reaction was a blend of visible shock and internal turmoil. Her eyes widened, her breath hitching in her throat as she struggled to comprehend the enormity of what Malcolm had just said. She took a step back, her hand instinctively reaching for support against the nearest surface.

"How could you do this to me?" Her voice quivered.

Wanting to explain everything to Kennedy, Malcolm didn't know where to start. He wanted to make her understand he was young and never cheated on her during their marriage, never lied to her, and never meant to hurt her. He wanted to make her see that he believed Eric was not a threat to their marriage and that he had a right to know his father.

"I'm sorry, baby. I didn't know. I didn't know he existed until today."

Kennedy shook her head. "That's not good enough. That's not good enough at all. Twenty-one years ago, you and I were seniors at Columbia University, dating *exclusively*. You cheated on me!"

In a fit of tears, she stormed out of the room and darted up the staircase.

Malcolm swallowed the lump in his throat. He looked at Eric, who stood there looking uncomfortable.

Malcolm chased after Kennedy, finding her in their bedroom. "Baby, please, we need to talk."

Kennedy sat on the bed, her cheeks soaked with tears.

"Kennedy, please, don't shut me out. I love you. I love you more than anything."

Kennedy wiped her tears. "If you love me, then tell me the truth. Who is Giselle Murphy? Why did you sleep with her? How long did you know about Eric?"

Taking a deep breath, Malcolm shared a painful revelation. "Giselle was a woman I met at a bar when I was twenty-one. We hooked up once, and I never saw her again. I only learned about Eric today. Hell, I only learned her name today."

Kennedy realized that Malcolm, much like many young men in their senior year of college, had displayed behaviors that others might categorize as "young, dumb, and full of come." Yet, she challenged him. "You expect me to believe that? You expect me to believe you had a one-night-stand with a random woman while we were dating in college, and she never once reached out to you, not even to tell you about your son?"

With his hands at his side, Malcolm peered at her. "Yes, I do. Yes, I expect you to believe every word coming out of my mouth. You speak as if you don't know me, as if you don't know my character. Do you really believe I would father a son and not take care of my responsibility as a man? I don't know whether to be pissed off or insulted by your reaction, Kennedy. You, outside of anyone else, know me better than that!"

Raising her hand, Kennedy shook her head. "Don't put this on me, Malcolm. You were the one traipsing around New York City, sticking your dick where it didn't belong."

Throwing up his hands, he shook his head and paced the floor. "For God's sake, Kennedy. I was young and foolish. I made a terrible mistake for which I'm truly sorry."

Kennedy's emotions surged, and she refused to accept his apology. "Sorry is not enough. Sorry doesn't change the fact that you have a son with another woman—a son you hid from me!"

He halted and faced her. "How the fuck can I hide something or someone I didn't know about? Now you're being foolish. The man told us that I didn't know about him."

Kennedy believed him, but her womanly emotions were all over the place. "How do you think all of this makes feel? How does it make me look?"

"I know how it makes me feel and look. I feel like a terrible person and a terrible father, like a liar and a cheater."

"Well, I won't argue about that!"

The painful exchange continued, and as far as Kennedy was concerned, she stood at the crossroads of her emotions as her heart and mind engaged in a tug of war over a twenty-one-year-old lapse in judgment. She believed Malcolm's explanation and trusted in the love they shared, but the thought of her man having sex with another woman gnawed at her soul. Immediately, her mind went to her earlier conversation with Zora. It was all too much for her.

Taking a deep breath, resolving to act on her instincts, Kennedy rose from the bed and moved toward the closet, retrieving a duffel bag.

Malcolm was now desperate to understand her intentions and feared losing the love of his life. "Babe, what are you doing?"

Kennedy ignored him, focusing on hastily throwing essential items from the drawer into the bag.

"Babe?"

"I need some time to think, Malcolm. I can't stay here right now; it's too overwhelming. First Zora and now you."

"Zora? Please. Let's talk about this. We can work through it together."

Pausing for a moment, she closed her eyes in quick meditation before turning to face him. "I know we can work through things, but I need space to process everything. This revelation about Eric has shaken me to my very core. I need to understand what it means for us, for Lindsay, and our future." She laid her vulnerability bare. "If we have a future."

Her words struck Malcolm deeply, but he knew he had to give her the time and space she needed. "I can't lose you, Kennedy."

"You're not losing me, Malcolm. I just—please, let me take this time to process it all in my way."

Nodding, Malcolm stepped toward her, and she stepped backward. "I'll be here when you're ready to talk."

With her duffel bag packed and hung over her shoulder, Kennedy took one last glance at Malcolm. "I'll be back. I just need some time to think. Please understand."

Malcolm nodded. "I'll be waiting. I love you, babe."

As Kennedy made her way to the bedroom door, she hesitated. "I love you, Malcolm, but right now, I need to love myself, too."

Malcolm's brow furrowed, as he thought, *What the fuck does that mean?*

With his head hung low, Malcolm made his way downstairs to the family room where Eric stood, a myriad of emotions flickering across his face, as Kennedy darted through the side door and into the garage. Eric couldn't help but feel like an intruder, an unexpected visitor to Malcolm's life, but the burning desire to know his father outweighed any reservations.

"I'm sorry, sir. I didn't mean to cause this conflict between you and your wife."

Malcolm laid a reassuring hand on his shoulder. "Hey, don't apologize. This is a lot to take in for everyone. It's not your fault."

"I just… I really want to get to know you, to have a relationship with you."

"I understand. I need some time to process everything, but I want to be a part of your life, too."

Eric smiled appreciatively and pulled out his cell phone. "Let's stay in touch." He extended the phone toward Malcolm. Accepting the gesture, Malcolm took the phone and added his contact information.

Deep down, though, he knew building a relationship with Eric—with his son—was the right thing to do. He only prayed Kennedy would accept Eric, too. He didn't want to imagine his life without her.

CHAPTER 27

By the time LaTonya pulled into the driveway, she'd stopped crying. She retrieved Keith's cell phone and deleted the text communication with Zora. She got out of the car and rushed to the front door. With shaking hands, she eased the key into the front door and stepped inside. She tossed her keys on the table and gripped Keith's cell phone. The urge to throw it against the wall heightened, but she chose against it.

When she walked into the kitchen, she saw Keith through the kitchen's back window. He was out on the deck, his back turned toward the house. He was leaning forward, his elbows balanced on the deck's railing as he puffed on a Cuban cigar.

LaTonya stood at the island and gazed out the window at the back of Keith's head. "How could you do this to me, Keith? With my friend, of all people?"

Truth is, the image was striking, as she always loved Keith's body. She supposed she could understand why any woman, even Zora, would want to be with him. He was handsome and an excellent lover, but to a friend of hers, he was off-limits. Zora had crossed the line and there was no way in hell she would get away with it.

Keith wasn't off the hook, though. She would leave him, file for divorce, and take him for every dime he owned, but what good would that do? She could've cared less about possessions. She'd invested too many years of her life in this man, and she would not allow this hiccup to end what she worked so hard to build. However, he would feel her wrath, though, and so would that backstabbing Zora Vaughn.

Keith turned around and looked through the window. He saw her standing in the kitchen, looking at him. He smiled and headed for the back door.

"You're back early." He closed the door behind him.

"Yeah, I know. I wasn't feeling too well, so I came back home." Of course, it was a falsehood. Physically, she felt fine. Emotionally, she was in critical condition. She felt like smacking the shit out of him, and yelling in his face, "I just sat across from your whore," but she couldn't let on that she knew. Not yet.

She set his cell phone on the island. "I couldn't call Zora." A knot formed in her stomach. "I had your phone. Unfortunately, I don't know her number off the top of my head, and I *doubt* if you have the number in your phone, so I didn't even look for it."

He peered at the phone, trying not to stumble over his thoughts.

She cocked her head, waited another moment, and then slid the phone across the island, stopping short of it falling onto the floor. "We need to talk."

"Sure, let me just—"

She palmed his face. "Not now. I want to take a shower. We have somewhere to be at ten o'clock." She grabbed her phone off the island, pivoted with a sway in her hips, and sashayed out of the kitchen, leaving Keith perplexed.

CHAPTER 28

As she stepped into her condominium, Zora found Maceo standing by the floor-to-ceiling window, leisurely munching on potato chips from a bag.

"Hey." Zora closed the front door, with her back against it, looking across the room and through the floor-to-ceiling window.

Maceo turned around, folding the empty bag in half. "I wasn't expecting you back so early."

Zora advanced into the living room, plopped down on the couch, and kicked off her shoes. "Yeah, same here."

Sitting down beside her, Maceo took his woman's feet and laid them across his lap, gently massaging them.

Zora moaned. "That feels so good, honey." She scooted down on the sofa and reclined her head. "LaTonya was in such a funky mood."

"Did she say why?"

"No, and I asked a few times, but all she said was 'Nothing.'"

"Maybe she and Keith had a fight or something."

"Maybe, I don't know."

"Well, give her a call tomorrow. Maybe she'll feel better then."

"Yes, maybe, but I am worried."

"About?"

Gazing into Maceo's captivating eyes, Zora hesitated, refraining from sharing what weighed heavily on her heart. She wondered if LaTonya suspected anything about her and Keith? It was true; LaTonya's behavior seemed remarkably out of character, as she had always been open and honest with her thoughts. To witness LaTonya's nonchalant demeanor, acting as if she wanted to avoid Zora's presence altogether, was an unprecedented and puzzling change.

Sighing, she smirked and looked out the window, into the darkness. "Nothing. I'm sure she's okay."

"Listen, babe, if it bothers you, why put off tomorrow what you can do today? Just call her. Better yet, I can call Keith to—"

"No."

"Why not?"

Reluctantly, she faced him. The look of defeat blanketed her face. "I really needed to talk to her."

"About what?"

She tilted her head and quipped, "None of your business."

He chuckled. "Girl talk. I'm sure she'll call you."

She sat up and pulled her knees into her chest. "I'm scared about having the mammogram, let alone a biopsy, and I wanted to talk to my friend about it."

Maceo wrapped his arms around her, pulling her into him and kissing her forehead. "I know you are." He reached over her and grabbed the phone from the sofa table. He placed it in her lap. "Call her."

She looked down at the phone. Reluctantly, she dialed LaTonya's house phone.

LaTonya answered on the second ring. There was dead silence.

Zora's stomach balled into the tightest knot; she thought she was going to be sick. She opened her mouth to speak, but words would not come out.

Then, suddenly, "Yes," came from the other end of the phone. LaTonya's tone was flat, borderline annoyed.

"LaTonya?"

"Who else would it be?"

"It's Zora."

"No shit."

"Oh," she paused, detecting an attitude. "Is everything all right? You left Stan's so quick, and I was worried about—"

"I wasn't feeling well, and I'd," she hesitated, sighing heavily. "I just needed to leave, that's all."

"Oh, I see. Well, okay then. Maybe we can get together—"

"Yeah, maybe, goodnight." She ended the call.

Zora tossed the phone next to her and looked at Maceo. "What did I do to her?"

"Hey! Let's watch that new *Sparkle* movie tonight."

"You mean the one with Whitney Houston?"

"Yeah, that's the one."

She sucked her teeth and sighed. "First, that movie has been out for years. Besides, I have plans."

"With whom?"

"Why does it have to be with someone?"

"Okay, what are your plans?"

"And why do you need to know my plans?"

Dumbfounded, Maceo stared at his woman with an open mouth. He couldn't understand why she was being so nasty toward him, as he knew he'd done nothing to receive such shitty treatment. Was she taking out her treatment from LaTonya on him?

"I'm going over to Kennedy's to have girl talk. I'm going to take a shower." She unfurled her legs, stretching them out before her.

"Want some company?"

"Did I ask for any company?"

"Goddamn it, Zora! What did I do to deserve all of this?"

"Other than breathing, I can't think of anything else."

"Wow," was all he could muster as he watched her sashay toward the bathroom. "What the fuck was that all about?"

CHAPTER 29

With the house phone in hand, LaTonya retired to her bedroom. Emotionally spent, she desperately needed to unwind. She dropped the phone on the bed and turned on the clock radio that sat on the nightstand on Keith's side of the bed. Charlie Wilson's "There Goes My Baby" blared through the tiny speakers, his voice wrapping around her like a comfortable blanket. She loved Charlie Wilson and was an even bigger fan of The Gap Band.

She bobbed her head, swayed her hips, and snapped her fingers as she sang along with Charlie. *"There goes my baby…there goes my destiny…"* Then, she sat on the bed with her head hung low. A knot formed in her throat and a tingling sensation took over her nostrils. Her eyes welled and the waterworks started up again. Laying down in a fetal position, she cried like a baby. It was something she needed to do. She needed cleansing before she could think straight.

Unlike most women she knew, LaTonya did not have a vindictive bone in her body. Revenge was not in her vocabulary. Although at that moment, she wanted to whip Zora's ass. *That bitch!* She wiped her nose with the back of her hand. After tonight, she would never speak to her again.

As she gathered herself, she sat up on the side of the bed, looked at the framed photograph of her and Keith, and reached for the phone. Teddy Pendergrass crooned, "You're My Latest, My Greatest Inspiration." LaTonya's head fell back, and she looked up at the ceiling, moving her torso to Teddy's voice. He was her favorite, too, and 96.3 WHUR was showing out as far as she was concerned. She wrapped her arms around her waist and sat up.

"Sing it, Teddy. Yes, Lord…they simply do not make music like this anymore. *You inspired me, inspired me,*" she sang, thinking that Keith felt that way about her once. What happened? She simply couldn't make any sense of it, and she wasn't going to try. Her marriage was over.

Looking at the digital time on the clock, it read 9:00 p.m. and The O'Jays "Used to Be My Girl" blared through the tiny speakers and Keith entered the bedroom.

"But as long as I live, she'll be my girl," he sang, wiggling his hips, snapping his fingers, and moving toward LaTonya.

She stood up and gritted on him harder than anything he'd ever seen. "Negro, *please!*"

The finger-popping ceased, and the hips were still. "Alrighty then." He looked at her back as she sauntered into the bathroom.

Once she crossed the threshold, she faced him. "We're leaving in fifteen minutes." She closed the door.

"Where are we going? What the hell is wrong with you?"

"Dinner and I'm fine," she yelled from behind the closed door. "Should there be something wrong with me?"

"No," he yelled, stepping inside the massive walk-in closet. "Kind of late for dinner, don't you think? I can make us sandwiches."

"I don't want a goddamn sandwich!"

Keith shook his head and decided against responding when the bathroom door opened. He looked over his shoulder and saw LaTonya standing in the doorway. Not in the mood for a fight, he returned his attention to sifting through the numerous buttoned-down shirts.

However, Latonya was ready for a knock-down, drag-out fight, but in due time. In all her naked glory, she pivoted and walked out of the bedroom and down the stairs, making a beeline to her cell phone. While in the kitchen, she had an idea. It was the best idea she'd ever had. It was dirty, nasty, revengeful, vindictive, and those other payback things wrapped up in a tiny ball of snow, rolling down a huge mountain, forming into the biggest avalanche that would crush those two cheaters!

A giggle escaped her as she reached for her cell phone. She felt devilish and was quite surprised that she loved how it felt. She'd been a loyal, dutiful wife and friend. Well, no more, damn it. Today was a new day, and revenge was going to be as sweet as the delectable, creamy cheesecakes from The Cheesecake Factory.

She scrolled through her Contact List until she came across the name she needed. She pressed *call* and held the phone up to her ear. Glancing over her shoulder, she escaped to the family room in the back of the house for privacy.

The male voice was deep and sexy. She typically never spoke to him on the phone, let alone called him, but she felt he needed to be involved, too.

"Hi, sweetie, it's LaTonya. How are you?"

"Hey, lady, I'm well. How about you?"

"I'm good. Listen, I can't talk long, but I need a huge favor, and we must keep this between us. Okay?"

"For you, anything."

"Can you meet me tonight in about thirty minutes?"

"Sure, just let me—"

"No, just meet me at the Safeway on Fort Washington Road. Come alone, and remember, it's a secret and a surprise for your boy!"

"Sure, I'll see you there."

"Great, bye!"

LaTonya dropped the phone in her purse and sauntered up the steps, bouncing boobies and all. Noticing the clock on the nightstand, she didn't have time for a shower.

"What should I wear?"

"Jeans will be fine. Hurry, we have to meet them at ten o'clock and I don't want to be late."

Keith looked at the digital clock on the nightstand. "It's already nine-fifteen. Them?"

"You need to get a move on then, honey bunny. Chop, chop."

CHAPTER 30

After her bath, Zora was quite anxious. She was going to see Keith. After all the emotional turmoil she'd been going through with the lump in her breast, deep in her heart—even though she knew it was the wrong thing to do—she could not end it with Keith. There was no way. He meant the world to her, and frankly, even though she didn't want to admit it, his dick meant more to her than her friendship with LaTonya.

What about Maceo? Simply put, he was not Keith. Of course, Zora loved Maceo, but there was a bond she had with Keith that she was not ready to break. Not for anyone. If she had to lose a friend, then so be it. If she had to lose Maceo, it would be a loss she would accept. She'd rather be with Keith than be without him. She fell off the turnip truck and lost her mind, but none of that mattered as long as she could be with the man she craved. The man she loved. The man she placed above all others. The man who did not return the same sentiments.

Stepping out of the tub, she quickly dried off, and wrapped herself in the towel, tucking it in under her armpit. She opened the bathroom door to darkness. There wasn't a light on in the condo.

"Maceo? You here?"

There was no response.

"Maceo!"

Moving slowly down the hallway, she pressed her palm flat against the wall, feeling for the light switch. She flipped on the light and nearly jumped out of her skin!

What are you doing?

"Ma'am?"

What do you think you're doing, Zora Lynette Vaughn? Her mother stood before her, seething with anger.

"I don't know what you mean, Mama."

God is not happy with you, Zora!

"God will get over it, Mama!" No longer surprised by the presence of the spiritual realm, she stormed past her mother's spirit toward the bedroom. She looked over her shoulder. "I love him, Mama." As she pushed the door open, her father's spirit sat propped up on top of her bed. "What in the hell?"

Watch your mouth and don't you talk to your mother that way.

"Daddy, I have to get dressed."

What has gotten into you, little girl?

"I'm not a little girl, Daddy."

You've got that right. You've turned into a trollop! her mother asserted, standing in the doorway.

Zora sighed heavily. "Whatever, I'm going to see my man and there's nothing you can do about it."

Zora, karma is a you-know-what, and everything you do will come back on you. We did not raise you—

"Yes, so you keep saying, Mama." Zora dropped her towel down around her feet, exposing her naked body.

Zora!

"Mama, please. Listen, as much as I love having you and Daddy around again, I really must get ready. I have to meet Keith at ten, and I don't have much time."

Fine! But let us leave you with this, Ms. Sleeping With Your Friend's Husband: when you die, and your time will come—trust me—you will have to answer for every single thing you've done here on Earth.

Yes, dear, your father is right. If you want to be with us in Heaven, then you must live your life right and stop this foolishness. You cannot continue to sin against God. He is not happy with you, and I cannot stress that enough to you.

"I'll go to church and pray about it on Sunday, Mama. Now, if you don't mind—"

You've been warned, Zora. Karma is just around the corner. You've been warned.

Zora shook her head in defiance and watched them disappear. Maybe everything they said had a ton of merit, but she simply did not care. She'd come too far to give up Keith. She loved him, and that was all that mattered. If God couldn't understand that, then she was simply sorry and willing to face the consequences.

CHAPTER 31

Standing at the foot of the staircase, LaTonya looked up at the top landing. "Darling, let's go!"

Keith rushed out of the bedroom and down the stairs. "I'm ready."

"Good. I'll drive."

"Well, that's a treat."

"Yeah, don't get used to it." She side-eyed him, thinking, *You cheating bastard.*

By 9:50 p.m., the Safeway parking lot was filled with shoppers on late-night runs for last minute junk food, meats, and condiments, bustling to complete their shopping lists.

LaTonya drove down each parking aisle before spotting the black Jeep Grand Cherokee Limited.

"There he is." She aimed her Lexus RX at him.

"There is—" The sight of Maceo caused Keith to choke on his words. He swallowed hard. "Maceo?"

"Yep!"

"What's he doing here?"

"Don't be silly. We're picking him up, you fool."

Keith's head snapped toward LaTonya, his eyes glaring at her in disbelief. He couldn't fathom the way she had been speaking to him tonight. A fleeting thought crossed his mind—could she be experiencing the effects of menopause?

Despite the shock evident on his face, Keith quickly composed himself, forcing a fake smile that concealed his true emotions.

LaTonya rolled down her window. "Hop in, honey. We're going to be late."

"Be late for what? What's going on, baby?"

She ignored Keith as Maceo opened the rear door and climbed into the back seat.

"Hey, Keith. What's going on, my man? LaTonya?"

Keith was dumbfounded. Something wasn't right. He had a funny feeling in the pit of his stomach, but he answered Maceo just the same. "I'm cool, man."

As LaTonya pulled out of the parking lot, Keith looked at her and then out the passenger window. "Where are we going, babe?"

"It is a surprise. We're going to meet Zora, too. Listen, I just wanted to surprise my friend, that's all." She gritted her teeth, trying not to choke on that word—*friend*. She swore to never associate again with Zora "The Cheater" Vaughn. "Do something nice for her. You know she's going through it with the lump in her breast and all. So chill, shut up, and enjoy the ride."

Maceo smiled. "Oh, cool. Zora said she had plans tonight with Kennedy."

"Yes, she does, hon. Yeah, Kennedy is on the surprise, too," she lied, quick on her feet. "They are meeting us, and I figured it would be nice if we all had dinner."

Keith looked at the side of her face. "But I'm confused."

"About?"

"You were supposed to have met her earlier, but you came back home because you weren't feeling well."

"Yes, that's what I told you. I told her that, too. Gosh, what's with all the questions? Can't you just shut up, sit back, and enjoying being in the passenger seat for once?"

Keith nodded, rolling his eyes. "Where?"

"Where what? And there you go with another goddamn question."

"Damn it, LaTonya, that's enough of this shit!"

"We're going to Rips. Are you happy?"

"Now, was that so hard?"

LaTonya chuckled, ignored him, and turned on the radio.

CHAPTER 32

It was a flat, moonless night. Route 301 was dark and deserted. The parking lot was like a ghost town and after waiting ten minutes for Keith, Zora decided to secure the room. She stepped inside the lobby of The Motel on 301. The night clerk knew her well as being a weekly visitor.

"Hi, pretty lady. The same room?"

"Yes, please. How are you tonight?"

"Oh, I'm fine, thank you." His smile was warm and inviting, as it was every single week. Truth be told, the clerk had a crush on Zora, and his heart smiled every time she entered the lobby. "Three hours?"

"Yes, please." Zora smiled, wishing she could have more time as three hours simply were never enough.

Just as he did every week, the night clerk slid the key under the thick plexiglass, and Zora slid him seventy-five dollars for a bottom-of-the-barrel room, in the middle of a wooded area, along Maryland's not-so-busy, dark-ass highway. Of course, this made for the perfect getaway.

"Have a good night."

As she turned on her heels, he admired the roundness of her bottom and chuckled, wishing he were the recipient of such a sweet piece of ass.

She looked over her shoulder. "You, too." She smiled at him. Aware of the secret affection he held for her, she added a little more swing in her hips.

Opening the door, she stepped out into the warm night. She was feeling good.

After looking up and down the dark highway, Zora walked to her car. Just when her hand grabbed the car door handle, she spotted headlights turning into the parking lot. Instantly, butterflies fluttered in her belly, excitement growing deep within her. Anticipation of what was to come built up, and she was extremely horny despite the hunk of a man she had at home.

When Keith saw the familiar sign, he desperately tried to maintain his cool, not understanding why they were pulling into the parking lot of his and Zora's sex den. But goodness, when he saw Zora, he damn near needed Depends as he was surely about to piss his pants. Yeah, royally fucked beyond his wildest imagination. His life and marriage flashed before his eyes. Now he knew why LaTonya acted so shitty toward him. She knew, and she was about to make this the most miserable night of his life. *I might as well just slit my throat*, he thought, because his life, as he knew it, was over.

Maceo sat in the back seat wondering why Zora was coming out of the office at The Motel on 301. By far, he was not a stupid man, as he noticed the change in Keith's posture and the wicked, devilish grin on LaTonya's face.

As LaTonya pulled into the parking space beside Zora's car, Zora's mouth turned upside down. All that was missing was the big nose, multi-colored Afro, and the big, red shoes because she felt like the biggest clown in the world.

Perplexed, Maceo remained quiet as he felt his heart slowly breaking.

"We're here, fellas. Let's get out. My, doesn't Zora look surprised? I told you we were going to surprise her." Facing Keith, she looked at him with a now-what-the-fuck-are-you-going-to-do look behind a curled top lip.

She climbed out of the car and walked toward Zora. "Hi there, *friend*. How are you?"

Zora didn't know what to say. She couldn't even move her feet. She was stunned and her father's words, *Karma is a you-know-what*, played repeatedly in her head.

Zora shifted her weight from one foot to the other. "Hey, LaTonya, what are you doing here?" That was a dumb question, as if she didn't know.

"I was going to ask you the same question, *friend*." LaTonya forced the phoniest smile she could muster while deep down inside, she wanted to haul off and knock the shit out of her so-called *friend*. Some friend, huh?

"Oh well, my car—"

Short of completing a lie about having car troubles and pulling into The Motel on 301 for assistance, she saw Keith getting out of the car and Maceo climbing out of the back seat. Her knees weakened, and she felt suffocated as if someone had tied a plastic bag over her head. She just knew she was about to faint. "Oh…my."

"Go ahead, Zora, 'my car' what?" LaTonya chided her.

"Well, um," she paused, nervously smiling, "my car was giving me problems, and I stopped in here for help."

A quizzical look smothered LaTonya's face. "You stop at a motel instead of the gas station down the road?"

Maceo approached Zora and looked from LaTonya to Keith. "Would someone like to fill me in on what the fuck is happening here?"

Zora looked perplexed. "Nothing's going on. Where were you guys heading?" She chuckled nervously. "I'm glad you guys came. Now I don't have to call a tow truck."

"Cut the bullshit, Zora. What room are we in?" LaTonya extended her hand, wiggling her fingers. "Key, please."

Zora looked at Keith pleadingly, but like a trained puppy, he looked down at the ground. "I don't know what you mean."

"Bitch, I don't have time for this bullshit. Give me the fuckin' key!"

Moving to stand between Zora and LaTonya, Maceo's stance was tall and firm. "Will someone *please* tell me what's going on here?" Now pissed, deep down, he knew exactly what was going on. He didn't just fall off the turnip truck. He looked Zora in the eyes. "Babe?"

"I don't—"

"Why, of course, I'll tell you, Maceo. You see, my *friend* and your *bestie*, Keith, over there, looking down at the fuckin' ground, have been fuckin' like rabbits. Ain't that right, Zora?"

"What the fuck is this bitch talking about, Zora? Make this shit make sense to me."

LaTonya frowned. "Bitch? Oh, I bring you into the light and you call me a bitch?"

Maceo shouted at Zora, "Is she telling me that you have been sitting on this motherfucker's dick? Look me in my face and tell me that this bitch is lying!"

"No, no. Let's not start yelling and shouting. We don't want to bring any attention to ourselves."

Maceo's head snapped in LaTonya's direction. "Attention? Bitch, you bring me here under false pretenses and you want me to be quiet? Fuck you! I want to know the truth about what's going on!"

Keith stuffed his hands in his pockets. "LaTonya, you've made your point."

Maceo glared at Keith; his face distorted. "Yo, you punk-ass motherfucker, you wanna tell me you've been fuckin' my woman behind my goddamn back?"

He was damned if he did, and damned if he didn't, so there was nothing else for him to do but confess and suffer the consequences.

"Yes." He looked down at the ground. "I'm sor—"

Maceo hurled an uppercut under Keith's chin, sending him flying against Zora's car, landing him flat on his back.

"Well, damn it!" LaTonya had not expected it. Sure, he would be angry, that much she figured, but right now Maceo looked as if he was ready to commit murder and Keith would be his potential victim.

Without warning, Maceo grabbed Keith by the collar and yanked him up to his feet, pulling him so close to his face, he could smell his breath. "What the fuck? Why my woman, dude?"

Barely able to speak because of the choke hold Maceo had on his collar, Keith whispered, "It—"

"Wrong answer, motherfucker!" Maceo spun Keith around like a rag doll and slammed him up against the brick wall.

Zora and LaTonya screamed, pleading with Maceo.

"No, Maceo, no!" Zora grabbed him by the arm.

With force, he jerked from her, sending her stumbling backward, and sneered at her. "Back up off me, you whore!" He returned his focus to Keith. "I should kill your punk ass right now!"

LaTonya's eyes widened like a deer caught in the headlights. She couldn't believe what was taking place before her, but really, what had she expected? This wasn't what she had planned, and if Maceo killed her husband, it would be something she'd have to live with for the rest of her life and that wasn't happening on her watch.

"Wait a minute, Maceo."

"Naw, ain't no 'wait a minute,' LaTonya. You fuckin' brought us here for a reason."

"Yes, I did, but not for you to kill my husband."

Keith squared his eyes on Maceo. "I'm sorry, man."

Tears streamed down Maceo's face. "Sorry? Sorry? Man, I trusted you with my life. We go back to the fuckin' sandbox, and this the shit you do to me? I brought your fuckin' ass up here from New Orleans to help you get on your motherfuckin' feet, you bitch-ass fucker! Sorry, huh? Yeah, well, fuck you, sorry motherfucker."

LaTonya gently grabbed hold of Maceo's wrist and peered into his eyes. "As much as I would love to see Keith suffer for his"—she glanced over her shoulder at Zora—"indiscretion, he is not worth it. Zora is not worth it. None of this is worth your jeopardizing your freedom." She gently squeezed his wrist. "Maceo."

Betrayed by the woman he loved more than his own life, Maceo stared at Zora for a few minutes, but it felt like hours. He shook his head. "No, you're not worth it. I'm done with you, Zora." With all his built-up anger, Maceo spat in Keith's face, grabbed him by the throat, and tossed him through the hotel room window, landing him on a table situated under the window.

In total shock, Zora and LaTonya stood motionless.

"Fuck the both of you broads! I'm out of here." Maceo gave Zora one last look and a disappointing shake of the head. "You ain't shit but a whore. No wonder you didn't want to marry me. You fuckin' that no-good motherfucker." Devastated and hurt beyond belief, Maceo stormed off the hotel property and ran north up Route 301.

With Keith sprawled across the table, LaTonya looked at him and made sure he was all right because, despite it all, he was still her husband and she loved him.

She turned to Zora, as she had a few choice words for her friend.

"You know, Zora, I loved you like a sister. I opened my life to you. I don't deserve this betrayal."

"I think—" Zora stopped short at the dagger look in her former friend's eyes.

LaTonya shook her head briskly. "You don't have shit to say to me. The best thing you can do for me is go straight to hell."

Zora looked at LaTonya with tears streaming down her face. "I'm so sorry."

"Go fuck yourself with your sorry, Zora. I don't want your apology, but I do want you out of my life, and take that sorry-ass motherfucker with you."

LaTonya turned on her heels to get into her car, but she briskly twirled around. "When your bitch wakes up, tell him I want a divorce!"

CHAPTER 33

Kennedy pulled into the graveled driveway, parking behind the shiny burgundy, 1979 Buick Regal under the *porte cochére* on Halifax Street in Emporia, Virginia.

Kennedy stared at the Southern one-hundred-plus-year-old brick house that held a mountain of memories. A tranquil pond filled with goldfish shimmered, surrounded by blooming magnolias. A wraparound porch embraced the house, the perfect spot for leisurely afternoons.

As Kennedy turned off her car and grabbed her satchel from the passenger's seat, she took a deep breath before climbing out. Her heart raced with a mix of anticipation and anxiety as she glanced at the familiar sight of her aunt Cynthia standing in the doorway of the sun porch.

"Lord, child, what are you doing here?" Aunt Cynthia stepped down onto the gravel driveway, hurrying toward Kennedy with open arms. They embraced, and Kennedy felt an overwhelming sense of comfort in her aunt's warm, loving embrace, succumbing to her emotions.

"Oh, Aunt Cynthia…" Kennedy's voice quivered as she tried to find the right words.

"What's the matter? Oh, honey, nothing is so serious that it cannot be fixed." Aunt Cynthia gently patted her back. "Why didn't you call to let us know you were coming?"

Kennedy wiped her tears and looked into her aunt's caring eyes. "I needed to get away for a while. I just needed to be here, where I feel loved."

Aunt Cynthia nodded understandingly. "Well, you're always welcome here, sweetheart. Come inside, let's talk over some sweet tea. We'll figure it all out."

As they walked toward the inviting wraparound porch, Kennedy felt a sense of relief wash over her. Being back there brought back a flood of memories, and she knew this was the place she needed to heal and find solace.

"It's such a beautiful night, Aunt Cynthia. Mind if we sit on a porch for a bit?"

Aunt Cynthia looked around. "Well, I guess so. Sure."

Sitting on the porch swing, while Aunt Cynthia went inside to prepare the sweet tea, Kennedy's mind wandered, her thoughts consumed by Malcolm's newfound son. She couldn't help but ponder the changes that had swept through their family since they last gathered here on this Southern porch. Just then, as a cool, October breeze carried the faint scent of fallen leaves, mingling with the rustle of branches under a canopy of twinkling stars, her cousins, Nicole and Angela, strolled up the walkway toward the porch.

They both shrilled in unison, their eyes widening with excitement as they spotted their cousin, whom they hadn't seen in several summers. "Kennedy?"

A smile spread across Kennedy's face, as she jumped up from the swing, her heart filled with joy at the sight of her beloved cousins. She ran toward them, her arms outstretched, ready to embrace the two women who had been like sisters growing up.

"Nicole! Angela!"

The trio collided in a warm, heartfelt embrace, their laughter echoing across the porch. Memories of summers past flooded their minds, of carefree days spent chasing fireflies and sharing secrets under the starlit sky. They had grown up together, bonded by love and the cherished traditions of their Southern upbringing.

As they finally pulled away from the embrace, Kennedy took a moment to look at her cousins, noting how much they had changed since the last time they were together.

"Look at you both! You look fantastic," Kennedy said, with a mix of pride and nostalgia in her voice.

Nicole grinned. "Time flies, doesn't it? But we've missed you, Kennedy."

Angela nodded in agreement. "Yeah, you've been off in the big city, living the life, while we've been holding down the fort here in good ol' Emporia."

Kennedy chuckled, feeling a sense of warmth and belonging. "I've missed you both, too, more than you know. But I needed to come back, to find myself again and to be with family, to be with y'all."

Nicole and Angela exchanged knowing glances. They knew this place, with its timeless charm and the love of family, had a way of healing even the deepest wounds.

"Well, you're back now, and that's all that matters." Nicole linked her arm with Kennedy's.

Angela added, "We'll stick together, just like we always have."

As the moon cast a serene glow over the fishpond and the verdant surroundings, the three cousins settled back onto the porch swing.

"So, talk to me. How are things?" Kennedy looked around. "I see not much has changed."

Nicole shook her head. "Everything's the same. Aunt Cynthia and Aunt Ruby are the same." She looked out into the yard and smiled, as if reflecting on a wonderful memory. "They still keep douche bags hanging up on the back of the bathroom door, under a fifty-year-old bathrobe."

The threesome bowled over with laughter.

"Oh my, God. Are you serious?"

Nicole held her belly with laughter, managing to get out, "Girl, you remember that door to the cellar that they never opened?"

Kennedy nodded, still laughing.

"Well, I asked Aunt Ruby what was behind that door. She opened it and three ghosts flew out!"

Kennedy howled with laughter and Angela joined her, wiping the tears from her eyes.

Nicole smiled. "I'm just kidding."

Once she gathered herself, Kennedy looked at her cousins. "Does it still smell like smoke and wood inside?"

Nicole looked at Kennedy. "You haven't been inside yet?"

"Just got here a few moments before y'all walked up. Aunt Cynthia met me at the door, and I wanted to sit on the porch while she makes sweat tea."

"More like kerosene," Angela said nonchalantly.

"What's 'more like kerosene'?" Kennedy asked.

"The house. Always smells like kerosene instead of a wood burning stove in the family room."

Kennedy and Nicole glimpsed each other and chuckled.

"Going to the bathroom scarred me for life," Angela reminisced.

Kennedy's brows furrowed. "What do you mean?"

"Girl, in that front bathroom, I saw a rat in the toilet. Scarred me for life, it did. Now, I look before I sit."

Nicole's laughter echoed through the air. "Was it dead?"

"I didn't stick around to find out!" With a straight face, Angela continued. "Remember how the aunts would make those curtains and slipcovers? Very talented. This house reminds me of *Mama's Family*."

"I have memories of plastic covers," Kennedy added.

Nicole nodded. "In the parlor, still plastic."

"In the family room, too," Angela added. "I remember falling asleep and sweating. I woke up wet!"

As the trio were barely able to keep it together through their uproar of laughter down memory lane, Aunt Cynthia came out onto the front porch, carrying a tray of sweat tea with a wide smile.

"I thought I heard two familiar voices."

"Hey, Aunt Cynthia," Nicole and Angela greeted in unison.

Nicole stood up to take the tray from Aunt Cynthia. "We came by to check on you and Aunt Ruby."

"Thank you, Nicole. I don't know what Ruby and I would do without you and Angela."

Aunt Cynthia sat across from Kennedy on a red-painted, metal chair.

In this Southern haven, surrounded by the love of family and the memories of her childhood, Kennedy felt at peace. The porch swing creaked gently, and the Southern breeze carried their laughter well into the night, reminding them that no matter where life led them, their bond would forever be rooted in the beauty and warmth of this cherished home on Halifax Street.

Over glasses of sweet tea, Kennedy no longer felt the weight of Malcolm's indiscretion. Aunt Cynthia's presence was a balm to her weary soul, as if her troubles had melted away.

The following morning, Kennedy awoke to the aroma of the wood-burning stove permeating the comforting ambiance of Aunt Cynthia and Aunt Ruby's house. A smile graced her lips as she recalled her cousin Angela's remark: "More like kerosene." With a nod, she thought, *She's absolutely right. How can wood smell like kerosene?* She chuckled.

It had been a few years since she last visited. She could not bring herself to face the people and the place that reminded her so much of her mother. Now, though, she needed to feel that closeness to her mother, surrounded by the family she knew loved her unconditionally.

As the sun peeped through the blinds, Kennedy stretched under the covers. She loved that comfortable bed, with the cool sheets and feather-stuffed pillows. Everything about the room had a smell and feel that she'd cherished as a child.

Even after a good night's sleep, she was not in the mood to answer any of her aunts' questions. However, she knew she would have to face their flurries of "whys" and "how comes" before she could sip her first cup of coffee.

Sighing heavily, she pulled back the covers and swung her legs over the side of the bed that she had to climb into because it was so high. As her feet dangled above the floor, she felt like a little girl again. She looked in the mirror attached to the oak wood dresser across from the bed. It was the same dresser that had belonged to her great-grandmother, Mattie. Yes, this was where she needed to be. Where her heart felt safe from any more heartbreak. Where the only tears she would shed would be from thinking of her mother, and not those from betrayal.

Before her feet could touch the floor, a tiny voice came from the other side of the door.

"Are you up?"

"Yes, ma'am, I'm up."

The door opened, and an angelic face peeped into the room. "Breakfast is almost ready."

Kennedy stretched. "It sure smells good."

"I put a towel and washcloth in the bathroom for you. You're going to do something to your head, aren't you?"

Kennedy chuckled and looked in the mirror again.

"Well, get yourself together and when you come to the table, we'll talk about why you showed up here out of the blue."

"Aunt Ruby, can't I visit my aunts?"

"What did that Malcolm do?"

Kennedy tilted her head. "What makes you think he did something?"

"I wasn't born yesterday. He's a man, isn't he?"

Kennedy stood up and walked toward the door. She looked into the face that favored her mother's. She warmly embraced her aunt.

Aunt Ruby regarded her with a hint of skepticism. "Well, we're pleased you're here."

"Thank you. I'll take my shower now and"—she glanced in the mirror—"do something to this bird's nest."

Her bare feet slapped across the cool hardwood flooring as she moved a few steps up the hall and into the bathroom. There was that smell, again. Caress. Convinced everyone in the family, except her, had stock in Caress soap, she turned on the shower and looked in the mirror as she peeled off the pink tee shirt and matching pajama bottoms. Piling the disheveled tresses atop the crown of her head, she searched the medicine cabinet for a hairpin. She reached for the longest hairpin she'd ever seen and secured her hair.

She stepped into the shower and, with her head back, allowed the warm stream to run over her face, down her neck, and over her full bosom. She reached for the Caress soap, inhaled, slathered it in the palms of her hands, and massaged her face. Visions of Malcolm and his newfound son clouded her thoughts. Then suddenly, her heart broke again. She leaned against the pink-tiled wall, hung her head, and silently cried.

Stepping out of the shower, she wrapped the towel around her, brushed her teeth, and headed back toward the bedroom. As she moved closer, her cell phone rang.

Seeing her daughter's name scroll across her phone, Kennedy clutched it in her hand, took a deep breath and answered. "Hi, honey!"

"Hi, Mom. How are you?"

"Oh, I'm fair to midland." Without further hesitation, Kennedy felt it was time to spill the beans. "Lindsay, I'm in Emporia and—"

"Emporia? My God, Mom, is everything okay with Aunt Ruby and Aunt Cynthia?"

"Yes, baby, they are fine.

"Then why are you there?"

"Honey, there's something important I need to share with you about your father."

Lindsay's heart skipped a beat. "What is it, Mom?"

Taking a deep breath, Kennedy closed the bedroom door. "Before your father and I married, he had an indiscretion. From that one indiscretion, he has a son—a half-brother you didn't know about."

Lindsay's eyes widened. "Wait, so I have a brother?"

Kennedy's voice carried a sense of understanding. "Yes, honey. I know this might be a shock."

"Why didn't I know about him?"

"We didn't find out until yesterday. Your dad didn't even know about Eric. It's complicated, but—"

"Eric? His name is Eric? Eric Ellis?"

"His name is Eric Murphy, and your father knows about him now and they're reconnecting."

Lindsay's thoughts buzzed as she tried to process the news. "So, I've had a brother all this time—wait, Mom. Dad cheated on you?"

"I said it was before we married."

"Right, but you met in college, correct?"

"Correct."

"So, that means he cheated on you, Mom!"

"Wait a minute, honey. That's not your concern. Now, your father was a young man in college, still feeling and sowing his oats. He had an indiscretion."

"What the hell does that mean, indiscretion?"

"Watch your language!"

"Sorry, but you keep using that word. I don't know what it means."

"Lindsay, honey, you don't know what a word means, use a dictionary. In short, your father had a one-night-stand with an older woman. He never saw her or heard from her again after that one night. Fast forward to today and you have a twenty-one-year-old half-brother. None of this changes who your father is; he's still the man who loves your stinky butt. He's still the man I married and love."

"Wow, Mom. Then why are you in Emporia? You left Dad?"

"Well…" Her daughter's question left her at a loss for words. Did she leave her husband because of something that happened when he was still wet behind the ears? "You'll understand, one day, honey. I love your dad. I just needed time to think. It's a lot to take in, I understand. But remember, this doesn't change anything between us. You're still my daughter, and I'm here for you."

Lindsay looked out the window of her dorm room. "I know, Mom. It's just…unexpected."

Kennedy's voice softened. "I get it, sweetheart. It's okay to feel overwhelmed. We'll get through this together."

"Thanks, Mom. I appreciate that."

"I love you, Lindsay."

"I love you, too, Mom." Lindsay felt a sense of connection even through the miles that separated them.

"Well, honey, let me get dressed and to the breakfast table."

"I wish I could have one of Aunt Cynthia's rolls! Do they have ham? I know they're going to have ham."

Kennedy smiled. "I definitely smell rolls. I saw the ham last night and I guarantee there will be fried corn in the mix."

Lindsay groaned. "Oh, and Mom?"

"Yes?"

"Don't you have one of those indiscretions in Emporia to get back at Dad."

Kennedy shook her head and smiled. "You have my word. Bye, honey."

"Bye, Mom."

Just as she'd expected, hot, buttered rolls, fried ham, butter-topped grits, scrambled eggs, country bacon, country sausage, fried apples, pear preserves, which were her mother's favorite, fresh squeezed orange juice, and piping hot coffee covered the table.

"Good morning, ladies!" Kennedy greeted her aunts in a singsong fashion, as she took a seat at the table next to Aunt Cynthia. "Everything looks so yummy!"

Aunt Cynthia patted her hand. "How did you sleep?"

"Like a baby." She looked around the dining room, which hadn't changed since she was a child. "I'd forgotten how peaceful it is here."

Aunt Ruby entered the dining room, carrying a large bowl of country-fried corn. She placed it on the table in front of Kennedy and took her seat.

"This is a lot of food."

Aunt Ruby opened the linen napkin and placed it on her lap. "Well, we don't get company often."

As Kennedy reached for a hot, homemade roll, Aunt Ruby looked at Kennedy and then at her sister, Cynthia. Although Kennedy kept her eyes on her plate, she was used to her aunts and how they went about retrieving information. Straight. Direct. To the Point. They had no cut cards. No matter the circumstances, flowery words were not a part of the family's genetics.

"So, he cheated on you, huh?"

"Yes, Aunt Cynthia, and I'd rather not talk about it now."

"With whom?"

Without looking up from her plate, Kennedy closed her eyes. "Aunt Ruby, does it matter?"

"Not really, but if you want to tell us, we'll listen."

Kennedy placed her fork on the table and rubbed her temples, knowing there was no way they were going to let up. "In college, Malcolm had an indiscretion and twenty-one years later, we find out he has a son."

The aunts showed no emotions, which puzzled Kennedy.

"Well, it goes that way sometimes." Aunt Cynthia delicately tasted a forkful of scrambled eggs.

Kennedy blinked a few times, unsure of what she had heard. "I'm sorry, but what did you say, Aunt Cynthia?"

Aunt Ruby interjected. "He was young, dumb, and what the young folk say, 'full of come.'"

"But I—"

Aunt Cynthia frowned at her sister. "The way you put that is so crass, but so true, sister. It happened to me once."

By the look on Kennedy's face, you could have sold her for a nickel.

"Yes, I remember that, Cynthia."

"Uh huh, and he had the nerve to tell me it was my fault because I told her, my best friend, how big his—"

Now flushed, Kennedy cleared her throat.

Aunt Cynthia blushed as she spooned country-fried corn on her plate.

Aunt Ruby peered at Kennedy. "What's the matter, child?"

Kennedy shook her head, blushing.

"Oh, honey, we have sex, too."

"Goodness, Aunt Ruby. Malcolm didn't cheat on me with my friend—"

"Well, what are you going to do, divorce him?"

"Well, I don't know…"

Aunt Cynthia looked at her sister, Ruby.

Aunt Ruby set her fork down and clasped her hands in her lap. "Is this his first offense?"

"Excuse me?"

"Is this the first time he's had an affair?"

Kennedy shrugged, a hint of skepticism in her expression. "As far as I know, but what does that have to do with the price of tea in China?"

Aunt Cynthia leaned forward in her chair, her eyes reflecting a blend of seriousness and warmth. "I don't know about no tea in China, but I do know that Malcolm is a good man, a good father, and a good provider. He loves you and Lindsay deeply. Yes, he made a mistake twenty-one years ago, back when he was in college, before you were even married. But Kennedy, you don't leave a man for one mistake, especially when he's grown into a better person since then. If anything, you find a way to be understanding."

Kennedy's gaze softened as she listened to her aunt's words, feeling a mixture of comfort and conflict within her heart. She leaned back, crossing her arms, and looked out of the window as if searching for answers in the swaying branches outside.

Aunt Cynthia took a sip of her orange juice, her eyes fixed on Kennedy. "That's right, sister, and remember, there's a third party involved here—his son. He's innocent in all of this. Imagine not knowing your father for twenty-one years, growing up without that connection."

Kennedy's thoughts drifted to Malcolm's son; a young man who had lived his life unaware of his true parentage. The weight of that realization settled on her, and she began to see the situation from a different point of view. She turned her gaze back to her aunt, a mixture of contemplation and uncertainty in her eyes.

"But what about us, Aunt Cynthia? What about our family?"

Aunt Cynthia's eyes were full of reassurance. "Kennedy, adding one more to your family doesn't diminish what you have. If anything, it enriches it. It's a chance for growth and understanding."

Kennedy took a deep breath. She realized her aunt's words were not just about Malcolm's past but about the future they could all build together—a future that embraced change and each other's flaws and strengths.

"I just… I need time to process all of this." Kennedy's shoulders sagged with the weight of her thoughts.

Aunt Cynthia smiled warmly, reaching out to place a comforting hand on Kennedy's. "And you should take all the time you need, my dear. Just remember that life has its twists and turns, but it's how we navigate them that truly defines who we are."

After breakfast, the morning was calm and sunny. Kennedy walked down Halifax Street to the corner store and bought her favorite snacks that she only ate when in Emporia: Now & Later, pork rinds, sunflower seeds, and peach soda. She felt like a kid again, as she crossed the road, making her way into downtown Emporia.

After a restless night of tossing and turning, Kennedy awoke the next morning with a knot of anxiety in her stomach. She stared at the ceiling for a moment, lost in her thoughts, until a gentle tap on the bedroom door drew her attention.

"Yes?"

"Are you up?"

"I am now, Aunt Ruby."

The bedroom door creaked open, and Aunt Ruby stepped into the room. Kennedy could see the worry etched on her aunt's face. Aunt Ruby walked over and leaned against the dresser; her gaze fixed on Kennedy.

"It's time for you to go home."

Kennedy blinked, her mind racing to catch up with the unexpected statement. "What?"

Nodding, Aunt Ruby's expression was unwavering. "It's time for you to stop running."

Kennedy sat up in bed. "Running? I'm not running, Aunt Ruby."

Aunt Ruby's eyes softened as she looked at her great niece. "Kennedy, I've known you all of your life. I can see it in your eyes, the way you've been avoiding facing things, avoiding going back home."

Kennedy shifted uncomfortably under her aunt's perceptive gaze. "I just needed some time to think, to figure things out."

Aunt Ruby sighed. "And you've had that time, darling. But sometimes, the longer we run from our problems, the bigger they seem to get. It's time to face what's waiting for you back home."

Kennedy looked down at her hands, her fingers picking at the edge of the crocheted afghan. She knew her aunt was right.

"I know it's not easy, but your husband loves you, and you two have a life together. Don't let one mistake define your entire relationship."

Tears welled up in Kennedy's eyes, and she brushed them away with the back of her hand. "I'm just scared, Aunt Ruby. Scared of what he'll say, of what will happen next."

Aunt Ruby stepped closer and placed a comforting hand on Kennedy's shoulder. "Life is full of uncertainties, sweetheart. Running away won't make them go away. It's time to face your fears and communicate with your husband. You both deserve that."

Kennedy looked up at her aunt, her vulnerability laid bare. "What if I can't forgive him?"

Aunt Ruby's eyes held a reassuring warmth. "Love has a way of healing wounds, Kennedy. You won't know until you try."

As the morning sun filtered through the curtains, Kennedy felt a mixture of apprehension and resolve. Her aunt's words echoed in her mind, reminding her that it was time to stop running. With a deep breath, she nodded at Aunt Ruby, grateful for the guidance and support she had been given.

"Thank you, Aunt Ruby. You're right."

Aunt Ruby smiled, her love and pride evident in her gaze. "You're stronger than you realize, my dear. It's time to go home."

Kennedy nodded again, her heart lighter than it had been in days. With her aunt's encouragement, she knew she was ready to take that first step toward healing and resuming what she had temporarily left behind.

As she was gathering her things to leave Emporia, Kennedy's phone buzzed on the nightstand. She glanced at the screen and saw that it was Zora calling. For some odd reason, her stomach knotted.

"Hey, Zora."

"Kennedy." Zora's voice was strained, and Kennedy immediately sensed that something was wrong. "Can we talk?"

"Of course." That knot in Kennedy's stomach tightened. "Is everything okay?"

"She knows."

Kennedy's heart skipped a beat. "About you and Keith?"

"Uh-huh."

"How did she find out?"

"I don't know, but my God, Kennedy."

"What happened, Zora? The short version, please."

"I was to meet Keith at the hotel and as I waited for him, guess who showed up?"

"LaTonya?"

"Yes, with Keith and Maceo!"

Kennedy sat down on the bed.

"Girl, all hell broke loose, is all I can say. Maceo picked up Keith and tossed him on the hood of LaTanya's car...and if that wasn't good enough, he tossed him through the hotel room window."

"Zora, how could you? How could Keith?"

"I know I messed up, Kennedy. I can't even begin to justify it."

"Zora, you've hurt so many people with this. This isn't just about you and Keith."

"I know, Kennedy. I'm facing the consequences of my actions."

"Where is Maceo?"

"I don't know. I'm at the hospital with Keith."

"Just a hot-ass mess, Zora!"

"Well, somebody had to bring him. His wife left him there, half his body hanging out of a hotel window. Girl, the manager was going to call the cops on us, but I gave him my credit card to repair the window, along with a little extra."

Kennedy couldn't believe what she was hearing, and she'd heard enough. "Well, listen, I've got to run. I don't have time to deal with your self-inflicted bullshit. I have my own shit to deal with."

"What's wrong?"

"Nothing to concern yourself with. You've really fucked up with LaTonya. You can hang that friendship up, for sure."

"I'm sorry, Kennedy."

"I'm not the one deserving of your apology, Zora. I doubt it would do any good anyway. Bye, girl."

Upon ending the call with Zora, a whirlwind of emotions engulfed Kennedy. Zora had become a source of betrayal, leaving behind a wreckage of shattered relationships and crumbled trust. As she held her phone in her hand, a sense of turmoil churned within her.

Zora's actions had created a tangled mess of feelings that Kennedy knew would take time to unravel. The bond LaTonya had shared with Zora had been tarnished, and the realization of the depth of this betrayal weighed heavily on Kennedy's heart. The friendships she had cherished with both women were now severed by Zora and Keith's exposed secret.

Staring at her phone, Kennedy grappled with conflicting thoughts. Should she attempt to repair the damage caused by Zora's actions? Should she try to mend the broken trust between Zora and LaTonya, despite the tangled web that had been woven? Or was this a situation best left untouched, a problem that wasn't hers to fix?

Zora and LaTonya were both dear friends, and the rift between them had put Kennedy in an awkward and uncomfortable position. The predicament was not of her own making, but the repercussions of Zora's choices had inevitably entangled her.

Kennedy understood there were no easy answers. Maneuvering the aftermath of such a revelation would require delicate handling and thoughtful consideration. While it might not be her responsibility to fix, she couldn't ignore the bonds she had with both Zora and LaTonya.

Kennedy took a deep breath before calling LaTonya. As the call connected, she could hear the strain in LaTonya's voice, and her heart clenched in anticipation.

"Hey, girlfriend. "

LaTonya's voice trembled. "Kennedy… I can't believe this is happening."

Kennedy moved from the bedroom, out onto the front porch, and into the swing. "I know, LaTonya. I'm here for you."

There was a pause on the other end, as if LaTonya was gathering her thoughts and emotions. "I found out about Keith and Zora, Kennedy. He betrayed me with her."

Kennedy closed her eyes. "I'm so sorry you're going through this, honey."

Tears flowed freely now, and LaTonya's voice wavered as she spoke. "I never thought he could do this to me, Kennedy. I trusted him, and don't get me started on Zora's raggedy, whorish ass."

Kennedy swallowed the lump in her throat.

"I'm done with Keith. I'm divorcing him. As far as Zora is concerned, well, she wasn't my friend anyway. She's trash. She's a tramp whore. She can go straight to hell. She can—"

Kennedy cringed and cleared her throat. "I won't say that I know how you're feeling, but Zora is my best friend."

"Yeah? Watch your husband around that bitch. She has a man, but that's not enough. She has to have everybody else's man."

Kennedy nodded. "You have the right to feel the way you feel, sis."

"I'm leaving him," LaTonya declared, her voice stronger now. "I can't forgive this."

"It's not an easy decision, LaTonya, but I support you no matter what you choose."

LaTonya's voice softened, her vulnerability showing. "I know, Kennedy. Thank you for being there for me."

Kennedy leaned forward, gripping the phone a little tighter. "Always, LaTonya. You're not alone in this."

They talked for a while longer, LaTonya pouring out her feelings of hurt, anger, and uncertainty. Kennedy listened, offering words of comfort and encouragement whenever she could, but refusing to share Malcolm's indiscretion. There was enough drama in this friendship circle. As the conversation came to an end, LaTonya's voice held a glimmer of hope.

"I don't know what the future holds, Kennedy, but I'm determined to find happiness again."

Kennedy smiled. "You're strong, LaTonya. You'll get through this, and you'll come out even stronger on the other side. Let's get together soon for dinner, okay?"

"Thank you, Kennedy. You're a true friend, and I'd like that."

As they said their goodbyes, Kennedy felt a mix of emotions. While she couldn't physically be there for LaTonya, she knew that being a listening ear and a source of support was important. As she hung up the phone, she silently hoped that LaTonya would find the strength and courage she needed to navigate this challenging chapter in her life.

As for Zora, while she couldn't condone her act of betrayal, she would be there for her, too.

CHAPTER 34

Lindsay eventually decided to call her father to discuss her feelings about the news of her half-brother and to gain a better understanding from his perspective. One evening, while Dorrie was out for the evening, Lindsay dialed her father's cell phone number. She took a deep breath as she waited for him to answer.

"Hello?"

"Hi, Dad."

"Hey, baby girl? Is everything okay?" While Lindsay was his baby, she was definitely her mother's girl. So, getting a call from her meant she either needed something or she was in trouble. He prayed it was neither.

"Yeah, everything's fine. I just wanted to talk to you about something."

"Of course, sweetie. I'm here to listen."

"Mom told me, and I've been thinking a lot about my half-brother, your son from before you married Mom."

There was a moment of silence on the other end, followed by a heavy sigh. "I understand this might be a lot to take in."

Lindsay nodded, and, from her bed, she looked out the window. "Yeah, it is. I want you to know that I'm not upset with you or anything. I just don't know how to process it all."

"I appreciate your honesty, honey. I want you to know that your feelings are valid, and I understand if you have questions or concerns."

"I do have questions. Like, how did you find out about him? And how are you building a relationship with him?"

"Honey, you're not a little girl anymore. So, I'll be frank. I was young, around twenty-one years old, and it was a one-night-stand with a woman I didn't know. I was in college. Things happen when you're young that can come back to haunt you when you're older. Remember that."

"Dad, do you regret it?"

"The only thing I regret is not knowing I had a son. I regret this young man, your brother, grew up without knowing he had a father or even a sister. It's not his fault."

"Is he nice?"

"Yes, he is. Baby, we have to open our hearts and our lives and welcome him with open arms. He's family."

"Does Pop-Pop and Gigi know they have a grandson yet?"

"I haven't told them yet. First, I have to square things with your mom. She's not happy with me right now."

"Give her space, Dad. You how Mom can be. She'll come to accept it. She loves you. She's not going anywhere."

"What makes you so sure and so wise?"

"Because I know you and because I'm your daughter. I love you, Dad, and I can't wait to meet my brother."

"I love you, too, pumpkin. How's school?"

"So far, so good. I seem to study all day and all night, but it's all-good."

"That's good. Hey."

"Yeah?"

"Thanks for checking on your old man."

"Of course. I've gotta make sure my favorite guy is good. So, you good?"

"I'm good."

By the end of the conversation, Lindsay felt a sense of clarity and relief. She thanked her father for being open with her and for sharing his experiences. They agreed to continue communicating about their growing family and to support each other in this new chapter.

CHAPTER 35

An emotional wreck, LaTonya walked over to the window. Her posture relaxed when Zora's car pulled up in front of the house. Her brow rose when Keith got out of the car. She wanted to get mad, but she was simply too tired.

The front door opened and closed.

She sat on the side of the bed, listening intently as Keith climbed the staircase, one step at a time. When he darkened their bedroom, he looked at LaTonya. His eyes asked permission to enter.

"You look like shit." LaTonya turned her back to him.

"I spent the night in the ER."

"That's good."

"LaTonya, we need to talk."

"I see your whore dropped you off." She moved toward the walk-in closet and flung open the doors.

"I had no other way to get home."

"Uber. Lift. Cab. Hitchhike."

Not wanting to debate that issue, as he knew he would lose, he ambled toward her and stood in front of her.

"I'm sorry. I never meant to hurt you."

She looked at him and pursed her lips tightly. "Well, you did!" She shouted that, in his face, at the top of her lungs, startling him.

"I know. Babe, I want to fix this."

"If I had a gun, I'd blow your fuckin' brains out." She was still screaming.

Her words stung. "I know you hate me."

"That's putting it lightly." She was irritated, angry, and pissed as hell. "Listen, you slut puppy—" she reached in the closet and pulled down the Louis Vuitton Keepall Bandoulière 50 bag "—for better or worse, in sickness and in health. Where in our vows did it say fuck my friend and your best friend's woman?"

"I fucked up, I admit that, but I never stopped loving you, LaTonya."

She spun on her heels and faced him. "Oh, go 'head somewhere with that bullshit! Couldn't you have found some other bitch to fuck instead of her?" She tossed the bag on the bed and returned to the closet, pulling out clothes and tossing them into a mound on top of the bag. "I don't doubt your love for me, oddly enough." She sighed and shook her head.

Keith was silent.

"Just answer me one question, Keith."

He nodded, looking at her with his hands stuffed in his pant pockets.

"Why wasn't I enough for you?"

He peered at her and shook his head. "You're all I need, LaTonya."

A stunned look crossed her face, amazed at the words that fell from his mouth, and so easily. "When did it happen?"

"No, LaTonya. I'm not going to rehash any of that."

"Oh, you will, and you will give me every fuckin' detail!"

"It was," he paused, carefully stringing his words, "during the adult party you had about five years ago. I was in the kitchen—"

LaTonya raised her hand and silenced him. "Five years? You've been fuckin' her for five years?"

He said nothing.

"Answer me, you no-good son of a bitch!"

"Yes."

Her legs weakened; her feet felt heavy. She plopped on the side of the bed. "Continue."

"Well, as I said, it was at your—"

"Yes, you said that already!"

"I was having a few drinks in the kitchen. I think I was about as inebriated as your guests were that day." He chuckled, but LaTonya found none of it funny as she looked at him like a scolding parent. He cleared his throat and looked down at the floor. "Well, Zora came into the kitchen and…one thing led to another…we had sex in the bathroom." He nervously rubbed his head. "After that day, I knew

I wasn't going there with Zora anymore, but she wanted more. She planned everything…she planned it all. She said she always wanted me. She was always attracted to me, and since you were her friend, it was okay for the two of you to share me."

Each syllable he spoke was like a knife digging deeper in her back. It was painful, and it burned deep down in her belly. She wanted to cry out, but she felt stifled. She couldn't breathe. Every nasty word of confession suffocated her.

"LaTonya, I never meant to hurt you. You must believe me, babe."

"Deep down in my heart, I do believe you, Keith. I believe you weren't thinking when you stuck your dick in that whore. I believe you didn't think about me at all when you hooked up with her again and again and again and a-fuckin'-gain for five years. But I will never, ever forgive you." She balled up the clothes and stuffed them in the bag.

"I know and I have no right to ask you for forgiveness, but Zora is devastated."

She whirled around a few times as if possessed. "Zora is devastated? Zora is devastated? Do you think I give a fuck about that trick being devastated? I like your gall, you asshole! I can't believe you dare to say some shit like that to me! Fuck, Zora!" She hung the bag over her shoulder, grabbed her cell phone from the nightstand, and headed toward the stairs.

Trotting down the steps, he followed on her heels like a four-month-old German shepherd. "Are you going somewhere?"

"You had a good thing going, Keith, but you fucked up when you fucked that bitch."

"I know."

Standing in the foyer, she snapped around to face him. "Stop fucking saying that before I smash you in the fucking head with a fucking lamp!" She snatched her keys and clutch purse off the foyer table. "The sight of you makes me want to vomit!" She opened the door and stepped out onto the front porch.

"Where are you going, LaTonya?"

She shot him a look that would kill him where he stood. "I'm going to none of your goddamn business. That's where I'm going."

He walked up to her. "Okay, you need some time away. I get that and I don't blame you."

"You *fucked* up!" Painful tears streamed down her face.

"Yes, I fucked up royally, but I don't want to lose you. I was wrong and I'll spend the rest of my life paying for it, that much I know, but if that's what I have to do to put us back together, then so be it."

"You should've thought about that five years ago. Damn, I can't believe you fucked that whore in our bathroom, and with me in the house. How…where in the hell did you find the balls to do such a thing, Keith?" She walked away toward her car. She yelled over her shoulder, "There is no fucking us!"

"LaTonya, where are you going in your pajamas?"

Opening the car door, she tossed the bag in the back seat and faced her adulterer of a husband. "Away from you, Keith."

Before getting inside the car, she took one more look at the man she loved so very much. Her heart ached not because of whom he cheated with, but because he cheated. Had he cheated with a stranger, the effect and pain would still be the same.

At one last attempt, Keith proceeded quickly toward her car. "LaTonya, don't do this to us, please."

"Don't do this to us? Keith, are you dense? What's happening to us—you can thank yourself for that."

She climbed in the car, started the engine, strapped on her seat belt, and took one last look at her home and the pitiful man she called a husband before backing out of the drive and peeling down the street.

Keith watched the taillights disappear down the street and around the corner, without stopping at the stop sign. With his head hung low, he sauntered into an empty house. Closing the door, he fell back against it and cried like a baby.

CHAPTER 36

After dropping Keith off, the drive to her condominium in National Harbor was a quick one. Once she pulled into the building's garage, Zora sat behind the steering wheel, staring off in thought. She wondered if Maceo was home. She looked around the garage. His parking spot next to the elevators was vacant.

She sighed heavily, grabbed her purse, and got out of the car. Before she locked the car door, she surveyed her surroundings and moved toward the elevator. She pressed the call button and waited patiently, still surveying her surroundings—not out of fear, but out of habit and safety. In the garage, it was dark, quiet, and lonely. She never liked that feeling regardless if it was morning or night.

When the door opened, she stepped onto the elevator and pressed 10 on the panel, followed by rapidly pressing the CLOSE DOOR button.

When the door closed, she should have taken a sigh of relief, but she held her breath instead, overwhelmed by nerves and anxiety. She had a strange feeling she was about to dance with the devil.

A bell rang, alerting her the elevator had reached the tenth floor. She squared her shoulders, inhaled, and breathed out heavily, but slowly. *With every action comes a consequence, Zora. Pull up your big girl panties and face yours*, she told herself as she stepped off the elevator, turned left, and sauntered down the hall. She stopped in front of her door; she paused before inserting the key, unlocking the door, and pushing it open.

It was quiet. No music was playing, which always meant Maceo was home. It seemed like he couldn't be without music.

She exhaled and closed the door. She dropped her purse and keys on the floor in the corner, kicked off her shoes, and pulled her tresses down from the tight bun that had given her a headache.

"Aspirin," she mumbled, "and a good nap will do me some good right now."

Rounding the corner into the kitchen, she stopped in her tracks, clutching her chest as if someone had knocked the wind out of her.

They stared each other down.

Her eyes held fear and a chill shot through her.

His eyes were void of emotion.

"Zora…"

Forcing a smile, she couldn't speak. Truth be told, she was afraid.

"Wasn't expecting to see me here, huh?"

She dropped her hands at her sides. "Well…"

"You didn't come home last night after that shit show." He opened the kitchen cabinet and pulled down two wine goblets. "Let's have some Champagne."

"No, thank you."

"Zora, I want you to have a glass with me."

"Maceo, I'm—"

"In a minute."

She nodded.

"Right now, I want to share a glass of Champagne with you. Can I do that, Zora?"

Now wringing her hands, she stumbled over her words. "Uh, yeah, sure…"

"I bought us a bottle of Cristal. Pull it out of the fridge and let's relax in the living room. Cool?"

Zora felt like she'd walked into some kind of time warp. This was not what she was expecting. He was too calm, cool, and collected.

Retrieving the bottle from the fridge, she followed him into the living room and sat in the chair next to the sofa on which he sat.

He patted the space beside him. "Right here, babe. I want you next to me."

Instantly, a rush of fear and the urge to pee washed over her, but she got up and sat beside him.

Maceo poured the Cristal and extended her a glass.

She accepted it, and before she was about to take a sip, he toasted.

"To us."

Baffled, her facial expression showed as much. *To us? What game is he playing?*

He chuckled. "I know what you're thinking."

"You do?"

"Yes. Listen, what went down last night…well, to be honest, I knew something was going on with you, but I just didn't know what. I feel relieved."

"Relieved?"

"Yeah. What's done is done. There's nothing you nor I can do to change it. You hurt me to the core of my core. I cannot imagine what this has done to LaTonya. You have lost that friendship, that much I'm confident of." His tone was still cool as a cucumber, which really was scaring the shit out of Zora, but she dared not show it. "As far as Keith, well, he's dead to me. If I don't think of him as dead, I will kill him."

Zora's mouth dropped. "Oh, uh…"

He sipped his drink.

"Have I lost you, too, Maceo?"

Nodding, his smile turned into a chuckle, which turned into shoulder-jumping laughter. "No doubt about it. I could never trust you again, let alone make love to you. You allowed another man to take from me."

"Maceo, I—"

"You were mine, Zora. In the ten years we've been together, I never—not once—looked at another woman. Sure, many women have approached me, but I only had eyes for you."

"Had?"

"I forgive you for your five-year indiscretion, Zora. What you did was sinful, so I forgive you because I want to move on with my life. I want to love again with a woman who deserves me, who deserves my love. If I don't forgive you, then I won't be able to do that." He got up and walked over to the floor-to-ceiling window and looked out on the harbor. Shaking his head, he sipped his drink. "I proposed to you on a day when you probably had just finished fucking my dude. Now I'm not surprised you turned me down."

"I didn't turn you down, Maceo."

He spun around and peered at her with a tilted head. "You didn't say yes."

"Keith, let—"

He reared back, his mouth gaping open, his fist clenched. "Maceo! I'm Maceo!"

His goblet whizzed past her head, causing her to duck. She jumped to her feet. "What the fuck is wrong with you?"

With his arms at his sides, he didn't flinch. Releasing a slight chuckle, he shook his head and moved toward the bedroom.

Zora didn't move, but she listened intently. What was he doing? She couldn't believe that, after all these years, she'd finally let Keith's name slip from her mouth around Maceo. She shook her head and palmed her forehead. "You stupid ass," she mumbled.

Maceo returned to the living room with a suitcase in each hand and a duffel bag over each shoulder.

Her eyes widened.

"No, Zora. You're not stupid. You're an intelligent, beautiful woman. Stupid? No. A trespasser? Yes."

Zora frowned. "A trespasser?"

Maceo moved toward the front door, setting down a suitcase. He opened the door and then looked at her. "Yes. 'Give us this day our daily bread as we forgive those who *trespass* against us.' I've forgiven you. Not so much for your sake, but for mine. I hope LaTonya can forgive you for trespassing against her."

After he picked up his suitcase and stepped into the hallway, he looked over his shoulder. "I loved you yesterday. I love you less today. Tomorrow and the days to follow, my love for you will lessen more, so eventually, I will love again."

When the door closed behind him, Zora stood speechless. *Well, damn.* She plopped down on the sofa and stared at the shattered glass on the floor. A semblance to her life.

CHAPTER 37

After a fifteen-minute mammogram at Capital Radiology, the technician escorted Zora to the waiting room, asking her to have a seat and wait for the doctor to come with the results.

An emotional mess, Zora busied herself with a magazine and her cell phone, scrolling her social media newsfeed, trying to get her mind off of the reason she was there. She closed her eyes, inhaled deeply, and exhaled, attempting to release all the built-up anxiety.

A few minutes later, the technician entered the waiting room. "Ms. Vaughn, you will need to have another mammogram. The doctor wants to have more films taken of the left breast."

She never thought there would be a second breast exam. Her heart was pounding. Her eyebrows slanted into a frown. "Is there something wrong?"

Noticing the concern on Zora's face, a look she'd become accustomed to seeing, the technician warmly smiled. "Let's not worry about things we do not know."

After the second mammogram, instead of going to the waiting room, the technician escorted Zora to a cold examination room. Sitting in the chair positioned in the corner, she had hoped this would be her last mammogram for at least a year. While waiting for the doctor, she wondered what would be next. She wondered, hoped, and prayed it was nothing serious.

After the soft knock at the door, the doctor came in to talk to her.

"Hello, Ms. Vaughn. There—"

"Zora, please." She faintly smiled. "If you're going to tell me my fate, at least do it on a first-name basis."

He nodded. "Zora, there were abnormal cells, in shape and size, showing in your left breast. I would like to schedule a stereotactic needle for tomorrow morning."

Staring into his mouth, she focused on his pretty white teeth, as if she didn't know how to respond. She was in total shock. "A stereotactic needle? What's that?"

"A stereotactic needle biopsy is a procedure used to take a small piece of tissue from your body. In this case, your breast. This tissue is then examined to determine its composition."

"Oh, okay…"

"It is better to err on the side of caution, Zora."

She nodded.

"I'll see you at nine-thirty tomorrow to prep and start the biopsy at ten." He smiled.

"Yes, thank you."

Inside her car, and after a good cry, she pulled herself together and drove home. She was facing a serious health issue, and she had nowhere to turn. She looked in the rearview mirror, hoping to see her parents nestled in the back of the two-seater. Lowering her head, she sighed heavily, and accepted her new normal: she was alone.

The next morning, Zora arrived at Capital Radiology at nine-fifteen for her biopsy. Despite fearing the worst, she experienced her first peaceful night's sleep since the altercation at the motel. As she walked through the door and approached the registration desk, her smile stretched wide, her resolve firm. She was prepared to confront this challenge head-on, knowing that she had to learn to navigate solitude, and this biopsy would mark her first step. The previous night, she had come to accept whatever fate awaited her.

"Good morning. I'm Zora Vaughn. I have an appointment."

"Yes, Ms. Vaughn. Please have a seat and I'll let them know you're here."

Smiling, she tilted her head in appreciation. "Thank you."

Two days later, Zora received a call from the doctor. "Ms. Vaughn, this is Doctor Jameson from Capital Radiology."

"Yes, Doctor Jameson. I hope you have good news for me."

"As a matter of fact, I do. The cyst is benign. We would like to see you in six months for a follow-up mammogram."

Sitting on the sofa, Zora was bent over in tears. "Thank you, God, and thank you, Doctor Jameson."

"You're welcome, Ms. Vaughn. See you in six months. Bye-bye now." Doctor Jameson hung up the phone with an enormous smile on his face, but it was not as large as Zora's.

Setting the cell phone on the end table, Zora lunged up and swung her fist in the air. "Yes! Thank you, Jesus." She wrapped her arms around herself. "God, you are good all the time, and—"

All the time, God is good!

Zora spun around at the familiar voice. With a wide smile and wide eyes, she stood still. "Mama?"

Yes, honey.

"Oh, Mama, it is so good to see you! I thought—"

Once again, you don't see anyone else?

Zora relaxed her stance and chuckled. "Yes, I see you, too, Daddy."

Zora, honey, you're right. God is good. He spared you, despite the terrible thing you've done to your friend and Maceo. She would have been by your side today, had it not been—

"I know, Mama! I know what I did. How many times—"

Hold on, young lady! Watch your tone with your mother.

Zora moved toward the window and looked out. "Sorry, Mama, and you're right. I've lost my friend."

You have to fix it, Zora.

"How do you suggest I do that, Daddy?"

Use carrier pigeon, or what's that thing young folks are doing now, honey?

Texting, dear, but it takes two to tango, and if LaTonya doesn't want to tango anymore, then so be it. Can you blame her?

Zora shook her head. "No, Mama, I can't. I wouldn't speak to me anymore, either."

With closed eyes, Zora heavily sighed and turned around to face her parents. Once again, she was alone.

CHAPTER 38

The aroma of grilled burgers, sizzling sausages, and barbecued ribs wafted through the air, mingling with the cheerful chatter and laughter of the gathered family members in the backyard of Kennedy and Malcolm's home. Colorful streamers fluttered in the breeze, and a banner hanging proudly read: WELCOME TO THE FAMILY, ERIC!

Underneath a vibrant canopy, a long table was adorned with an array of mouthwatering dishes, from juicy watermelon slices to creamy potato salad and a mountain of corn on the cob.

Malcolm's father, Lionel Ellis, and Kennedy's father, Parker Rhodes, swapped stories and jokes, and stood by the grill, their faces lit up by the contagious energy of the celebration.

Nearby, Lindsay and Maxwell playfully bickered about who would win in a game of Cornhole, their laughter harmonizing with the festive melodies playing from a nearby speaker.

As the family mingled and shared stories, Eric stood at the center of it all, a mixture of awe and gratitude etched across his face. He was being introduced to a world that was suddenly his, welcomed with open arms by his father, stepmother, half-sister, and grandparents. They chatted animatedly, sharing fond memories of their own family gatherings.

"Eric, would you like to try my famous potato salad?" Parker Rhodes flashed a mischievous grin.

Eric chuckled. "I'm excited to try it!"

Helen Ellis chimed in, her eyes twinkling. "You're in for a treat, young man. Kennedy's father has a way with food."

Laughter bubbled up from the group, and Parker gave an exaggerated bow. "Well, I do what I can to keep everyone's taste buds dancing."

As the feast continued, Kennedy approached Eric with a plate piled high with food. "Make sure you leave room for some of my dad's famous ribs." She handed him the plate.

Eric grinned, his eyes reflecting genuine happiness. "I'll definitely save some space for those!"

Lindsay and Maxwell cheered and high-fived as Lindsay successfully tossed the bean bag into the hole. Their friendly competition added a vibrant spark to the festivities. Then, Lindsay wandered over to the edge of the backyard, where a cozy set of chairs sat in a small circle. She settled into one of the chairs, joining Eric with a friendly smile.

"Hey there." Lindsay's voice carried a mix of curiosity and friendliness.

"Hey." Eric's smile mirrored hers. "This is quite the gathering, huh?"

Lindsay nodded. "Yeah, it's definitely a full house. But I'm glad everyone could make it. And I'm especially glad you're here."

Eric's expression softened with gratitude. "Thanks for saying that. It means a lot."

Lindsay leaned back in her chair, letting out a contented sigh. "So, Eric, tell me a bit about yourself. I mean, other than the fact that you're my brother."

Eric chuckled; his ease was apparent. "Fair enough. Well, I'm an architect. I love sketching, and I have a soft spot for classic rock music."

Lindsay raised an eyebrow playfully. "Classic rock, huh? I've always been more into R&B."

Eric grinned. "Oh, we can have a friendly music debate anytime."

Lindsay was feeling a sense of camaraderie forming. "Deal. What else?"

Eric's eyes crinkled as he thought. "I love traveling, and my goal is to see as much of the world as I can."

"That's awesome. Any favorite places so far?"

"Italy was incredible. The history, the culture, the food… It was like stepping into a different world."

"I want to travel, too. Maybe one day."

Their conversation flowed effortlessly, as they shared stories and laughter. They talked about hobbies, favorite movies, childhood memories, and even about his deceased mother. Lindsay felt a sense of kinship with Eric.

"So, Lindsay, tell me about you." Eric's eyes were full of genuine interest.

"Well, I'm a freshmen at Hampton University, majoring in engineering, minoring in literature. I have a passion for writing, and I'm a bit of a bookworm. I'd like to be a novelist, someday."

Eric grinned. "Ah, the literary type. That's cool."

As the evening air grew cooler, Lindsay wrapped a shawl around her shoulders. They continued to chat, their conversation touching on deeper topics like family, dreams, and their shared journey of discovery.

"I have to admit," Eric said with a smile, "I was nervous about coming here today. But meeting you, it's been really great."

Lindsay smiled warmly. "I'm really glad you're here. I'm glad I have a big brother."

Malcolm and Kennedy leaned against the porch railing, their eyes fixed on the small circle of chairs where Lindsay and Eric were engrossed in conversation. The couple exchanged glances, their smiles carrying a mixture of pride and contentment.

"Look at them," Malcolm murmured, his voice filled with a warmth that mirrored the scene before them.

Kennedy nodded, her gaze fixed on Lindsay and Eric. "It's like they've known each other forever."

Malcolm's smile deepened as he watched his daughter and newfound son share stories and laughter. "Yeah, it's pretty amazing how quickly they've connected."

Kennedy's expression was soft as she leaned into Malcolm. "I'm so proud of her."

Malcolm wrapped an arm around Kennedy's shoulders, a tender gesture that conveyed his agreement. "Me, too. It takes courage to navigate this kind of situation, and she's handling it with grace."

As Lindsay and Eric continued to talk, their laughter carried on the breeze, intertwining with the music playing softly in the background.

Kennedy squeezed Malcolm's hand. "Our family is expanding in unexpected ways."

Malcolm nodded, his gaze never leaving the scene before them. "Yeah, and I couldn't be happier about it." Facing his wife, Malcolm cleared his throat, his expression a mix of gratitude and sincerity. "Babe, there's something I want to say."

Kennedy looked at him, her eyes attentive. "What is it?"

Malcolm took a deep breath, his gaze unwavering. "I want to thank you. Thank you for forgiving my indiscretion, for understanding that I made a mistake in the past. That I was young and stupid."

Kennedy's expression softened, and she placed a hand on his arm. "Malcolm, we all make mistakes. It's how we grow and learn from them that matters."

"I know, but your forgiveness means the world to me. It's allowed us to move forward, to build something strong together."

Kennedy smiled gently. "We've faced challenges before, and this one is no different. Like always, we've come out stronger on the other side."

"And I'm grateful for that, Kennedy. I'm grateful for you."

"I'm grateful for you, too, honey."

As they stood there, the weight of their shared history and the depth of their connection hung in the air.

Malcolm took a moment to gather his thoughts before continuing. "There's something else I need to thank you for."

Kennedy looked at him curiously. "What is it?"

Malcolm's gaze turned toward the gathering, where Eric and Lindsay were sharing a laugh. "For accepting Eric into our family. For embracing him and making him feel welcome."

Kennedy's smile was warm and genuine. "He's family, Malcolm. He's *our* son. Besides, I know what it feels like to be motherless."

"Seeing the way you've welcomed him, the way you've supported both of us—it means more than I can express. And I can't imagine how difficult it must have been for you, losing your mother."

Kennedy caressed his cheek. "Eric's going to need me."

"He will?"

"Yep. You see how fine he is? Looks just like his daddy. I'll have to help him ward off the women."

Malcolm beamed. "I love you, wife." He passionately kissed her. "I promise to always cherish what we have."

Tears shimmered in Kennedy's eyes. "I love you, too, husband. Our journey has brought us to this moment, and I'm excited for our future."

They stood there, hands entwined, and hearts connected. He pulled her into an embrace, and they kissed with heated passion, tongues playing.

"Get a room!" Lindsay shouted at her parents from across the yard, captivating everyone's attention, causing an uproar of laughter.

As Kennedy looked out at the gathering, she was devastated by the rift between her two best girlfriends, LaTonya and Zora. While she had hoped to have them both present to welcome Eric into their circle, she declined to bring them together due to their conflict. Moreover, the ongoing drama had prevented her from sharing the news about Eric, or her husband's indiscretion, with them. Regarding the latter, Kennedy firmly believed that matters between spouses should remain private and not be divulged to friends.

As the evening progressed, Kennedy's father, Parker, known for his storytelling prowess, regaled the group with tales from his own adventures, punctuating them with uproarious laughter. Malcolm's parents, Lionel and Helen, shared stories of their early years together, painting a vivid picture of their journey as a couple. The mingling of generations and stories created an intricate tapestry of memories that Eric was now a part of.

Lindsay and Maxwell joined the conversation with lively tales of their own escapades. They recounted childhood mishaps and triumphs, trading playful jabs and drawing laughter from the family. This, too, was a form of them still getting to know each other.

With dusk settling in, the sounds of music and laughter mingled, inviting impromptu dancing and swaying under the starlit sky.

Eric found himself embraced by the warm camaraderie, his earlier apprehensions melting away with each shared joke and hearty laugh. He felt an overwhelming sense of belonging as he conversed with Kennedy, Malcolm, and the rest of his family.

At one point, Lionel stood up, raising his glass high. "To new beginnings and to family, both old and new!"

The sentiment was met with a chorus of clinking glasses, and the air was filled with cheers and well wishes. Eric's heart swelled with gratitude, his eyes briefly locking with Kennedy's, who offered him a reassuring smile.

As the night wore on, the bonfire crackled to life, casting dancing shadows and warm hues across the faces of the family members. They gathered around the fire, toasting marshmallows for s'mores and sharing ghost stories that sent shivers down spines.

As the clock struck a late hour, the exhaustion of the day's festivities began to catch up with everyone. The family reluctantly began to disperse, exchanging hugs, promises to meet again, and declarations of newfound bonds.

Eric turned to Malcolm, with gratitude evident in his eyes. "Thank you, Dad. This means more to me than I can express."

Malcolm clapped him on the shoulder, a smile lighting up his face. "You're family, son. You belong here, with your family."

CHAPTER 39

Spring of the following year had hit its stride, as Zora stood in the bathroom mirror looking fresh in a cream linen jacket and pant ensemble. She had pulled her hair back into a ponytail, leaving loose ringlets to fall around her face. She smeared chocolate glaze lip-gloss across her lips, puckered and slouched. She was beginning to love the person looking back at her again.

Exiting the bathroom, she escaped to the kitchen, where she topped off a thermos of hot coffee. She picked up a prepackaged bag of snacks and the thermos and headed into the living room.

Zora looked around her condominium. The movers had traveled her belongings several days earlier to Los Angeles, California. Next month, she would begin her new job as the new hospital administrator for Los Angeles County Hospital. For most, moving to a new place was exciting, but for Zora, it was depressing. She had burned every bridge built in Maryland and had lost every friend who'd ever cared about her. Even Kennedy steered clear of her. It had been quite some time since she'd spoken to her. So, it was time to start anew. When she learned of the position, she didn't hesitate to apply. Within a week, she flew to Los Angeles for the interview. Before her return flight could descend into Maryland, the hospital had offered her the position.

She hadn't spoken to Keith or LaTonya since the night her life spiraled out of control at The Motel on 301. She attempted many phone calls, but to no avail. After months of soul searching and weekly therapy sessions, she wanted to talk to LaTonya and tell her how sorry she was, but she knew an apology would not have been sufficient. She had accepted her responsibility and the consequences behind her actions, so all Zora could do now was pray that LaTonya would find it in her heart to forgive her someday.

One last time, she looked out the floor-to-ceiling, wall-to-wall window—the main feature that sold her on the condominium in the first place—taking in the Woodrow Wilson Bridge, Northern Virginia, The Washington Monument, and the National Harbor. She smiled at the airplane descending into Reagan National Airport.

"I'd always loved the view from here."

She spun around to Maceo standing in the doorway, her luggage propping the door open.

Startled, she gasped. "Sweet Jesus…"

"Hi, Zora."

"Maceo."

"How are you?" He stepped across the threshold.

She smiled and gently nodded. "I'm good."

He looked around the empty condominium. "What happened to your furniture?"

"I'm taking over a new hospital in Los Angeles."

"Yeah? That's good to hear. Congratulations."

"Thank you."

"I still had my key." He extended it toward her. "I guess you'll need this back."

A little more of her died as she hesitantly approached him, taking the key. "Thank you. I'll see that the new owners get it."

There was a long moment of awkward silence. They both quickly spoke, and then stopped, chuckling.

"You go ahead."

"No, you first."

"Zora, I don't hate you."

"I still love you."

He smiled, nodding. "I just wanted to come by, drop off your key, and say goodbye." Although his emotions were telling him to steer clear, he inched closer to her. Something about her still drew him to her.

She stood frozen. She loved Maceo and wanted to feel his touch again. Knowing she could never do or say anything to right the awful wrong she had done to him, she hoped that one day he would give her a second chance. Maybe today would be the day.

Looking into each other's eyes, there was silence between them. Then he thumb-stroked her chin.

"Thank you for breaking me. I never understood it before, but I get it now. Only a lover can wound so deep, cut to the very core. While you were so-called loving me, you were breaking me, watching me bleed. I loved you hard, Zora. Your lies and manipulations, increasing the level of cruelty as you went, shredded my heart. So, thank you, because now I have a strong heart. Thank you for breaking my heart."

"I'm so sorry, Maceo. I didn't mean to hurt you. Please believe that."

He nodded. "I believe you. You were being too selfish to recognize you were hurting anyone, especially LaTonya." He leaned in and inhaled the scent of her hair. Closing his eyes, he wrapped his arms around her, pulling her into an embrace.

Her pulse was tripping because she wanted him badly. She wanted to feel love. She wanted someone—anyone—to love her again.

He broke their embrace and stepped back. "I'm getting married, Zora."

Staring at Maceo blankly with her mouth open, Zora was at a loss for words. Really, what could she have said?

She cleared her throat. "Married? We just broke—"

"She's someone I've known for years." He beamed as he spoke of his new love, which shattered any remnants of Zora's heart. "She's been bringing her car into the shop for years."

She tilted her head. "Maceo, you were having—"

"No." He shook his head. "I don't have the heart to do to anyone what you did to me."

Blinking a few times, she closed her mouth and licked her dry lips. "Wow, uh… Okay, uh…Well, it didn't take you long."

"Thank you, Zora."

"For?"

"For teaching me the difference between a good woman and a bad one."

Now broken beyond repair, Maceo had crushed her to nothing. She was okay with it, though. It was part of the consequences.

With a lone tear falling over her cheek, she meekly smiled. "Have a good life, Maceo. I wish you all the happiness your heart can hold." She headed toward the door, never looking over her shoulder.

"You, too, and safe travels." Knowing he would never see her again, deep down in his soul, he was okay with it.

The End.

About Jessica Tilles

A native of Washington, DC, Jessica Tilles is a highly acclaimed, award-winning publisher, national bestselling author, ghostwriter, and accomplished businessowner.

In 2000, Jessica founded Xpress Yourself Publishing, welcoming talented authors and expanding her roster to over eighty authors. Her dedication and excellence were recognized in 2008 when she was awarded the esteemed title of "Independent Publisher of the Year" by the African American Literary Awards Show. Subsequently, in 2015, she redirected her focus toward her literary career and downsized her roster.

Also in 2000, she established TWA Solutions and Services (formerly known as The Writer's Assistant), a comprehensive creative design firm providing a range of services including book publishing, graphic design, web design, editing, and ghostwriting. Through TWA Solutions, she offers invaluable guidance and mentoring to authors navigating the complex realm of book publishing, empowering them to navigate every aspect of the publishing process with confidence and success. Her personalized coaching approach ensures that each client receives tailored support and strategic advice to realize their literary goals.

Beyond her professional achievements, Jessica is also a valued staff writer for Black Men In America. Her contributions extend to various publications, including the notable article "Third Shift Blues" in *Black Romance Magazine*. She has been honored with accolades such as the Rising Star award from the Memphis Black Writer's Guild and the Outstanding Contributor to Literature award from the Jackson, Mississippi Reader's Club. Additionally, she holds a place of distinction in Heather Covington's *Top 100 Literary Divas*.

Jessica currently resides in Maryland alongside her cherished fur companions: Piccachu, Chelsea, Chanel, and Cinnamon.

Visit Online:

www.jessicatilles.com
www.twasolutions.com
www.xpressyourselfpublishing.com
www.literaryghostwriter.com

Follow on Social Media:

Facebook: @JessicaTillesAuthor
Instagram: @JessicaTilles
Twitter (X): @JessicaTilles
LinkedIn: @JessicaTilles
Goodreads: @JessicaTilles

Publicist:
F.A.M.E. PR & Multimedia
c/o Adrienne Lillette Harris
813-340-1300
Email: info.famepress@gmail.com

9 780985 248499